Queen of Fae and Fortune

FAE OF REWYTH BOOK 5

EMILY BLACKWOOD

Copyright © 2023 by Emily Blackwood

authoremilyblackwood.com

All rights reserved.

No part of this book may be reproduced in any form or by any electronic or mechanical means, including information storage and retrieval systems, without written permission from the author, except for the use of brief quotations in a book review.

Cover Design by Moonpress *www.moonpress.co*

❦ Created with Vellum

The Time Of The Saints

The Saint of love awoke tired. She had been tired, she realized, for some time. Not the typical kind of tired, not physically dreary or simply worn out from a busy day. Tired? No, she felt exhaustion in every ounce of her body, in every bit of her being.

The Saint of love was quite done.

Gone were the days where Anastasia would walk the gardens in the morning, admiring the blooming white roses or the warm sunrise. Gone were those peaceful songs the birds sang, that light breeze from the mountain wind.

Now, Anastasia woke with a familiar feeling of dread in her heart. She sat up, looking around her pristine bedroom.

"Go back to sleep," Erebus, the Saint of death, whispered from his silk pillow.

She had to admit, they were an odd match. The Saint of life and the Saint of death. But they were equals, in many ways. In more ways than they were opposites, she supposed. She had seen that familiar light in him that he tried so desperately to hide, and he had seen that darkness in her.

Many did not understand their relationship. *She should hate him,* they would say. *And he should despise her.* But that could not have been further from the truth.

"I can't sleep," she replied, turning her attention to him. He would have slept all day, if she had let him. He was always so relaxed, so confident. Even if their world was ending today. "I'm worried. How can you be so sure that we are doing the right thing?" Anastasia picked at the lace hem of her nightgown.

Erebus groaned, but eventually sat up, propping himself beside her.

Anastasia's stomach flipped, like it always did, at the sight of him and his dark, unruly hair in the morning.

"Right or wrong," he started with his scratchy voice, "it has to be done. Magic is not what it used to be, Anastasia. If we let things continue as they are, we will have nothing here. This world is a corrupt one, and even I can see that."

Anastasia leaned her head on his shoulder. "You're right," she admitted. "They can't control themselves anymore."

"We must end it now until the peacemaker is born," Erebus said. He leaned back in the bed, closing his eyes and covering them with a lazy arm.

They had agreed on these terms months ago, along with the other Saints. They would peacefully pull most of the magic from the lands, leaving just enough for only a few fae and witches to wield. Once that was done, the Saints would retire from the lands, pulling away completely to let the world heal from the aftermath.

And eventually, when the peacemaker was born—someone strong enough to avoid the temptations of the darkness, someone pure enough to not abuse such power—they would allow the magic to come back.

Anastasia liked this plan, she did. But they were putting a lot of faith into someone who did not even exist yet. This person would be expected to sacrifice everything for the greater good, and Anastasia knew how hard that could be.

"Right," Anastasia said after a few moments. "We will wait for the peacemaker."

Hours later, after Erebus and Anastasia had crawled out of bed to meet with the other Saints, Anastasia found herself picking the ends of her golden hair.

"Is everyone ready?" Phodulla, the Saint of air, asked.

Anastasia nodded, feeling Erebus's hand fall onto her shoulder. She had to be ready. She had no other choice.

The others nodded, too. *Ready or not, this was ending today.*

"Good," Phodulla continued. "Erebus, you may begin."

Erebus stepped forward, entering into the small circle they stood around. As the Saint of death himself, Erebus would be the one to pull them all from the world, taking most of their magic with them.

Anastasia was not afraid of this next step in her life. She knew that whatever happened, she would be with him. That was enough for her.

But the rest of the world? The fae, humans, and witches they were leaving behind?

She worried for them. She worried deeply.

Erebus closed his eyes and held his hands out before him. The shadows of death leaped and skipped from his palms, infiltrating the air around them.

The lanterns flickered out.

A small thrill of excitement stirred within Anastasia. She always felt this when Erebus drew on his magic, it was their deep soul connection that allowed her to sense these emotions of his.

"On this day, we sacrifice ourselves so that this world we now inhabit may know peace. Our magic has brought joy, greatness, and influence to those who have needed it for many years, but those days are over. Where our magic brought light, it now brings darkness. Where our magic brought peace, it now wages wars."

Silence fell upon the Saints at the weight of his words.

"With these items, we extract the magic from this world until the one who may wield it all arrives."

Erebus opened his eyes and signaled to the other Saints.

Anastasia pointed at Erebus's feet, starting a small fire before him. This was the part of the ceremony where the magic would be trapped within these items, stored until the Saints themselves allowed it to be released.

They had each chosen something special. Anastasia had chosen a small pendant, one with a carving of a small flower to remind her how delicate life could be. Erebus brought a dagger, Phodulla a pipe, Detsyn a ring, and Rhesmus a horn.

One by one, they brought these items to the fire.

Anastasia was surprised that nobody objected, nobody even seemed to raise a brow as each item sat in the fire.

Erebus backed up, regaining his position in the circle.

Rhesmus was the one to speak next. "Join hands," he demanded. They obeyed, joining the circle around the sacred items. "Repeat after me. Together we rise, together we fall. Until the peaceful one arrives, the power shall be no more."

Together we rise, together we fall.

Anastasia repeated those words, squeezing Erebus's hand a little tighter.

They repeated the words over and over again, until the flames leaped through the shadows Erebus had sent into the room, until the items on the floor began to rattle with magic, until the entire room began to overflow with the influx.

This was the power of the world returning home.

Her vision darkened, her ears rang. This would be their last time walking on these lands, living in this world.

She shut her eyes tightly, waiting for the transition. Waiting for the end.

It would be thousands of years later when she would see those objects again, see the world again, feel that power again.

For when the peacemaker was born, the magic could return.

CHAPTER 1
Jade

My father ate without speaking. Every meal with him for the last two weeks had been that way—silent. I wasn't sure why it surprised me. He had never been a talkative person, and even when he did speak, it was usually nothing I wanted to hear.

Until now, anyway. Now, I wanted nothing more than to talk to him, than to hear what he was thinking. Every few moments, when he wasn't busy pushing his food around his plate, he would steal a glance at me, probably hoping I wouldn't notice. I figured one of these times he would build the strength to say what he was thinking, to get his feelings off his chest.

But it had been two weeks in Rewyth, and my patience grew thinner with every passing day.

My curiosity could no longer be contained.

"I must say," I started, attempting to strengthen my shaking voice, "I didn't expect you to protect me when the Paragon brought war to Rewyth. That was a shocking turn of events, to see you on that battlefield." *Saints*. In the silence of the room, my voice nearly echoed off the stone walls.

His shaking leg froze beneath the long wooden table, but his eyes remained glued to the food in front of him. "You are my daughter," he replied matter-of-factly. "Of course I protected you."

The silence filled the room again, although I was sure he could hear my heart racing in my chest. I hated that after all these years, I reacted to him this way. I cared.

I had been replaying those moments over and over again in my mind. Weeks ago, when the Paragon had been fighting us in our own kingdom, my father saved my life. He had jumped from nowhere to attack one of the Paragon members that nearly killed me, and I still had no clue how he managed to escape with his own life.

For me. He did it all for me.

It had been years since my father cared about my life. In fact, I was convinced he wouldn't care at all if I had died back home, all those years yelling at me and fighting me.

"Well," I said as I cleared my throat, "you could have died."

He dropped his fork, metal clacking. "I do not care if I could have died," he said. His voice came out in a rushed whisper. "We are family, Jade. They were going to–" He pressed a closed fist against his mouth before continuing. "They were going to *kill* you. And I couldn't lose you, too. Not after everything."

Family. The word hit me like a punch. There were many people I considered to be my family, now. Once, it had only been Tessa. She was my only family for as long as I could remember, even when we lived in the same house as our father. He was never there. Was never protecting us. Was never looking out for us. That was the purpose of family, wasn't it? To protect one another against any enemy? To help each other get by?

Now, I had Adeline. She was just as much of a sister to me as Tessa was. She had even managed to fill that dark, endless pit of sorrow that sometimes became much too heavy to bear alone. Serefin, too, who also lingered around, constantly uplifting the mood of any room. He had started in my life as Malachi's most trusted guard, and I now saw him as my brother.

Then there was Cordelia, half-witch, half-fae who was prickly and sharp and temperamental, but she would defend me in an instant. She had defended me, too, over the weeks. Anytime I needed her, she was there. She had my back.

There were others that I now considered part of my family. Malachi's brothers had their moments, but I no longer needed to watch my back when they were in the room. Over the weeks, we had even begun to enjoy each other's company. Eli had a great sense of humor, and even made Adonis and Lucien laugh once or twice in the last few days. They were all always there, one step behind me, protecting me.

And then there was Malachi, who had become so much more than family to me. He was my other half, my sanity. I needed him like I needed air, and I was quite sure I would be buried in the ground somewhere if it weren't for him.

That was my family.

Sitting across from my father, though, watching him

swallow down emotion that he had likely been carrying alone for weeks in this kingdom filled with people he once saw as his enemies, I paused. *Did he fit into that group of family?* His furrowed brow was permanent now, almost as if his face froze in worry. His hair was more gray than anything else, and even though he ate more than he ever had at home, his arms grew thinner with each passing day.

"Adeline told me you wanted to come with us to the Paragon's temple when we left," I said.

His jaw tightened as he picked up his fork once more. "Yes," he said. "It all happened so quickly, I tried to follow you but they...they..." His foot tapped under the table again, shaking the floor slightly with each nerve-igniting movement. "They would not let me follow you. I tried, Jade. I didn't want you to go without me."

My father actually wanted to go with me to the Paragon?

"I'm sorry," I blurted out. "I'm sorry I left you here, father. You're in a kingdom that is not your own, surrounded by strangers. That could not have been enjoyable for you while I was away."

He huffed. "I don't care about the kingdom or the fae," he said. "None of that matters. Not anymore. What I cared about was your safety, Jade. I could not help you from here. I did not know what they were doing to you. Adeline explained that they tested you? That they made you complete some trials?"

His eyes searched my face. He had never looked at me like that before, like he cared. Like he would be sad if he lost me.

He had never looked at me like a father.

"They did," I said. I brought both hands to my lap and

clasped them together as I searched for my next words. "They made me pass trials in my mind. They wanted to see how strong I was."

He cursed beneath his breath, shaking his head. "Those ignorant bastards. They have no idea who they're dealing with. They don't know how strong you really are."

I watched in awe as my father began eating again. This was not the drunken, idiotic man who cared about nothing but himself. This was not the fool that stumbled home just minutes before the sun rose, nor was it the same fool who bartered away any extra coins Tessa and I managed to collect for food.

My father sat before me today with dignity. With purpose.

In a wicked, dangerous way, it gave me hope. Hope that he could grow, that he could actually become part of this messed up family. Hope that I wouldn't lose the last piece of home I had left.

I looked into my father's tired eyes. "You really think I'm strong?" I asked before I could stop myself.

His foot stopped tapping. "I do."

"Why?" I asked. "What's changed? You never saw me as strong before. You never saw me as powerful."

He shook his head again, his eyes flickering to the room behind me. "I was too selfish," he said. Saints, even his voice had changed. "I did not see you for the woman you truly were, Jade. I saw you as her daughter, and it broke my heart every time I looked at you."

My mother.

"She had to have been pretty strong, too," I said,

treading each word like new territory. "Did she know? Did she know I would become this person?"

Esther had told me once that she knew my mother. She knew my mother would give birth to the peacemaker, the changer of worlds and the breaker of curses.

"My memory of her had been tainted for so long. Sometimes I can't even remember her face. Some memories are clear, but others I can't even trust are real."

I swallowed. "Like what?"

My father smiled softly, his mind going somewhere far, far from that dining hall. I let him sit in silence, reveling in whatever memory had come to his mind. I couldn't remember the last time I saw him smile that way.

"She was always speaking of the Saints. Always wanting them to approve of her. Their history fascinated her. She would do whatever it took to learn more about them, to hear more of their stories."

She spoke of the Saints? "Did she ever speak to you about the prophecy? Did you know that she was friends with Esther?"

His eyes darkened. "Your mother...she was brilliant. She was always smarter than me. She always knew what to say, what to do next. When she found out she was having you, she was so happy. I had never seen her happier. But she had a dark side, too. She had secrets. She sometimes snuck away into the night and would not return for days." My father's smile faded until it disappeared entirely.

"You never asked where she went?" I asked. My heart sped up in my chest. "You never followed her?"

He only shrugged. "She had her dark side, Jade, and I had mine. That's what made us such a great match.

Without her, I..." He tore his gaze away again, only looking back at me to say, "I know you want answers from me. I want answers, too. But the truth is, your mother was very good at hiding. She hid secrets. She hid another life. It's possible that she knew of your destiny from before you were even born."

We ate the rest of our meal in silence. That was the most he had ever talked about her. That also might have been the longest conversation we had without either of us growing angry or storming off.

It was progress. And progress was good enough for now.

CHAPTER 2
Malachi

I smelled her before I saw her. Cinnamon—sweet and alluring—filled my senses as the bedroom door creaked open. I remained facing the window, looking out upon the rising sun that filled the fae kingdom with a cascading sheet of gold light.

"Enjoy breakfast with your father?" I asked, not bothering to turn around. Her footsteps approached, followed by the warm sensation of her hands sliding up my bare back, gently grazing the base of my wings.

"Always," she replied with a long sigh. I admired her for wanting to spend time with her father. She was certainly kinder than I could ever dream of becoming. It was her idea to eat with him every morning. I didn't question her. Her father had attempted to save her life, after all. No matter how much of a drunk he had been, no matter how bad the things he had said to her were, he was still her father.

At least he tried.

"You amaze me with your kindness, you know," I whispered. Her forehead came to rest on my shoulder as she wrapped her arms around my waist from behind. I immediately felt stronger with her near. I always did.

"I'm not sure sitting in near silence for an hour every morning constitutes kindness," she replied. "Although he did talk about my mother today."

"Really? Anything specific?"

She hummed in thought. "Nothing much. He doesn't remember anything useful, other than the fact that she had secrets. That much I could have guessed on my own."

It didn't surprise me that her father couldn't remember much. He had drank his life away for the last fifteen years. That would damage anyone's memory, much less a human's.

Grief would do that to a person.

Jade's father now faced the nearly impossible task of digging himself out of that hole, of repairing this relationship he had ruined.

"With time, he might remember more," I suggested. "I'm surprised he talked about her at all."

"Yeah," Jade replied with a long exhale. "Me too."

We stayed that way for a few minutes, watching the sun rise together over the kingdom. *Our* kingdom. This had become a habit for us. Jade would return from breakfast, and the two of us would take a few minutes each morning to simply *be*. Together. Just us. Before we had to resume the role of King and Queen of Rewyth, before we had to deal with politics and war. Before we had to speak of Saints and secrets and prophecies, we could simply be us.

Jade and Malachi.

It quickly became my favorite part of each day.

But no amount of time with her would be enough. No

number of sunsets or sunrises would be enough. Each day, the dream would come to an end. Jade would step away from me, leaving a cold breeze to replace where her body had just been standing, and we would have to put on those crowns.

"Come with me to town today," I blurted out, grabbing her hands and pulling her tighter around my waist.

"Town? What for?" she asked.

"For nothing, for fun. To escape for the day."

She laughed quietly, the vibrations of her rumbling through my back. A feral heat washed over me.

"Is that a good idea?" she asked. "What if we get caught?"

"We'll conceal our faces," I said. "Besides, we are the rulers of this kingdom. It should be nothing but a mundane task for us to wander through the towns of Rewyth."

Even as she grew silent in thought, I knew her answer would be yes. That was one of the parts I loved most about Jade. She had always been rebellious; she had always been willing to take risks. I knew that from the first time I saw her, fighting those wolves in the forest of her home.

Jade had a dark side, and it lit up even the coldest parts of my soul.

"We have to be careful," she said after a while. I spun around in her arms, pressing my lips to hers in a long, delicate kiss.

"We will be the two most careful people in this world," I said after I pulled away. "I need one day with you away from this damn castle or I might not make it to one more court dinner."

She smiled, the familiar light flickering in her eyes.

"Come on," she sighed. "Those dinners aren't so bad. Serefin and Adonis fighting, Lucien telling Cordelia to shut up. They've been entertaining, at least."

"You are the only thing that makes them bearable," I said. "Discussing politics all day was exactly what I dreaded taking over the throne for."

"Well," she replied, her body pressing flush against mine as she closed the small distance between us, "it is your kingdom. If you don't like the court dinners, you can always change them."

I growled quietly, holding her body to my chest. "Tempting, but I don't know if having an uprising so soon after becoming King will help our efforts."

"They could try to rise against us," she said, "but they would fail."

Her words hung in the air between us. They were true words, of course. Nobody could rise against Jade. She had become the most powerful person in existence. Stronger than Silas, stronger than me.

Stronger than anyone.

She had no need to prove herself over the last two weeks. After her show of power to the Trithen army, she earned everyone's respect. Nobody doubted her. Nobody questioned why I had protected her for so long.

Jade had wanted to be one of us for some time. Even now, though, she wasn't. Not really. Other fae looked away as she walked through the halls of the castle. They dropped their heads as she spoke to them.

Each time I saw it, my chest warmed.

To Jade, though, I knew it was different. Jade wanted

this to be her home. She wanted power, too, but not any more than she wanted to belong.

"Grab your cloak," I suggested. "If we sneak out now, perhaps nobody will notice us leaving."

"Escaping your own castle," she replied. "I like this mischievous Malachi."

"Mischievous," I repeated, catching her wrist as she tried to pull away. "I like the way you say that word."

She let me pull her body back to mine. "I am the King of Shadows, you know," I said, brushing my lips softly against hers as I spoke. "There's plenty more mischief where that came from. You just have to stick around long enough," I said.

"I like the idea of that," she mumbled back to me.

"The idea of what?"

"Of sticking around."

She pushed herself up onto her toes and kissed me, the warmth of her sending a thrill of adrenaline down my spine. I kissed her back, wanting more of her. Always wanting more of her.

She was smiling when she finally pulled away. "We better get going. Cordelia is always wandering the castle in the morning, and I don't care to have her digging around in our minds while we're sneaking off into town to avoid our problems."

"After you, my queen."

CHAPTER 3
Jade

After running into Serefin in the hallway and convincing him we would be back before the day was over, Malachi decided flying us to town would be faster than walking. I didn't argue with him on that, and I wasn't about to decline a chance to fly through the morning sky in his arms.

It still amazed me—how strong his wings were. How powerful his muscles were as he shot us into the sky, the wind brushing through my hair. I instinctively tightened my arms around his neck. A low laugh from him told me he felt it, too. He was never going to let me fall, though. Never.

The stone white castle disappeared below us, replaced by the thick forest that surrounded the kingdom. Even with the chilled air of the cold season, the greenery thrived below us.

"It never gets less beautiful," Malachi said. His warm breath against my neck created a deep contrast with the cold air around us as we flew. "At least we'll always have that."

Malachi—the deadly, feared fae with the power to kill

anyone he wanted—admired the beauty of the castle in a way that made my stomach drop. I always loved that about him. He was terrifying to most, but not to me. I saw through that tough exterior. He could be frightening when he wanted to be, yes, but he always had my best interest at heart.

And he would always, always protect me.

We flew like that for a few minutes before Mal brought us to the ground, just behind the tree line of the forest.

"We'll walk from here," he said, setting my feet on the ground. He reached toward my head and pulled my hood around my features. "Keep this up. With any luck, nobody will know who we are."

His hope was admirable.

"And what if they do recognize us?" I asked.

The corner of his mouth twitched upward. "Then we'll hope they're fans of ours. Or else things might get ugly."

I smiled back at him, ignoring the warning I felt in the pit of my stomach.

Malachi took my hand in his and walked us toward the bustling town below. I had been here before, the most recent time being with Adeline and Tessa. I remembered it so clearly, how happy Tessa was that Adeline had bought her a dress.

Her face lit up like a thousand suns. It was the smile that came to mind every time I thought of my sister.

I remembered Adeline's face, too. She was equally as happy to be the one providing for Tessa.

Saints. There were so many times in my life that I hated the fae. Before I met any of them, all I knew were the dozens of stories I had heard about how terrible they were. How dangerous they were, how predatory. I heard stories about how they would kill any human they came into contact with just for fun. Some even thought they would disguise themselves as humans and crawl over the wall that separated the human kingdoms just to torture them.

How ridiculous all those stories were. I knew that now, these fae wouldn't do that.

Most of them wouldn't, anyway.

Adeline wouldn't. She was even kinder than most of the humans I knew. Her intentions were pure, I could tell just by looking in her eyes.

"Hey," Malachi said, pulling my attention back to him. "Are you with me?"

"I'm with you," I replied. "I was just remembering the last time I came here."

He nodded, eyes widening as he suddenly remembered. "We can go back to the castle if you don't feel comfortable being here," he said. "I completely understand."

"No," I interrupted. "These are our people. It shouldn't be a problem for me to walk through this town. It's...it's a happy memory, anyway. One of the last times I saw Tessa smiling before she died."

Malachi smiled softly, but it didn't reach his eyes.

He knew what it was like to lose a sibling. Close to it, anyway. Fynn hadn't been blood-related to Malachi at all. That became clear to us when we learned that Silas was actually Malachi's father. But still, they had grown up together. They weren't nearly as close as Tessa and I had been, but they were family.

I guess we had both lost family.

"She would be proud of you," Mal said in a hushed

voice. We were entirely out of the cover of the trees now, and the sun beat through the chilled air to warm the small amounts of exposed skin on my face. "Tessa would adore the woman you've become, Jade. I know it."

I shook my head. "Maybe," I said. "Or she would be terrified. If she knew that the Saints communicated with me, I think she might never speak to me again."

"People fear what they do not know," Mal replied. "Tessa may have feared you once because she did not understand. Once she truly understood you, though, and once she truly understood your power, she would be nothing but awestruck. Just like the rest of us."

I gave him a reassuring smile and squeezed his hand, suddenly grateful that he was holding on so tightly. Tessa and I hadn't always seen eye to eye. Saints, there were times over the years when it felt like we were never going to get along.

Right before she died, though, things changed. *Tessa* changed.

The memory of her brought forward the memory of the trial, too. My mind couldn't separate the two; couldn't keep reality away from those twisted tests from the Paragon. The sound of her heart-shattering scream was always there, lurking in my thoughts. I could no longer think of my sister's perfect, shining hair without that ugly sound ruining it all.

Sometimes I wondered if I would ever remember her the same.

The narrow dirt path turned to scarce cobblestone. I kept my chin tucked, not daring to make eye contact with anyone who passed us on the path. Malachi did the same, although I knew he used small amounts of glamour to keep us hidden, too.

Over the last two weeks, I started to notice how his magic felt. Through our bond, I could feel him using even the slightest amount of glamour. His death magic felt like a strong force of nature in my soul, like he demanded it from the world. But small amounts of glamour were much, much harder to detect. Whenever he used it, it felt as though a jolt of light tickled my heart, right below my chest.

It was still such a bizarre thing, to be connected to him this way.

"In here," Mal whispered. He tugged my hand, and we ducked through a small wooden door that led to what appeared to be a tavern. We were the only ones inside, other than a young fae who busied himself with drying ale mugs across the room.

His eyes lit up when he saw us, but the pull on my chest told me Malachi had just increased the glamour he was using to keep us disguised.

"Two mugs of ale, please," Mal ordered. We took a seat at a table near the far wall, one that was half-hidden in the shadows of the morning sun.

"Of course," the man replied. Mal sat directly next to me, blocking me from anyone who might walk in through the front door.

I pulled my cloak a little tighter around my shoulders. "Isn't it a little early for drinking?" I asked him.

Mal shrugged. "I think we make our own rules today," he said. "Besides, who knows how long we'll have until we're needed back at the castle? We might as well take advantage of it."

The fae brought the two mugs to our table, taking the coins from Mal, before he bowed his head and walked away.

I held the overflowing mug in my hands. "Please tell me this isn't laced with more fae magic," I said.

Malachi just smiled at me as he brought his own mug to his lips, taking a long drink without breaking eye contact.

"Great answer," I replied.

"Even if it did," he said, "I'm not sure you would feel it the same."

"Why's that?"

"Remember the wine we drank with Cordelia at the Paragon's temple? The night before your trials began?"

Of course I remembered. The three of us drank the wine while we all pretended we weren't living for Silas's twisted entertainment. "The human wine, right?"

He smiled again. "Except it wasn't human wine, Jade. You just never felt the full effects."

My mind raced. I wasn't a mere human anymore, that much was clear. I had powers that nobody else could explain, and the Saints spoke into my mind. "You're telling me that was fae wine? And I didn't start hallucinating?"

He nodded. "And I must say, you acted much differently from the last time you drank fae wine."

I recalled the festival in Trithen, when Adeline and I had drank until we had nothing left to do but dance our hearts out in the crowd of fae.

My problems had been much simpler back then.

"I don't recall you having a problem with the way I drank the fae wine back then," I said, bringing my voice to a hushed whisper. "In fact, I remember you quite liked the way we danced."

Something dark crossed his expression. He took another drink of the ale. "I'd much prefer you dancing for me that way in the privacy of our bedroom."

His words held a joking tone, but the heat that pulsed through my body was very serious. Just like his magic, I had begun to sense his emotions within my own body, too.

The heat that I felt wasn't entirely mine, but a wickedly tempting mixture of both mine and Malachi's emotions.

And damn, it made me want him that much more, knowing he wanted me just as badly.

I gained the courage to break eye contact with him, finally bringing my own mug of ale to my lips and taking a long sip.

And I nearly spit it out.

Malachi laughed as he watched me struggle to swallow the liquid. "Not your favorite?" he asked.

"Saints," I muttered. "Why does anyone drink this? I much, much preferred the wine."

Malachi reached across the table and brought a thumb up to the corner of my lip, wiping the foam that lingered there. "You'll get used to it," he replied. "And once you drink that whole mug, it'll start tasting a lot better."

"That, I don't doubt," I said.

I took another drink of the liquid, holding my breath this time as I swallowed the bitter ale.

Malachi and I fell into the comfortable silence together as we turned our attention to the sounds of the bustling town outside. The citizens were just beginning to awaken. Footsteps, hushed voices, and carriage wheels all began to fill the air.

It reminded me of home. Although back home, most

humans kept to themselves. Nobody even bothered saying hello to their neighbor, or partaking in any sort of conversation. We were simply focused on surviving, one day after another.

Here? The fae actually seemed to be enjoying themselves. They were...pleasant.

"Do you ever miss it?" Malachi asked, breaking through my thoughts.

"Miss what?"

"Your home. Your house. Your human town."

I shrugged, but stopped myself to really consider his words. "I miss some things," I answered honestly. "I miss Tessa, mostly. She was what made most days bearable. Although half the time, she really made my life more difficult." I couldn't help the smile that spread across my face. "I miss having to hunt in the forest every day. Well, I suppose that isn't entirely true. I miss being in nature all the time. I miss the dirt under my bare feet as I washed up in the stream. I miss the morning air, before anyone else in the town had awoken."

I looked up at Malachi to find him staring at me with intense eyes across the table.

"What?" I asked.

"I've been thinking," he said. "About the humans. About how unfairly they've been living."

"You don't need to worry about that," I said. "You have enough to worry about as it is. We both do."

He leaned in, propping both elbows on the wooden table. "I know you think about it, too, Jade. About how things could be different for them. Things could be easier."

I shrugged. The truth was, I hardly let myself think

about it. Humans had lived in poverty for centuries. Compared to the witches and the fae, humans didn't deserve luxuries. They were the scum, the pests that had to scavenge to survive.

For a long time, I fell into that role. I hated the fae, just like all humans, because they didn't care about us. They didn't care if we had enough food to eat, or if our land produced enough crops. They didn't care if the animals had migrated away right before a rough winter, or if a bad storm had taken most of our houses from us.

The fae lived in their own prosperous lands. They took the best resources for themselves. They always would.

I didn't see life any other way.

"Things will never be easier for humans," I whispered back. "They'll never be as powerful as the fae. They'll never be able to defend themselves."

Mal's eyes grew wild. "But what if they didn't have to defend themselves, Jade? What if *we* could protect them?"

I scoffed. "There are treaties that protect the humans," I said. "Even those are no use. I'm not sure what else we could do."

We both leaned back in our chairs, taking another long drink of the ale. My head was already beginning to feel lighter.

"What if they lived here, with us?" he asked. His voice had grown so quiet, I barely heard him.

"You mean, bring humans to the fae kingdom?"

He shrugged again without looking at me. "It could work."

"Or, it could end in disaster. You saw what happened to

my sister, Mal! The power divide is too great! Humans like her don't stand a chance against the fae."

"But that was before you, Jade. You've changed everything for us! For them!"

"It won't work," I said. "I'm not a human anymore. To them, I am just as dangerous as the fae."

"But you *are* a human, Jade. In here," he pointed to my chest, "you're just as human as any of them. You'd fight for them. You'd protect them. You'd stand up for what's right."

"And what is right?" I asked. "What's the end goal here?"

He swallowed, and my eyes trailed his throat before meeting his dark eyes. "Peace," he said. "Peace is the end goal. It always has been. It always will be."

That's what we've always wanted, that smooth, feminine voice in my head said. Anastasia, Saint of love, had been speaking to me more and more often. It seemed as though I couldn't get away from her, could never quiet her when she decided to show up.

I picked up the mug of ale and swallowed as much as I could.

Malachi's eyes widened as he watched me.

"You okay?" he asked.

I nodded. "Everything's fine," I replied. "*Peace.* That sounds almost too good to be true."

Concern hardened his features, but it quickly passed. He hadn't asked me about the Saints that spoke to me, although I could tell he wanted to.

That was a conversation for another time.

Today, we were pretending those problems didn't exist. We weren't talking about Saints today, not here.

I took one more drink of the ale, starting to get used to the taste of the bitter liquid as it fell down my throat and into my stomach, creating a warm knot there.

"This will all be over soon, right?" I asked, more to myself than to Malachi. "Once I fulfill my destiny as the peacemaker, we can put this all behind us."

He leaned in and placed a hand on my knee. "I'll make sure of it," he said.

CHAPTER 4
Malachi

Jade handled the ale much better than I expected. Two full mugs gone, and she only began to slur her words slightly. I loved seeing her this way, this relaxed. Not worried about being the peacemaker, not worried about the weight she held on her shoulders. It had been ages since we'd been able to strip ourselves of the responsibilities of the castle.

Even if that's what seemed to trace each of our conversations. Even if this freedom from our duties was only temporary.

I was about to ask the barkeep for another round of ales when the front door of the tavern burst open. The wooden planks smacked against the wall behind us, causing Jade to practically jump out of her seat.

Whatever peaceful getaway we had been experiencing was about to come to an end.

I had been using glamour to disguise my black wings. To any other fae, they would look silver. Normal. I even pushed my magic further and gave Jade a matching set of silver wings, although she couldn't see them.

Over my shoulder, I could see two fae entering. Not casually entering, either. No, they sauntered into the tavern like they owned it. Like they belonged there. Like they ran the place, and they were astonished that anyone else had dared to enter.

"What's goin' on here?" one of the men asked. He wasn't talking to us. He barely gave us a glance before turning his attention to the barkeep, who appeared equally as surprised as we were.

"Nothing," the barkeep said after finally finding his ability to speak. "Nothing's going on."

"Really?" the fae asked. He had dark hair that he pulled into a knot right above his neck, and he wore a long, clean cloak. Clearly, he thought he was important enough to upkeep his appearance. In this part of town, that was a rarity.

Just as much of a rarity as a clean cloak.

"Is there a problem?" I asked casually from my seat at the bar.

The two men slid their attention back to us, as if they were surprised that I would speak up at all. "No problem," one of them said. "This barkeep owes me, that's all. He can't serve customers here without paying me my share."

I expected some sort of argument from the barkeep, but he only dropped his shoulders and glanced down at his feet.

"And why's that?" I pushed. "Isn't this his bar?"

The two fae looked at each other and began to laugh. The one with the clean cloak—who I now began to realize was the one in charge here—stepped forward. "I don't think that's any of your business," he said. His eyes scanned my body quickly before his attention slid to Jade.

That was the first mistake he made.

I pushed my bar stool back and placed my body between him and Jade, blocking his gaze. "I'm asking, which makes it my business," I demanded. "Now answer my question. Why are you taking his money?"

This fae's nostrils flared. His hand fell to his hip, reaching for a weapon.

That was the second mistake he made.

My power unleashed on him in an instant, just enough to send him to the ground screaming in pain. I let his companion watch in horror as he slowly backed away from the scene unfolding.

"I said, answer me."

"Who are you?" the fae on the ground asked. "What do you want?"

Jade's hand fell onto my shoulder. "I believe he told you he wants an answer," she said, her voice slicing the air like a sword.

All eyes in the room fell to her. She commanded that, she demanded that respect.

It was like we could all feel what she was capable of, primal and powerful.

The fae on the ground tried to scramble to his feet. Another pulse of my power sent him back down. His clean cloak now dusted the dirty floor of the tavern.

"We have an arrangement," his companion managed to spit out. "The barkeep pays us a portion of sales, and in return, he receives our protection."

"Protection from who?" Jade asked. "Why would the barkeep need to be protected in his own town?"

Silence fell over the room. With the two cowards stuttering for words, I turned my gaze to the barkeep.

His wide eyes and messy hair made him appear even younger amidst the chaos. "Who are they protecting you from?" I asked. He did not look away from me. Instead, his jaw tightened. I noticed the way his fists balled at his sides.

Nobody. This barkeep didn't need protection from anyone besides these two bastards.

"Great," I said, not needing the barkeep to confirm anything else. "You're telling me that you walk into this young fae's establishment, bully him into giving you money, and you have the nerve to tell me that you're *protecting* him?"

The fae on the ground squirmed again. "It's not like that!" he yelled.

I always hated that—how men would lose all sense of pride when they faced death. He could at least pretend to have strength. To have dignity.

But they were all cowards. I had known plenty of men just like him in my life; men who preyed on the weak. Men who took whatever they wanted from those who didn't have anyone to help them.

Men like my father. Men like Silas. It made me sick.

They would never stop. They would take and take and take, and the evilness would never end. Why should it? Nobody stopped them. Nobody put them in their place.

Until now, anyway. *Until us.*

I pulled the sword from my hip, the weapon they didn't

realize I carried until I moved my cloak aside. Cowards were always ignorant, too. Unprepared.

It made them fools.

The fae on the ground began to stammer, began to beg for mercy.

"Please, don't do this! You'll never see me here again! I'll never enter this tavern again!"

"No," I said, holding the sword in front of me. "You won't."

I did not hesitate to kill him. With a steady hand, I pierced the sword directly through his heart. His friend's scream was the only sound accompanying the thud of his body falling back onto the floor.

"What about you?" Jade asked the companion. He sauntered backward, glancing between us and the barkeep. "Do you still think this man owes you anything? Or perhaps you'd like to ask the barkeep for it yourself instead of letting this fae handle your dirty work?"

Jade took a step forward, narrowly missing the pool of blood that now formed around the dead body, the heels of her black boots clicking the wooden floor as she moved toward him.

The man backed up until he could not back up any further, his eyes in a frenzy as he glanced between Jade and myself. As if I would help him. As if I would stop her. The wooden wall of the tavern kept him there, ready to meet his fate. "Please, Miss," he begged as Jade stopped before him. "Please don't do this. Have mercy!"

Show no weakness. Yield no mercy.

Jade lifted her hand, palm facing the sky, as torturously

slow tendrils of her magic escaped her, dancing in the air until they landed on their target.

The man's face contorted in pain, but only for a moment. Seconds later, he was on the ground next to his friend.

Also dead.

"Saints," the barkeep muttered. Jade turned to look at him, but I kept my eyes on her, unable to look away from her beauty.

From her power.

I could feel it inside of me, how much more she was capable of. The fact that she now controlled her power so well was merely a sign of how strong she was getting with every passing day.

Did she realize what she just did? Did she realize what just happened? Without a sword, without a weapon, without hesitation, she had killed him.

The power of life, taking what was rightfully owed to her.

The peacemaker, the judge.

Without so much as a drop of blood on her hands, she stepped away. Although I knew as well as anyone that the blood still stained that perfect skin of hers. It wasn't visible to the eye, but it was there.

And that was just as dangerous as being drenched from head to toe.

"Who are you people?" the barkeep stuttered. He was fearful, his eyes wide with caution, but he did not back away. We had just solved the biggest problem he had.

Jade looked at me and held my gaze as she answered,

"We are Jade and Malachi Weyland, King and Queen of Rewyth."

I dipped my chin to her, giving her the respect she deserved.

The barkeep sucked in a sharp breath before falling to his knees. "Please, forgive me," he stammered. "I had no idea." He began digging in his apron for the coin I had paid for our ale. "Here," he said, holding it out as he bowed his head. "You need not pay for anything in this tavern."

"Keep it," I said, stepping forward and grabbing Jade's hand. "And if you have any other problems in this place, send word for us. Nobody takes your money. Nobody unwanted steps through those doors. This is our kingdom, and we're here to keep it safe. Is that clear?"

He lifted his head to look me in the eye, his mouth hanging open. "Thank you, King Weyland. Thank you."

I tugged on Jade's hand lightly, pulling her in the direction of the door. "We'll send men to dispose of the bodies," I added as we stepped over them.

A few seconds later, we were out of the tavern and back in the bustling streets of the town.

"Saints," Jade mumbled. "That was insane, wasn't it? I mean, how dare they act that way! That poor barkeep was trying to run a business."

I reached up and pulled her black cloak further around her head, covering her face. "They're cruel," I said. "But they won't be a problem anymore, and that's what matters."

She looked away and her jaw tightened. "They deserved to die," she whispered.

Was she trying to convince *herself* of that?

"Yes," I replied. "They would have kept stealing from him, and who knows how many others they were doing the same to? We did the right thing, Jade. This kingdom is a better place without them."

"Right," she breathed.

I squeezed both of her shoulders before placing a finger on her chin and forcing her to meet my eyes. "These weaker fae cannot protect themselves," I reminded her. "We're the ones who must do it. We're the ones who keep the balance. Things will only get worse after the peacemaker ritual is completed tomorrow. What if a fae like him gets power? What if the balance is disrupted even more than it already is? They need us, Jade."

I ran my thumb across her lower lip. She closed her eyes, leaning into my touch.

"You're right," she said after a few seconds. "Thank you, Mal. It just felt so…"

"Wrong?"

"No," she said, shaking her head. "It didn't feel wrong at all. It felt good, actually." She blinked a few more times, her throat bobbing as she swallowed. "And that's what scares me."

I pulled her body into me and wrapped my arms around her, using my wings to block us from anyone who passed. "You have nothing to fear," I whispered. "We're in this together, Jade Weyland. You and me. Do you know how many times I thought I had lost myself to the darkness? That's what this power does, Jade. It makes you think that it's taking over, but it's not. It never will. Do you know why?"

She pulled away just enough to look into my eyes. *Damn, she was beautiful.* "Why?"

"Because you're here. And I care about you, and I know you love me. And that keeps me here. That keeps me sane. When I think I've lost it all to the darkness, you're right here, fighting for me. And you always will be."

She smiled.

"I don't know," she started. "I'm half-tempted to believe that you'd be just as willing to dive into the darkness."

I smiled back. "If darkness swallows you whole, I won't hesitate to dive in after you. But I'll pull you back, Jade. I'll always pull you back."

We stayed there for a moment, reveling in each other's arms, before sneaking out of the town and back to our kingdom. Back to our duties. Back to being royal. Back to politics and war and enemies.

But we had each other, and that made it all worth it.

CHAPTER 5
Jade

The next morning, back in the confines of our royal castle, Cordelia's fists pounded on the door, barely louder than my heart beating in my ears.

Today was the day I performed the peacemaker ritual. Esther had been preparing everything, gathering witches to help her in whatever needed to be done.

It was finally time.

"Are you sure about this?" Malachi asked. He rolled his shoulders back and took a deep breath. Saints, he looked so noble. Each time he put on his formal court clothes with black leather strapped across his chest and his dominant wings tucked behind his shoulders, I couldn't take my eyes off him.

He looked as if he were born for this.

I, on the other hand, felt too small in the grand ball gown I wore. The neckline covered my right shoulder but my entire left arm was bare. The thick, black pleats fell in waves down to the floor, making each step more difficult than it needed to be. It wasn't much exposed skin compared to what I had worn in Rewyth before, but *Saints*.

It felt much, much too vulnerable.

I nodded anyway, letting Mal know I was ready. I knew he could see the lie, knew he could see right through my barriers, right through the walls I had in place after spending so much time with the fae.

He could see how terrified I was. I could see the fear in his eyes, too. Dark yet barely there, mixed with dozens of other emotions I didn't have the time to name.

"Good," he sighed. "Let's get this over with, peacemaker."

The weight I had felt for this moment seemed to dissipate. Days of waiting, days of wondering. Ever since the first whisper of *peacemaker*, I had been longing for this day. Somewhere in the back of my mind, I always knew it would come. I would have to face this, face my duty.

I tensed at the thought. *Duty.* How ridiculous, that after all this time it was my *duty* to fulfill this prophecy. It was my *duty* to restore power to the fae.

Malachi's hand fell onto my back, warm and confident. "You were born for this, Jade Weyland. You have nothing to fear. If anything, it's everyone else in this damn kingdom that should be afraid. But not you. Never you."

I smiled, a real smile this time. Not a fake smile full of pleasantries and lies. Malachi's words...they felt real. They felt like they were true, like everyone in the kingdom really should be afraid of me.

The last couple of weeks had certainly proved some of that. Between court meetings, training with Cordelia—which I really didn't think was still necessary, but I kept my mouth shut about that—and all of my other duties as Queen of Rewyth, I felt as if I finally had a place here. I had a purpose.

The fae of Rewyth did not dismiss me. They did not roll their eyes as I walked by. No, they nodded with respect in my direction anytime I passed. They even bowed to me on occasion when I entered the dining hall or when I exited the room after a court meeting. It felt odd at first, but day after day, I grew into the new position in court.

By Malachi's side, it felt so natural.

Malachi was more than accommodating. I had been the Queen of Rewyth in *his* eyes for some time now, but not to me. Not to everyone else. He was just as surprised as I was to see the overwhelming change of attitude from our people.

Even my father, surprisingly enough. The fae began to respect him more, too. Although I wondered how much of that had to do with his lack of drinking and how much of it had to do with the fact that his daughter was now Queen of Rewyth.

I didn't mind, though. Malachi came with me to most of my training sessions. Cordelia began to test his magic, too. After learning that he was a descendant of a Saint, we figured he had boundaries to push. Unlimited power could live somewhere inside of him, he only needed to let it out.

And my power...

To say that my power had grown stronger would be a disrespect to it entirely. No, *strong* wasn't the word. *Unstoppable,* maybe. *Undeniable.* I wielded my power easily; it took little to no effort to blast an entire stone wall or turn any object—big or small—to ash.

And late at night, after Malachi had drifted into an endless sleep beside me, I often thought about how powerful it would feel to turn bone to ash. To burn flesh away as if it never existed.

And that voice...

You have the power of life, the voice said in my mind. *Give it. Take it. Do as you must. Your wishes are divine, Vita Queen. Whatever you want is yours.*

I stopped being annoyed by the voice that visited my mind. I stopped being annoyed because I liked the things this Saint said. I liked the confidence she had in me, in my power. Always in my mind, always telling me to want more. To burn more.

But none of that mattered. Not really. Because I had a duty to uphold.

"I am not afraid," I answered Malachi. It was an honest answer now, one that rolled off my tongue with ease.

"Good," he replied, opening the door to Cordelia. "Because no matter how much power is restored to the fae, you are our queen. You are our light, Jade."

Cordelia looked between us, hand cocked on her hip with her thin eyebrows raised, as if she had been waiting on us for hours.

I liked that she never lost her attitude. It was beginning to grow on me.

"You two finally ready?" she asked. "I was starting to think you ditched us and were halfway to the sea by now."

I pushed past her, brushing her shoulder with my own. "You wish you could be so lucky," I teased.

Cordelia and her power to read minds, though, knew the truth, knew I secretly liked the small friendship developing between us, no matter how much of it had been hidden in punches to the face and sneak-attacks with my magic.

The half-witch was actually not so terrible.

The three of us walked the hall in silence, our footsteps synchronizing as we grew closer and closer to the ballroom.

Esther would be waiting for us there.

The energy shifted as we walked through the large, wooden doors. I had been in this room many times now. My wedding was the first. Countless dinners. I remembered the way those bodies hung from ropes when Malachi strung them not so long ago.

Although it felt like a lifetime ago. We were so, so different now. I was not weak. I was not afraid.

For once in my entire damn life, I felt peace.

Of course, the peace did not always last. All it took was that one voice—the voice I liked to pretend didn't exist—to talk in my mind. To tell me something big was coming. To tell me I had to be ready to fight.

Vita Queen, she would call me.

Queen of life. What a joke. Apparently, the Saint hadn't realized just how much I craved death and destruction these days.

"Welcome," Esther said as we walked in. "We've been waiting for you."

I quickly scanned the room, taking in the witches that Esther had been working with to prepare the ceremony. They weren't from her bloodline, but they did have some magic running through their blood. Esther was able to send messages out to old friends, and I was surprised by how many people wanted to help.

But I was the peacemaker, after all.

The three women, Esther included, stood with their hands crossed in front of them. Waiting. They wore white dresses, simple and pure. I wasn't sure if it was part of the ceremony or not, but the sight of it made the hair on my arms stick up.

The rest of the dining hall remained empty. We wouldn't have an audience for this. Wouldn't need one.

I approached Esther and began to kneel before her, next to a small fire that burned inside a golden bowl. Malachi grabbed my arm, pulling me to him.

"You don't have to do this," he hissed in my ear. "Do it or don't, but let it be your decision. This is your life, Jade. You choose your destiny."

Saints, I wanted to believe him. I really, really wanted to believe him. But we both knew I couldn't walk away from this.

Vita Queen, that voice said again, as if warning me. As if pushing me. *You're about to learn how powerful you really are.*

No, running wasn't an option. I placed my hand above Mal's hand and squeezed gently. "I'm ready for this," I said, feeling more truth in the words this time. "I'll be okay."

He held my gaze under those heart-wrenching thick lashes before nodding and letting me go.

I knelt. Both knees hit the stone floor beneath my thick dress. My hands shook—barely enough to be noticeable. I wasn't sure why I was nervous, though. Esther had walked me through it dozens of times.

First, the witches would draw upon the power of the Saints. This required relics, relics that they had apparently been hiding all these years. Gifts from the Saints. One necklace, belonging to Anastasia. One dagger from Erebus. A beautiful air pipe from Phodulla. A small, stone ring from Detsyn, and finally a horn from Rhesmus. These were not any relics. They were special relics, ones that held the remaining power of the Saints before they left this world.

Secondly, I would have to swear my oath. I didn't ask too many questions when Esther explained this. I think she understood, too. I would swear the oath, no matter what I had to swear to. I wasn't backing out. We both knew that.

Lastly, a sacrifice was required. A sacrifice of my life. Since I had already died, though, Esther explained that the Saints would accept my blood.

I silently prayed that she was right.

"Peacemaker," Esther began. She held the five relics in her now open palms as she stood over me. I could have sworn the fire to my right flickered with a flare of life. "We are here today to fulfill your duties as the chosen one. Chosen—not by us, but by the greater powers. The Saints that used to walk these lands. They have chosen you, blessed you, and tested you. You, child, are the one to fulfill the prophecy that they began many centuries ago."

Malachi sucked in a breath behind me. His nerves became a ball of fire in my own stomach, mixing with my emotions and fueling the power that ran hot in my veins.

"What now?" I whispered, although my voice practically echoed across the room.

"Give me your hand," Esther ordered. I held my hand out before me. She lowered the relics and knelt on the other side of the small altar, holding my hand in hers with my palm facing upward.

"This may hurt," she said. I nodded anyway, giving her the permission to do what she needed.

She picked up a small blade, no bigger than my hand, and sliced the skin on the center of my palm.

I instinctively flinched away, but she gripped my hand tighter, holding me there.

Malachi's presence became a comforting force behind me, although I knew he couldn't touch me. I had to do this entirely on my own.

Blood began dripping off my palm, smacking against the silver bowl beneath it. Esther flipped my hand over, squeezing until blood had covered the bottom of the bowl.

"Close your eyes," Esther demanded.

I obeyed, letting my head fall back as I shut my eyes, blocking out the room.

"I'm going to call the Saints forward," she explained. "Accept any messages you receive, Jade. Open your heart, open your soul. They will come forward with what they need from you."

Unable to speak, I nodded.

"Let's begin," Esther said. The witches began to chant, repeating words in a language I did not understand. I kept my eyes shut and tried to focus on what I was feeling, searching for any signs from the Saints.

Come on, Anastasia. Don't be shy now. Come forward. Tell me what to do.

The chanting grew louder and louder until I could no longer hear my own heartbeat, could no longer feel Malachi's presence behind me. The words became all-encompassing, caressing my body as if I were part of the air myself.

The voices of the witches, some of the strongest to exist, echoed through my mind, through my bones, through every inch of my body.

And then, all at once, it stopped.

My eyes shot open, searching to see what had happened to Esther and the witches.

The room was nothing but darkness.

"Esther?" I whispered. Instead of echoing off the walls as it did before, my voice carried endlessly into the dark void.

"Esther isn't here," a voice responded. Anastasia's voice, smooth and calming.

"Anastasia?" I asked. "What's happening?"

Then, in the midst of the darkness, a woman appeared. She wore a white lace dress that rippled in the air around her. A light illuminated her body, but I didn't know where it came from.

She was the only thing in the darkness, the only thing that mattered at all. My attention pulled to her like an instinct, I had no choice but to stare at her with wide eyes as she stepped forward.

"Jade," she said, smiling. Her white teeth glistened as she tilted her head and scanned me with her golden eyes. "I'm so happy you are here."

"Where am I?"

"You're with the Saints, my dear. The witches have sent you to us just as they were instructed to do."

Panic crept into my chest, morphing my senses and igniting my power, until Anastasia's small, pale hand landed on my shoulder. Warmth immediately radiated from her touch, covering all those feelings of fear and panic, and replacing them with something else.

Something pure.

"You do not need to fear," Anastasia said. "You will be back in your kingdom soon enough. First, however, we must discuss something with you."

"Who is *we*?" I asked, scanning the darkness around Anastasia's golden light. "Are the other Saints here?"

A silent beat passed. "They are."

I blinked once, and when I opened my eyes again, Anastasia was not the only figure standing before me. No, four more now joined her.

The five Saints, all standing before me in a vision I could hardly look at straight on.

Pure beauty, pure excellence, pure power.

I instinctively dropped my head, bowing before them. "Apologies," I said. "I did not know I would be meeting you all personally."

"Rise, child. We have business to take care of."

I stood up from my bowed position and finally, one by one, looked them all in the eyes. It felt wrong to stare at such power directly. I wanted so badly to look away, but I forced myself not to.

"You all have chosen me to be your peacemaker," I said, trying to steady my voice. "Can I ask why?"

The five figures before me glanced at each other, smiling.

"You question our decision?" The one Saint with black wings stepped forward. I knew immediately who this Saint was, and the chill that crossed my body only confirmed it.

Erebus, Saint of death.

"No," I said, holding his wicked stare. "I'm only curious."

Anastasia stepped beside him. "We knew for decades who you would be when you were born, Jade. We knew before your mother even grew you that you would be the one."

"But why? What makes me special?"

A small smile grew on her face. "The fact that you think you are not."

Her wings, silver with gold flecks, spanned multiple feet on each side of her body. Her skin even seemed to glisten in the light that shone down on the group of them. Pure, lean muscle sculpted her body, the body of a warrior. The body of a fighter. Yet she held an enormous amount of grace. Even her words brought me comfort.

"I have the power of life," I said. "Same as you."

Anastasia nodded. "Yes, dear. You do."

"And Malachi," I stole a glance at Erebus, "the gift of death." I could have sworn I saw him smile, but it was quickly replaced with the cold, emotionless surface.

"I was wondering when you might mention him," Anastasia said with a soft voice.

"I'll be your peacemaker," I said, unable to swallow the sudden wave of desperation that clawed at my chest. "I'll do whatever you need me to do, but I won't hurt him. I'll protect Malachi to whatever end."

Anastasia stepped forward, caressing a warm hand across my face. "Oh, I know you will," she said. "You and I have a lot in common, you know. It's part of the reason this decision was so easy."

I bowed my head. "I'm ready."

"Good," Anastasia said. "You must swear an oath to us, an oath of protection. An oath of peace and of power. If you break this oath, Jade Weyland, your life is ours. Your soul is ours, to live in our realm alone for the rest of eternity. Do you understand this?"

I blinked. "Yes."

"Then let it be done. Phodulla, please continue."

The Saint of air stepped forward, chin high and shoulders back. She contrasted Anastasia greatly, with pale skin and midnight black hair. Her bright green eyes held a promise in them, a promise of power. A promise of vengeance. She held a mightiness that at first seemed similar to Erebus's, but in a more subtle way.

I did not want to be on her bad side.

"Peacemaker, born Jade Farrow, married to Malachi Weyland, and chosen by the Saints. You will fulfill your duties as the peacemaker to us, you will uphold our values and our truths, you will keep peace among fae, humans, and witches. You will not let any one entity overpower the others, and you will be fair in all your ways. You, Jade Weyland, will be the most powerful individual walking in this realm. You will carry yourself as such, never taking advantage of those weaker than you. You will feel a strong pull to this power, as all of us have, but you must not give in. You must not let this power break you, peacemaker. If you do, you will have failed your destiny as our peacemaker, and power will become uncontrollable across the lands. The weak will die. The powerful will reign. You must succeed, Jade Weyland. Accept this oath and become who you were born to be."

The words hit me with the force of a punch, creating an entire new reality right before me.

I had no option. Failure was not a choice. Succeed or die.

Succeed, or sacrifice my soul to the Saints.

"I accept this oath," I said. Delight flashed through Phodulla's features.

"You already have Anastasia's gift, the gift of life. Life magic. You will now receive the gifts of the rest of us, so that you may control the power that flows across the lands."

I nodded, trying to calm my rapid heart.

This was really happening.

I stood, frozen, as each Saint approached me.

Phodulla came first. The Saint of air. She stepped forward and blew, releasing her breath and something much, much stronger into my face, blowing my hair back over my shoulders and nearly knocking me off my feet. Her power buzzed through my body. And then it was over. The wind stopped, she stepped back.

Detsyn, the Saint of love, was next. She grabbed both of my hands, interlocking our fingers and leaning forward to place a kiss on my cheek. I did not flinch away, even as a welcoming, overjoyous warmth washed over me and did not leave.

Rhesmus transferred his power to me by gripping my shoulder. Tightly. It was not as delicate as the others, but the power of war suddenly filled my awareness, settling like a heavy weight at the bottom of my stomach. With a nod, he released me and stepped back.

Anastasia came next. She smiled at me like she always did,

radiating a light from her hands and placing it directly onto my chest. I had known this power, had felt it in my body before, but never so forcefully. A new stream of magic ignited within me; Anastasia's full powers awakened in my body.

Erebus was the last Saint to give me power. I expected something harsh and painful, as he was the Saint of death. But he stepped forward and tilted my chin up with a finger under my chin. His eyes were dark, his brows drawn together as he lowered his head and pressed his forehead against mine. It was not pain that came next, nor was it a coldness. Instead, a familiar warmth washed over me, very similar to the way Anastasia's power had. It settled in my chest, right next to her power, and pulled on each of my senses.

All five Saints, all five sources of power.

Now, it was all mine.

Phodulla cleared her throat, regaining my attention. "It was our plan for you, Jade Weyland, to die. The peacemaker must die and be renewed as a stronger, unstoppable force. However," the Saint looked back at the other four. "We witnessed your death once. The witch called to us, and we answered."

My heart raced uncontrollably in my chest. "What does that mean? I don't have to die again?"

"You are strong, peacemaker. Stronger now than you were before, are you not?"

I nodded.

Erebus stepped forward in the corner of my eye. I tried not to look at him, tried and tried until he stood directly in front of me, gently pushing Phodulla aside.

"Death," Erebus started, his voice as thick as stone, "is

very fickle. Death is what forced us to remove magic from the free lands. But you know that already, don't you?" He stepped forward again, coming uncomfortably close as his breath tickled my cheek. He towered over me, his powerful body blocking my view of the other Saints. "You have been close to death many times," he said. "You have witnessed it. You have given in. You have craved it."

My blood turned to ice.

"Yes," I breathed.

"Good," he said. I jumped at the boom of his voice. "Then you know the consequences. We did not expect the human that would eventually fulfill the peacemaker's destiny to be so familiar, so we have decided to make an exception."

I finally dared a glance at his eyes, black as night. I said nothing.

The Saint of death continued. "We will accept this previous death of yours as your sacrifice to us." He reached down and grabbed my hand, pulling it into the space between us. His touch was cold and warm all at once, filling my body with a strange sense of both belonging and danger.

"I've already died," I said, though I wasn't sure why I said it.

A smile grew on his face, one that put a chilled knot in the pit of my stomach. "Yes, child," he said. "Your blood is not the blood of a mere mortal any longer. You are now something different. Something stronger, stronger than even a fae."

He used the edge of his fingernail—though I didn't notice it being that sharp or long—to slice the skin on my wrist. Blood dripped down, wrapping across my palm and slipping off the edge of my fingers.

It didn't hurt. It didn't sting. It just fell, drop after drop, as a dark numbness spread up my arm.

Instead of letting me go, Erebus tugged tightly on my arm. I stumbled forward, but he caught me with a hand on each side of my face. He pulled me up quickly, and for a quick, torturous second, I thought he was going to kiss me.

But he didn't. Instead, he blew a breath of air into my face.

Except it wasn't air. Not entirely, anyway. What came out of his mouth felt like air, but it danced with black shadows that spread across my vision and around my body.

"What is this?" I stuttered.

"This is what is owed to you by death," Erebus half-growled into my ear. I heard a gasp from one of the other Saints, I assumed it to be Anastasia, but I couldn't quite tell.

He finally let go of me, letting me stumble backward as I wrapped my mind around what had just happened.

"That wasn't part of the plan," one of the Saints said to him.

"She was to get all of our power by fulfilling this. She is strong. She can handle a hint of death, as well."

"She's had plenty of death already, Erebus," Anastasia argued.

"The boy does not count," Erebus replied.

"He is your descendant, mind you!" she hissed.

"He is, and he is powerful. But now they can share this gift, be one with it." Erebus argued as if he had just given me something great, but the look on the other Saints' faces told me otherwise.

"What was that?" I asked again.

Phodulla stepped forward. "Erebus has given you a touch of death, child. Seeing as you have already died, this shouldn't affect you much."

"I can handle it," I said confidently.

"Yes, you can," Erebus growled.

"The last step is for you to decide, peacemaker. You have seen the witches. You have seen the fae. It is up to you to decide which species is to be gifted the free flow of power. Which is the most deserving?"

I shook my head. I knew this was coming, but I didn't think the decision would be so hard. Witches were born for magic, they thrived on it. They had been able to survive since the Saints had taken their power, but barely.

And the fae...the fae were powerful and fierce, but I had seen so many abuse their power. The entire Paragon, for instance.

But did that mean Malachi did not deserve his power? Did that mean the rest of the fae who possessed gifts did not deserve them?

"I don't know," I said. "I can't decide."

"It is your destiny to decide, child."

I didn't dare look at the Saints. Any of them. I didn't want to see any sign of regret lingering on their faces.

"They all deserve to have magic back," I said under my breath. "I cannot choose one species over another, because they are equally deserving." I finally lifted my gaze. "The truth is, when you took most of the power from these lands, you stripped them of who they were, of who they could be."

"What are you saying?" Anastasia stepped forward.

"I'm saying I cannot choose if just the witches or the fae gain their power back. They both deserve power. If you are going to revive magic in the lands, give it back to everyone, and let it be done."

The Saints all looked at each other again. I was really starting to feel like the outsider here, like they all had some sort of hidden communication between them.

"That is it, child," Anastasia announced. "You now carry the power of the Saints. All the Saints." She tossed Erebus a sideways glance. "It is now your duty to keep the balance on earth, to stay true and right and pure no matter what the circumstances. We're trusting you, peacemaker."

A flash of light, so bright that it encompassed everything I thought I knew and everything I thought I was, spread throughout the room. And then there was nothing.

※

Malachi knelt over me when I woke, panic and desperation flashing through those dark eyes of his. "Jade?" he breathed. His fingers dug into the skin on my shoulders, as if he had been shaking me to wake up for some time now.

"I'm okay," I breathed. I thought I might have been confused or somewhat disoriented from my visit with the Saints, but I wasn't. Not in the slightest. I saw very clearly what had just happened to me, and I knew deeply what I had to do. What I had to carry.

"It is done," Esther announced from the other side of the dwindling fire. "If all has gone accordingly, your wife now carries the power of the Saints. They have sworn her in as the peacemaker, and she has agreed to fulfill her destiny to them."

Malachi didn't take his eyes off me. "Jade? Is that true?"

I let him pull me into a sitting position. "Yes," I breathed. "They asked me to pick, Mal, and I couldn't."

His eyes searched mine for an answer I didn't have. "What are you saying?"

"I chose both. Magic will be returned to witches and fae, both."

"Well," Cordelia chimed in from behind me, not sounding the least bit surprised. "What happens now?"

Esther stopped what she was doing and looked at me. Not at Malachi, not at Cordelia, at me. She stared into me with a fierceness I had never seen before, a fierceness that held the strength of an entire coven, a fierceness that reminded me of who she really was and where she came from. "We wait for the magic," she said. "And we pray to the Saints that Jade is strong enough to control it all."

CHAPTER 6
Jade

"You're sure you did it right?" Adonis asked. "Because I don't feel any different."

"I'm pretty sure, Adonis," I replied. Lucien and Eli joined him, lingering in the back of the study as Adonis questioned me. Serefin and Adeline remained relaxed, observing the interrogation from the other side of the large wooden table.

"How do you know?" he asked, taking a few desperate steps forward. I couldn't help but stare at the dark circles under his eyes. He hadn't slept much either, it seemed.

"Stop questioning her," Malachi barked beside me. "If she said it's done, it's done."

We had been at this for over an hour, sitting in this room waiting for...well, I wasn't sure what we were waiting for. A magic bolt of lightning to hit the room? The Saints themselves to arrive and grant everyone their magic gifts?

"Wouldn't that be nice," Cordelia said as she entered the room, reading my thoughts like she always did. Although I was starting to get used to it. Dragon followed tightly behind her as the study doors closed. "And I'm not a babysitter."

Dragon stepped out from behind her. He looked much different now, even a bit younger without his ripped clothing and dirty face. I hated that I barely talked to him since we left the Paragon's temple, but I trusted that Cordelia and Esther were watching over him.

Which I now realized might have been a mistake.

"We're a little busy, Cordelia," I said, trying to keep my voice level as I gave Dragon a smile. He seemed ignorant of the tension in the room, though, as he walked forward and helped himself to a seat at the large dining table next to Adeline and Serefin.

"I can see that," Cordelia replied. "And thank you for the invitation to this little meeting, by the way," she added. "It's been absolutely riveting listening to your thoughts from halfway across the castle."

"Seriously?" Adonis asked. "How are you allowed anywhere near us with that gift of yours? I'm surprised they let witches like you live."

"I'd like to see anyone try and kill me, prince boy," Cordelia replied.

I tried to hide my smile. And failed.

Adonis accepted his defeat and eventually retreated, joining his brothers at the back wall of the study.

"Dragon," I said, willing to do anything to change the subject, "how have you been enjoying your time here in Rewyth?"

His eyes lit up with so much excitement, I nearly felt it myself. "I like the trees," he explained. "And the food."

Adeline laughed beside him. "Good," she added. "You

need some more food in you. It will help you grow big and strong."

An emotion I began to recognize as Malachi's twisted in my chest. It was...it was guilt, so sour that I nearly doubled over.

"They treated him like he was nothing," Malachi whispered in my ear. "I can't believe they would starve a child like that."

"He's out of there now," I reassured him. "And that's all that matters. He'll have a better life here."

"Because of you," Malachi said, running a finger up the inside of my forearm as he turned his back to the rest of the room. "You fought for him to get out of that wretched place. You never cease to amaze me, my queen."

His eyes flickered down to my lips, and in that moment, I didn't care if the entire room saw. I wanted him to kiss me. I wanted to feel those lips on mine, and so did the power that burned in my center.

"Peacemaker," Dragon's young voice cut the air, breaking any tension that lingered between Malachi and I.

Mal smiled, which was more like a promise, before backing away.

I took a few steps toward Dragon, who now attempted to braid Adeline's hair in a way that reminded me so much of Tessa.

"Yes?"

"I knew you could do it," Dragon replied, not taking his attention off Adeline's perfect cherry hair. "They always knew it, too. Even if they did not want to tell you."

"Who?" Malachi interrupted. "Who didn't want to tell her?"

Dragon finally looked at us. "Everyone at the temple. I heard them whispering about her when they thought I wasn't around."

"I find it hard to believe that anyone in that temple believed in what I could do," I said. "Especially Silas."

Malachi flinched before quickly covering it up with a blink. I instantly regretted bringing him up.

That was the second father Malachi had to kill. It had to be done, I was the first person to understand that. Still, Malachi's hands were covered in so much blood, I sometimes wondered how he didn't drown in it all.

"Did Silas ever speak to you?" Adeline asked. She had a gentleness about her that felt so comforting, even for me. I was glad she was here, I was glad Dragon had her, too.

Dragon shrugged. "Sometimes. He told me not to talk to anyone else, though."

Now he had all of our attention.

I glanced at Cordelia, who would no doubt be reading his thoughts and digging around in his memories, but she just stared at him with a raised brow.

"What?" Lucien asked. "What's so surprising about that?"

"Silas wanted to keep him a secret?" Serefin questioned. "Why?"

Malachi stepped closer, looking at Dragon as if he were looking at him for the first time. "I don't know yet," Malachi replied. "But I'm starting to question what exactly was going on in that mountain. Cordelia?"

Attention in the room slid to her. "Don't look at me," she said with her hands raised. "Like I said, I'm not a babysitter."

"Can you search his mind? Find out what was so special?" I didn't care if it sounded like an invasion. If something interested Silas, we needed to know. Especially since we had practically kidnapped him to raise in our own kingdom.

She cleared her throat and dropped the hand that propped against her hip, focusing all of her attention on Dragon. To my surprise, he didn't even squirm. Just looked at her with his head tilted in curiosity.

And for the first time since I had known her, Cordelia looked truly clueless. "No," she said, hardly over a whisper.

"No what?" Mal asked.

"No, I can't read his mind."

"It's been hours," I announced. "Surely it's safe for us all to go to sleep."

Most of our company had left us, leaving only myself, Malachi, Serefin, and Adeline in the room waiting for magic to manifest. I enjoyed their company, I really did, but exhaustion was beginning to take over.

Malachi insisted that we stayed awake until the magic began to show, but I was starting to doubt, well, everything.

"I agree," Adeline added. "If we start to get magical powers, we'll come find you!"

Malachi shook his head. "It's dangerous," he added. "What if our people begin to manifest gifts and lose control? What if we need to maintain the peace?"

"We will," I added. "But I can't maintain anything if I'm half-asleep."

Serefin quit pacing. I could see the tenseness that lingered in his shoulders. "I agree with Malachi."

"Of course you do," Adeline retorted. "He's your king."

"I'm your king, too," Mal added.

Adeline gave him a soft smile. "You were my brother, first."

"Well, I'm not anymore. We know that much for sure."

Hurt flashed across Adeline's face, and I reached out to grab her hand. She quickly covered it with a smile of pity.

They were raised like family, but they were never blood related. That became very clear now that we knew who Malachi's real father was.

And Adeline was nothing like the Saint of death.

"We never got to talk about what happened under that mountain," Adeline said softly. "Just between the four of us."

"There's not much to talk about," I said, knowing Adeline would see right through the words. "Malachi saved my ass before the Paragon could kill me."

"I still can't believe they would do that to you," Serefin added. "After everything you've been through. You were chosen from the Saints, and they doubted you even then."

"Yeah, well I don't think they doubt me anymore."

Adeline squeezed my hand. "What happened to you in there, Jade? We were worried sick every single day that you were gone. Saints, I wanted to storm into those mountains and kill them all myself for taking you."

They knew. Of course, they would know what Malachi went through under that mountain, but I doubted anyone else knew. Maybe his brothers, but that was it.

I looked at Mal, who gave me a reassuring nod. We could trust them.

"The trials were rough," I started. "Malachi warned me what they would be like, but..." I was grateful for Adeline still holding my hand, because I was sure they would be shaking. "It felt so real."

"You don't have to tell us if you don't want to," Serefin chimed in. "You don't need to relive it."

"No," I said. "It's okay. It wasn't real, right? I can't bury those images in my mind. I need to get them out." Serefin nodded, his jaw set. I continued. "I saw Tessa, I saw my father. I saw...I saw a lot of deadlings. Nobody survived, though. There was so much death..." I remembered what Erebus had said to me during the ceremony. Surrounded by so much death. He was right about that. "I had to kill him," I added.

I didn't need to explain who I was talking about. Adeline sucked in a sharp breath. "Oh, Jade," she whispered.

"That's not the worst part. Because of our magic connection, he was affected by what happened in my mind. When I killed him in the trial..."

"Saints," Ser mumbled.

"And my power somehow brought him back to life."

Adeline snapped her head in my direction. "You're joking."

"She's not joking in the slightest," Mal said, placing a warm hand on my shoulder. I instantly felt reassured, safer. He was here. He was alive.

That was all in your mind.

"Jade has the power of life," Malachi added. I waited for

some sort of reaction from the two, but they stared at me with wide eyes, waiting for more.

"Just as Malachi has the power of death."

And then slowly, in a way that put a fire in my stomach, they both smiled. "What a damn pair you two are," Serefin said.

"Yeah," Malachi said, giving my shoulder another squeeze. "What a damn pair."

We sat like that in silence, letting another half hour tick by as we waited for something. Anything. The castle was silent at this hour, right before dawn. It came to my attention that we had been there all night, waiting for something we weren't sure was coming.

Can you at least give me a hint? I silently thought to the Saints. *When exactly is magic going to be restored?*

A beat passed with no response. It's not like I was expecting a response, anyway. They hadn't said anything to me since I saw them in the ceremony, and I was half-convinced that they were done speaking to me altogether. I knew what I needed to do. There was nothing else for them to say.

Patience, peacemaker, a voice spoke back to me. But it wasn't Anastasia this time. The voice was low and fiery, and I recognized it immediately. It was Erebus who spoke.

Where is Anastasia? I asked.

We're all here, Anastasia spoke back. *You can channel all of us now, if you wish. We are all here to help you, if you need us.*

Can anyone else speak to you? I asked, making eye contact with Malachi, who stared back with a raised brow.

Not yet, Erebus replied.

Yet? I asked. *What does that mean?*

Apparently, they were done with our social hour. Nobody spoke back to me. Nobody explained. Nobody answered my questions.

"You okay?" Mal whispered, leaning over the wooden table and dropping his voice.

I nodded. "Just trying to get some answers."

"And?"

"Patience, peacemaker," I repeated, imitating Erebus's deep voice.

Mal's eyes widened, realizing what that meant. "That wasn't Anastasia speaking to you that time, was it?"

I waited for a second, half-tempted to lie so he wouldn't worry about me. But it was no use. Malachi would know if I was lying, would know any emotion I felt now because of our bonded magic.

"No," I answered bluntly. "It wasn't."

A flicker of something swam in his deep eyes before he blinked it away. Even though I could feel his concern as deeply as I would feel my own, I knew he wouldn't show it. Not if it meant suggesting something was wrong. Not if it meant suggesting I wasn't strong enough to handle the Saints speaking to me.

And Malachi knew I could handle it. Deep down, he knew.

"Alright," Adeline said from the large stack of books she had attempted to busy herself with. "I'm exhausted, and I love you both dearly, but I need sleep."

I stood, unable to fight the exhaustion any longer. "Me too."

"Go with her," Malachi ordered Adeline. "I don't want her to be alone."

"I don't need a babysitter," I snapped. "I'm fine, Mal."

He stood and walked around the table, placing both hands on my shoulder. "I know you're fine," he said, brushing a soft kiss onto my forehead. "Do this for me, please? So I can at least attempt to not worry about you every second we are apart?"

My chest tightened. I let myself melt into him for a second, leaning into the pine and warmth and smoke that was so incredibly *him*.

And then I pulled myself away. "Okay," I said. "But just for one night." *Even though it was practically already morning.*

"Come on," Adeline said, reluctantly throwing her arm around my shoulders as we turned our backs on the two of them. "I've been dying to have a slumber party."

"You two be careful," Serefin yelled from the far side of the study.

"Always are," Adeline teased.

I let myself think of Malachi until we made it to Adeline's room.

"Promise me if you start melting the castle with some crazy fire magic, you'll wake me up," I said to Adeline. My voice had grown groggy and tired.

"Only if you promise me that you'll put the fire out with whatever magic the Saints have given you."

"Deal," I said.

We fell onto her white, silk sheets, and slipped into a deep, deep sleep.

CHAPTER 7
Malachi

Vita Queen.

Four entire days passed with nothing peculiar happening. We met with our court, we discussed politics of the kingdom and of neighboring kingdoms, we ate, and we slept.

There were no odd instances of magic. There were no Saints showing up among us. There were no rebellions of magic and newly gifted power breaching the walls of our kingdom.

None of that.

The only change I noticed among any of us, was the change I saw in Jade.

"You're getting slower," she teased. The wind snapped her hair around her face and blew the trees in the distance. We had been outside all day, the warmth of the sun beginning to heat the frigid air.

She swung forward with her fists once more, and I barely dodged in time to miss her punch.

"You're getting faster," I rebutted.

"Please tell me you're not going easy on me because I'm a woman," Jade hissed.

Saints. I wished that was the case. The reality was that Jade was strong. Our normal sparring sessions that typically left her breathless were leaving me sore and gasping for air. Each punch she threw hit a little harder. Each maneuver I dodged took a little more effort.

Focusing on her stance, I anticipated the next kick. When she swung her foot toward my upper leg, I caught it, pulling her body forward so she had no choice but to fall against me.

I caught her with one arm while using the other arm to pull her leg around my waist. Her face came inches from mine, breathless and wild.

"That's a dirty move," she whispered. Her arms came to rest atop my shoulders as she relaxed against me. Sweat glistened across her forehead and dripped down her neck.

"Trust me, my queen," I replied, letting my gaze fall to her plump, inviting lips as she continued to pant for air. "You haven't seen *dirty*."

I closed the short distance between our mouths and kissed her, rough and needy. We hadn't taken much to delicacies lately, but rather stole these kisses in the passing moments of our busy days.

Jade kissed me back, tightening the leg around my waist and lifting herself up so both legs secured around my body, just below the base of my wings.

Made for me. Mine. Forever.

My power flared in response, and I couldn't control the short tendrils of my power that lapped around us, momentarily shading us from the sun as I fought to keep control.

"Careful, killer," Jade mumbled into my lips. "Don't want to hurt anyone."

The tickle of delight I felt in my chest was her power, flaring equally as wild as mine. Though she could hide hers a bit better, I still felt it. I felt nearly every emotion she felt now, and it had only gotten stronger since the peacemaker ritual had been completed.

But with that slight, delightful flicker of Jade's life magic came a darker sensation of lust, a feeling that was never there before the ritual.

It felt familiar, yet so unlike her.

Whatever it was, though, whatever had changed deep inside of her whenever she agreed to fulfill the peacemaker's destiny, my power was pulled to it like it belonged there all along. Like it deserved to be there, like it was made to be together.

Like we were made to be together.

"Your power is growing," I said. Jade continued kissing me, running her lips along my neck. I gripped her hips harder, holding her to me. "Do you feel it?"

"Mhm," she hummed against me, not pausing her mouth for even a moment. Her hands wound through my hair, lightly pulling and holding my head up.

"I'm serious."

"So am I. I'm serious about this," she said, kissing my jawline. "And this," she mumbled against my neck, my earlobe.

Damn it all. This conversation could wait.

My mouth found hers in the daylight of the field, kissing her like I had wanted to for days. My fingers tightened around her, but she only moaned against my mouth in response.

I half-walked, half-flew us to the nearest tree, pinning her body against it for support as I pulled myself toward her, getting as close as possible to my wife. Nothing but forest surrounded us to my right, and to my left, the castle was nearly out of view.

Still, I pulled my wings out, spanning them against the sun that beat down through the trees.

"Mal," Jade murmured against my mouth. "Mal, Mal, Mal."

Shit. The way she said my name sent my power into an unstoppable frenzy, and I was suddenly grateful that nobody was near us to be injured.

Jade did that to me. Against everything, even my wild temper, Jade was the only thing that made me lose control. And I loved every bit of it.

I pulled her tunic down past her shoulder, exposing the skin of her neck so I could kiss her there. She tilted her head back with a gasp, easily giving me access to everything I wanted.

"I love you, Jade," I found myself muttering. "I've loved you since before I even knew you, and I'll love you forever. Long after I'm gone."

"Don't talk like that," Jade said, pulling her face down to meet mine. "You're not leaving me. Not now, not ever."

All I could do was nod in agreement, and her lips found mine again, dancing together in the same wildness that I felt inside of me. That my power felt within.

"I love you, too," Jade said after a while, long enough that I had forgotten I even said it at all. "I love you more every day, so much that I'm not sure I'll be able to handle it sometimes."

I knew that feeling. I knew it very, very well.

Every damn second I spent with Jade gave me more of that feeling I never thought I could get enough of.

Jade clawed at my clothes now, needing to be closer to me. Each slight scrape of her fingernails ignited more of a fire within me, pain mixing with pleasure in a way that only Jade could satisfy.

"I hate to break up the party," Cordelia's voice split through the air, freezing any heat that may have still lingered. "We're waiting for you two."

"Really?" Jade sneered, still partially on top of me. "You choose *now* to interrupt us?"

I didn't have to look at Cordelia to know the way she stood, glaring at us with her hand cocked on her hip. "Why?" Cordelia replied. "Something important happening over here?"

"Saints," I mumbled, reluctantly pulling away from my wife. "You have no idea where you aren't wanted, do you?"

"Oh, I have plenty of ideas," Cordelia sneered. "Would you like me to tell them to you?"

"No!" Jade and I yelled in unison.

Cordelia stared at us for a moment longer before turning on her heel and walking back through the field toward the castle.

"That was short-lived," I whispered, giving Jade one more quick kiss.

"But worth it," she whispered back.

She slid her hand into mine, and with our hearts still

beating like wild animals, we followed Cordelia back through the field.

Today was not just any other normal day in Rewyth.

Today was our last morning here. We were leaving for... well, everywhere.

CHAPTER 8
Jade

An hour later, we were ready to set off on our tour of the surrounding kingdoms. I couldn't deny that it was necessary. I would be the peacemaker, the one responsible for maintaining the power of these lands. The least I could do was show my face, to let them know I wasn't their enemy.

"I'm not sure who decided that you could join us," I hissed to Cordelia. "Don't you have enough torturing to do here in the kingdom? Or have you exhausted all your new toys in Rewyth?"

She laughed dramatically, kicking her somehow *always* clean boots onto the wooden ledge of the carriage. "I'm always up for an adventure, peacemaker," she replied, looking aimlessly out the small window of the carriage door. "Besides, all the interesting people are coming with you. I'd be bored here all alone."

She was right about that. Malachi and I weren't traveling the kingdoms alone. Along with plenty of his guards to travel with us, we were accompanied by his brothers—Eli, Lucien, and Adonis—along with his sister, Adeline, and his most trusted guard and companion, Serefin.

Some of the other court members wanted to come along, too, but Malachi insisted we keep the group small.

If that's what you'd call this.

Adeline piled into the carriage next, giving Cordelia a dirty look before sliding onto the carriage bench beside me. "I see you're riding in the carriage with us *royals*," Adeline sneered, emphasizing the last word. Cordelia would not care, though. She cared very little about making friends here, especially with Adeline, and that was made clear from the second we arrived back in Rewyth.

Adeline didn't seem to care that much about Cordelia, either.

I didn't blame her. They were complete opposites. Adeline was always so gentle and kind, and Cordelia, while she was kind in her own ways, was anything *but* gentle.

Maybe this trip would help them bond.

"Ready in here?" Malachi asked, peeking his head into the carriage. He had insisted on riding one of the horses, along with the rest of the men accompanying us on the trip. He wore his royal uniform, one made of black fabric and gold emblems, fitting snugly across his sculpted muscles. His black wings never ceased to amaze me, either. They drew attention to him everywhere we went, always a reminder of the death that came with him.

And damn, it was sexy.

"We're ready," I said back. He stared at me for a second longer, scanning his eyes down my body before shutting the door to the carriage, leaving me inside with the other women.

"Wow," Cordelia said, pursing her lips. "He might as well undress you right now. He practically already did with his eyes."

Adeline gasped in surprise. She wasn't as used to Cordelia's *fun little comments.*

But I was.

"I'd be careful with your suggestions," I snapped back. "Would hate to make you ride a horse all the way to Paseocan while Mal and I occupy the carriage."

Cordelia squinted at me.

Adeline rested her forehead against the carriage wall and exhaled. "This is going to be fun," she mumbled under her breath.

Cordelia turned her head to Adeline. "Don't even get me started with you and the handsome guard," she teased. "Am I the only one here without someone keeping me warm at night?"

Adeline's cheeks flushed red in the corner of my eye. I tried not to smile. Her relationship with Serefin was certainly not public knowledge, though Mal and I had known about it for quite some time. Mal didn't mind. If anything, it brought him comfort that Adeline was being watched over. But that was Adeline's secret to tell, not Cordelia's.

"Don't worry," I said before Adeline could muster a response. "I'm sure you'll draw in plenty of willing suitors with your warm attitude and kindness. It's a very attractive quality."

Adeline snorted beside me.

The carriage jolted into motion, and we were on our way.

The entire day passed before the horses needed to stop for a break. Adeline and Cordelia were both already asleep on the wooden carriage bench, slumped on either side of the walls. At least they weren't up bickering, which took the majority of the afternoon.

The silence had been welcomed, to say the least.

"We'll stop here for the night," Malachi announced. "There's an inn through that path. It's small, but it is discreet and safe. It will do just fine while our horses rest."

I pushed the carriage door open and jumped out, my stiff muscles practically screaming at me from the long trip.

Malachi made his way in my direction. "Enjoying the journey so far?" he asked, placing a hand on my lower back and guiding me toward the path.

"Oh yes." My voice dripped with sarcasm. "My favorite part has been Adeline and Cordelia arguing about which of your guards is the tallest. It's riveting."

Malachi laughed. "Once we're in familiar territory, you can ride one of the horses."

"I'm not sure why we need to wait," I pushed. "It's not like I'm any safer inside the carriage."

"A stray arrow can't hit you inside the carriage. Assassins can't jump from trees and take you out. You're not even with us, as far as anyone else knows. You're hidden, and that's not a bad thing."

His arm fell around my shoulders. "Everyone in this inn is about to discover that I'm here."

I watched as glamour fell over him, turning his black wings silver to hide any identifiable traits. Even so, he looked tall and strong. He held himself like a king would, and anyone could see that.

"We'll see about that," he whispered, lips brushing my ear.

We approached the inn, which was no more than a worn down, wooden building. A few lanterns lit up the windows on the second level, but other than that, it was silent.

Eerily silent.

"It's okay," Malachi whispered. Surely, he could feel how nervous this place made me. "I know the owner."

That wasn't entirely enough to ease my nerves, but I trusted him. Malachi wouldn't put me in danger.

Knowingly.

A couple of his guards walked in first, another holding the door open for us to enter. They bowed their heads as we passed through.

And before I could think about how the hair on the back of my neck stood up, we walked inside.

The building inside was just as bland as the outside, with planks of wood propped up to create tables and a bar on the far end. An older woman sat near a lantern next to the door.

"What do we have here?" the woman asked, standing from her stool behind the rickety table. "Tell me that's not–" she walked toward us a few paces before she stopped in her tracks. "Saints, it is you!" Her face lit up as she took in Malachi.

"We're on a low profile here," Malachi interrupted before she could say anything else. "I don't want anyone to know who we are."

The woman looked past me and peered out the door we had just walked through. "With all these men?" she asked. "And all those horses? You might as well have announced your arrival, boy."

Boy? They must have known each other well if she was comfortable enough to call the King of Rewyth *boy*.

"If anyone asks about them, tell them it's one of my brothers."

"Will do," the woman replied. Her eyes finally slid to me, raking me up and down. "And this must be…"

"Yes," Malachi said, cutting her off again before she could say my name. "It is. Do you have rooms available for us tonight? We'll be out of your hair by sunrise."

The woman stared at me for a beat longer, and I almost thought she wasn't going to look away at all. I wanted to squirm under her attention, but Malachi's warm hand on my back kept me standing tall.

I didn't have to prove anything to this woman.

She eventually broke her stare, scurrying back behind the table. "Oh, don't be silly," she said, waving her hand. "You are welcome to stay as long as you need. A few of the rooms are occupied, but I'm sure we can make this work."

She and Malachi went back and forth for a few moments before he dropped a small bag of coins on her table.

"Ready?" Malachi whispered against my ear. I nodded,

and he led me through the nearly empty bar and up the wooden stairs in the back of the room.

To my surprise, the few bodies at the bar remained focused on whatever conversations they were already having. Nobody even glanced in our direction.

Maybe Malachi's glamour worked better than I thought.

"Don't worry about them," Malachi said as we reached the top of the stairs. "Nobody here cares enough to acknowledge who we are."

They don't care? "Don't you find that a little odd?" I asked as Mal pushed the key into one of the doors at the end of the hall. "That they don't care?"

Malachi just shrugged. "For tonight, I think it's our best-case scenario."

Okay, he had a point there. Being in and out of this place was better than drawing any sort of attention to us, good or bad.

After wiggling the key in the lock for what felt like an entire minute, the knob finally twisted open. I stepped inside, taking in the room. It wasn't much, which was to be expected. A bed, one I'm sure Malachi wouldn't even fit on, sat in the corner of the room. A dresser pushed against the wall with a small, dusty mirror resting atop it. The room did, to my surprise, have its own washroom, which was a blessing of its own.

I silently sent a thank you up to the Saints.

Don't thank us just yet, Erebus hissed back in my mind. *Stay close to him.*

Like I was going to leave him and wander around a strange inn by myself anytime soon.

"Do the others get rooms?" I asked as I made my way to the window that overlooked our horses and carriage.

"I secured a room for Adeline and Cordelia, but the rest can fend for themselves with whatever's left."

"Wow," I sighed, "that's awfully generous of you."

Malachi came up behind me, pulling me back to him with his hands on my hips. "That's what they say about me, you know," he said. "Generous, deadly, and incredibly sexy."

"Oh really?" I asked, spinning in his arms. "Who, exactly, says that about you?"

The raw pull of attraction in his eyes was the same I felt deep in my stomach every time he and I were alone together. "You, for starters," he mumbled, bringing his lips down to my jaw and kissing me there, hot and slow.

"Well, I suppose that's not entirely a lie," I mumbled back, my voice giving way to the rush of emotion that filled my veins.

But all of that emotion, all of that heat and need I felt for Mal, faded quickly when my stomach rumbled. Loudly. Loud enough for Mal's pointed ears to flicker.

He froze mid-kiss, pulling away to look into my eyes. "You need to eat."

I pulled on his neck, attempting to bring him back into the moment. "I will later," I said. But my stomach rumbled again, louder this time.

Saints, I really was hungry.

"Stay here," he said. "I'll get you something from downstairs."

Go with him, Erebus's voice boomed in my head, more

demanding than before and forceful enough to make me jump.

I didn't argue. "Let me come with you," I said to Mal.

"No way," he said. "I don't want anyone down there to recognize you. It could cause more trouble than we need tonight, and I'm too exhausted to kill everyone who touches you."

No, he's not, Erebus said.

"Then I'll kill them all if they even give us a second glance," I said. It was mostly a gesture, but *damn*, the words felt good leaving my mouth. Because for once in my life, I was confident that was actually true. And a small flicker of my power told me I was more than capable of protecting myself.

We would be just fine.

He eyed me for a second, squinting slightly, before turning to the door. "Don't talk to anyone," he whispered. "Don't even look at anyone."

"Got it," I replied. I followed him down the hallway, now littered with Mal's men fighting over who would get which room, and descended the stairs.

Glamour still hid his black wings, but there was no hiding the sheer height of him. The sheer power that turned heads to him like a beacon.

I followed closely behind him as we approached the bar on the far side of the room. "Dinner for two, please," Malachi ordered in a low voice to the middle-aged man who worked behind the counter. Mal glanced sideways at the others who sat at the bar before adding, "Quickly."

"Coming right up," the barkeep replied.

Before Malachi could even pay the man, he was pouring two large mugs of ale and setting them down on the bar.

Mal turned slightly, shielding me from the few men that sat at the far end of the bar, while he raised a brow in question.

I answered by reaching across him and picking up one of the mugs. *Saints*, we would need more than a mug of ale to get us through this trip.

Careful, Anastasia spoke in my mind. *You need your senses to be on guard at all times.*

Really? I thought back. *Now you decide to speak to me? After all this time?*

Only I didn't say the words silently. Malachi's eyes snapped to mine. He grabbed his own mug of ale before ushering us to a small table in the corner of the room, hidden in the shadows. "They're speaking to you? Right now?"

I glanced over his shoulder, making sure nobody was eavesdropping, before I nodded. "Nothing important, though."

"What are they saying?" His eyes searched mine desperately. I knew what he really wanted to ask. I could feel it. *What did Erebus say?*

"He told me not to leave your side tonight."

"What? Why? Does he think something will happen?"

I shrugged. "Not that I know of," I said, taking a sip of the golden liquid. "Although they're very picky about what they do and do not choose to tell me."

"This place is safe," Malachi said, although I wasn't sure who he was trying to convince. "I've been here multiple times before, decades ago. We can trust these people."

"Everyone here is fae," I guessed, looking at the wings around the room. Malachi wasn't using glamour to give me wings like he did last time, just using enough to hide his own. "Won't someone notice that I don't have wings or pointed ears?"

Mal shrugged. "Like I said, everyone here is too busy caring about themselves to pay us any attention. For all they know, you're a witch and I'm your human escort."

I nearly spit out my drink. "Wouldn't that be a sight," I added.

A wicked smile spread across his face. "Perhaps Erebus knows that, too."

I shook my head. I had my own reasonings for why Erebus might want us to stick together. Either he thought I was helpless and needed my husband to protect me—which was a ridiculous thought considering he had literally blown the essence of his magic into me—or he thought Malachi, his descendent, could use some of my protection.

Which also seemed strange, considering I had no idea how to use any of the powers they had given me.

I could feel it, though. When I needed to use them, they would be there, ready for me to wield. I had worked for this, trained for this.

And I would protect Malachi at all costs. The Saints knew that more than anyone.

"Could it be that Erebus wants to protect his bloodline?" I asked in a whisper. "Maybe he cares about *you*, Malachi. He knows I'll do anything to protect you."

Malachi shook his head, shaking the thought from his own mind. "Not possible," he replied. "He didn't seem to give a damn about Silas. I'm sure he has hundreds of other descendants around here that he doesn't even know of."

I tilted my head. "Hundreds?"

He took another sip of his ale. I watched as his throat bobbed, swallowing the liquid in one big gulp.

"Let's talk about literally anything other than how many possibly related fae may be running around here."

I fought a smile. "Fine."

We sat there in a comforting silence until Cordelia came into view, pulling up a chair and plopping herself down at the table. "There you are," she said. "I've been looking everywhere for you two."

"Everywhere?" I asked. "Because we're not exactly hidden."

She grabbed the ale out of my hands and took a long drink. And then another.

"Everything okay?" Malachi asked.

She finished a couple more gulps before wiping her mouth with the back of her hand. "How could everything not be okay?" she asked, leaning forward with her palms on the table. "We're in a strange inn with strange people in the middle of nowhere. I've been kicked out of my own room by your bodyguard and his little girlfriend, and I'm starving."

The barkeep decided that was a good time to bring our plates of food to our table, a large serving of meat that was still steaming.

Cordelia moaned.

"Here," I said, pushing my plate between us. "Share mine."

"Serefin and Adeline kicked you out?" Malachi asked.

Cordelia shrugged. "Well, they didn't exactly force me out the door," she started, "but I'm not really into observing."

Mal and I both rolled our eyes.

"You shouldn't be alone here tonight," I said. "You can't share a room with one of the other guards?"

She scoffed. "I'd rather take my chances, but thanks."

The three of us sat there, sharing our dinner with Cordelia, while the rest of the inn buzzed around us. Adonis and Lucien were nowhere in sight, and a few of the other guards Malachi had brought with us lingered casually around the bar.

An hour later, after three mugs of ale and as much food as we could possibly eat, I was ready for bed.

"Be careful, Cordelia," I warned.

"You're cute when you worry," Cordelia teased. "But I'm a powerful witch, remember? You're the one who needs to watch your back."

At least I tried to be nice.

"Come find me if you need anything," Malachi added, although I couldn't tell if it was a serious offer or not. Either way, Cordelia would never take him up on it. They had been cordial over the weeks we had spent together, but never even *close* to friendly.

I think that was as good as it was going to get.

Mal followed tightly behind me as we left the bar and wandered back to our room. The warmth of his body radiated through the thickness of our clothes. He reached around my body to unlock the door in front of me before pushing it open and following me inside.

And then, finally, we were alone.

The slight buzz of the ale and the exhaustion from the trip washed over me, like my body was waiting for this moment to finally let its guard down.

Mal did the same, shoulders sagging in exhaustion in a way I was sure only I would notice.

Sleep. Sleep was exactly what I needed.

Arms groped down on my body, pinning me backward. The familiar feel of metal on my throat made me freeze.

"Scream and you die."

CHAPTER 9
Malachi

My sword was in my hand before I could even blink, spinning to Jade while every single one of my senses focused on the body behind her. Silver wings, but none that I recognized.

Fae, but not from Rewyth.

"Let her go," I growled.

His blade pressed against her throat, but if he wanted her dead, he wouldn't be hesitating.

"I just want to talk," the attacker said. Sharp features reflected the lantern light, giving me small glimpses of his face.

"This isn't a great conversation starter," Jade mumbled. Any fear or shock she had been feeling was replaced by anger; each of her features now held a promise I knew she would be keeping.

She didn't let the intruder say another word. I watched —every one of my senses on guard and ready to act—as Jade sent a sharp elbow into her attacker's ribs. Hard.

He grunted and doubled over, immediately losing his

grip on her. Jade quickly stepped toward me until I pulled her the rest of the way behind me.

Safe at my side, Jade drew her own weapon. Her anger burned with mine, mixing together in my chest in a way that made it difficult to control my power.

"What do you think you're doing?" Jade asked, her voice bewildered.

The man dropped his dagger and held his hands up in surrender, still catching his breath from Jade's hit.

Good girl. She really *was* getting stronger.

"I came here to see you," he managed to choke out.

"Obviously," Jade snapped. "Would you like to inform me why you thought holding your weapon to my neck was a good idea? Or should I kill you now and get it over with?"

Cordelia burst into the room, using her black boots to kick the door open. "What's going on here?"

"Saints," I mumbled. She stormed in, eyes frantically searching Jade and I with our weapons out. She didn't need to ask, though. She had probably heard our thoughts from her table downstairs.

"That's exactly what we're trying to figure out," Jade answered.

A dark, amused smile contorted Cordelia's sharp face. "Well," she said, clasping her hands in front of her. "Isn't this exciting? These two don't like company, buddy. I've already tried."

"There's going to be an attack!" he blurted. "I came to warn you!"

"Warn us?" I replied. "Is that what you call that?" I took a step in front of Jade.

"There's few that don't like what's happening. They don't want their magic to be controlled."

"What's that supposed to mean?" Jade asked. "They're planning on killing me so they can use magic? Do they think I'm forbidding the use of magic?"

The man shrugged.

This was a mess. If anyone was actually planning an attack on Jade, we needed to know about it. But there was absolutely *no way* I was going to trust this stranger, when just seconds ago, he had his hands on my wife.

"Sit down," I ordered him.

His eyes snapped to me, and I recognized that familiar shine of fear lingering.

Good. He should be afraid.

He did as I ordered, sliding his feet over to the worn-down, wooden chair in the corner of the room and taking a seat.

"Assuming you *are* telling the truth," I started, "why would you warn her? Why would you want to help us?"

He shrugged. "She is the peacemaker," he said. "There have been many times in my life that I have wanted power, but now is not one of them. These fae...they'll take over. They'll create unease and they'll destroy everything to get what they want. Please, you have to believe me!"

He began leaning toward Jade with his hands out, pleading.

"That's enough," I barked. I turned my attention to Cordelia. "Is he telling the truth?"

She cocked her head sideways, like he was about to be her new form of entertainment. "From what I can tell, yes," she said. "Although he's leaving something out." She took a few steps forward, passing Jade, and knelt before the man. He looked terrified now, shaking where he sat with eyes wider than ever.

But why would someone so afraid be willing to put their hands on the peacemaker?

"Who's planning the attack?" Cordelia asked. "And how do you know about this?"

He answered without hesitating. "A group of rebels. I overheard them when I passed them on the road. I saw one of the royal crests on your horses and I knew it had to be you. Please, I would never do anything to hurt the peacemaker. I only wanted to warn you!"

I glanced at Jade, who now looked annoyed at the entire situation. "How are we supposed to know you aren't lying to us?" she asked. "How are we supposed to know you won't run directly to them and tell them the peacemaker is here at this inn?"

"I won't!" he stammered. "I swear to you, I won't!"

Cordelia glanced up at us. "Your call," she said.

To kill him. Jade was right, we could let him go and risk the fact that he might be lying, or we could kill him and eliminate the threat.

I looked at Jade. She was the one who was at risk here. It would be her decision to make.

She nodded, understanding what I was thinking.

"Well," she said, taking a step forward and kneeling next to Cordelia. The man glanced between Jade, Cordelia, and me as if one of us would show him mercy. As if one of us were good.

As if one of us would hesitate to kill him.

Stupid, stupid man.

"I'm not a fan of strangers putting their hands on me," Jade started, whispering into the man's face. "And neither is my husband here."

I lifted my chin.

"Unfortunately for you, you've got things wrong," she continued. "You think of me as weak. You think you can put your blade to my throat and survive." Jade laughed, harsh and bitter. "You were wrong."

Cordelia stepped back, just an inch, but I saw it. Right before the magic inside of me lit up with anticipation, recognizing the power inside of Jade rumbling to life. Life force, with the ability to kill.

And Jade was done with him, done with threats, done with feeling weak. I wasn't surprised when the tendrils of her magic escaped her outstretched hand, wrapping around the stranger like warm rays of sunshine, before he stilled entirely—mid scream—and slumped back in the chair.

Dead.

"You made the right choice," Cordelia said. "Although I have to say that was entertaining."

"Go find Serefin," I ordered. "And keep this to yourself." She waited a second more, glancing at Jade one more time, before nodding and leaving the room.

Following orders for her was rare. She knew how serious this was.

"Are you okay?" I asked as soon as Cordelia was out of earshot. Jade stood, still not taking her eyes off the man before us who grew paler with every passing second.

"I'm fine," she whispered. "More than fine, actually."

I stepped forward, sliding my hand into hers, shocked at

the cold I found there. "He deserved to die," I said. "He should have never entered this room."

She blinked, holding her eyes closed for a few seconds before opening them again. "I know," she replied. "Do you think any of that was true?"

"We can't expect everyone to be happy about you being the peacemaker."

She laughed under her breath. "Even though I'm the one who allows them to have their power restored. I'm really feeling the love there."

I tugged gently on her hand, pulling her from the dead fae. "That's why we're doing this," I reminded her. "To show everyone who we really are. To show them that they don't have to be afraid of you."

Her eyes snapped to mine. "You think they're afraid of me?" she asked. Suddenly, we were back in those woods, fighting off a pack of wolves that wanted Jade's meat.

"Yes," I answered honestly. "I do."

I expected Jade to feel bad, to feel embarrassed. I wasn't sure why, though. Jade had spent so much of her life afraid of the fae, it served them right to be afraid of her now. Even if she wasn't human anymore. Even if she could kill them with the simple command of her power.

Damn. I should definitely not have found that sexy, but I did. *I really, really did.*

What was even sexier was the smile that flickered across Jade's face. "Good," she said. "They should be afraid of me. Of us, I mean. The wicked will fall, Malachi. Finally, the wicked will fall."

Serefin helped a few of the guards get rid of the fae's body. After ordering a couple of my men to stand guard outside my door to stop any more unwelcome visitors, Jade fell fast asleep in my arms.

Her voice repeated in my mind until I, too, fell asleep with the rising moon.

The wicked will fall.

CHAPTER 10
Jade

The next day had me wishing someone *would* attempt an attack on our carriage. At least that would be interesting.

The low hum of the carriage wheels on the dirt road only added to my exhaustion, and based on the way Adeline and Cordelia slumped on the bench across from me, I assumed it added to theirs, too.

I couldn't stop my mind from wandering off, thinking about the fae who snuck into our room last night. Why would he sneak all the way through the inn just to get himself killed? Why risk it?

Unless he knew something we didn't...unless he was holding onto more secrets than he let on...

I barely had to try to kill him. Death came easily, easier than I ever thought it would. It was no longer difficult for me to summon my power. It hadn't been, I realized, for some time.

Because it belongs to you, Erebus's voice echoed in my mind.

I jumped in my seat.

Erebus was nothing like Anastasia. I could feel the calmness in Anastasia when she spoke in my mind, like a warm bath or a cool breeze. Nothing harsh, just smooth words softly echoing in my own mind.

The Saint of death did not come and go with that same grace. He held a rigidness that made the hair on my arms stand up whenever he spoke to me. Anastasia sounded powerful, too, in a way that I could feel deep in my bones whenever she made herself known, but Erebus could command me without even speaking. His presence in my mind simply put a small, life-altering amount of fear inside of me.

The closest way I could describe it was a *thrill.*

Any hints on when everyone else will get their magic back? I thought back.

When they are ready, he said.

Great. That's very helpful, thank you.

You can sass me all you want, child, but that won't make the magic manifest any sooner. Why are you in a rush, anyway? You're the one who didn't want any of this to happen.

I stared at Adeline and Cordelia, both ignorant to the conversation I was having in my own mind. It's not that I cared, but some small part of me somewhere was concerned, just slightly, for how our little group would change.

How the world would change around us.

Adonis, Lucien, Eli. How would they change when they got magic? Would they grow power-hungry? Try to throw Malachi off his throne?

No, Erebus's voice boomed. *They will not remove the death-fae from the throne.*

I snorted. *You sound so certain.*

Silence. The sickening sound of the carriage wheels over the terrain re-captured my mind.

Until...

Did you know Malachi was your descendent? I thought when he didn't reply. I pictured Mal's harsh features, his black wings. He even looked a little like Erebus, with the same distinct features and curled hair.

Surely, one of the most powerful creatures to exist knew who his descendants were.

That's none of your concern! Erebus replied, sharper this time.

It is when his life may be at risk. How can you be sure another descendant isn't planning on taking over his title? He may not be your only heir, which we learned very quickly with Silas.

Dark laughter filled the space in my mind.

What's humorous about that?

Do you see any other fae walking around with black wings, child? Have we allowed any other fae to carry around the death-gift? Did we allow Silas that same courtesy?

Shit. I hadn't thought of that. The Saints had... had *let* Malachi have his black wings?

But why? Why would you want him to stand out? I asked.

Because, Erebus replied. *You are the peacemaker, and you are fated to him. Light and dark, just as you have been told. We knew this for longer than you have been alive. We have known his fate for some time now, child.*

So what? So you gave him black wings?

We gave him the ability to protect you, and you to protect him.

My heart sank. Erebus, the Saint of death, gave Malachi his power of death, gave him those midnight-black wings and cursed him in his world, so he could protect me? So he could be with me?

I pounded my fist on the carriage door. "I need a break!" I shouted. "Stop the carriage!"

A few shouted orders from Malachi, and we were rolling to a stop. Erebus said nothing as I tried to control my racing heart, tried to calm myself from the truth he just imparted on me.

Thank the Saints.

I needed to stretch my legs, I needed water, I needed…I needed…

Serefin opened the carriage door, allowing sunlight to flood into the space. I threw a hand up to cover my eyes as I slid toward him on the wooden bench.

"Everything alright?" he asked, holding his hand out for me to step out of the carriage. His eyes, though he always tried so carefully to hide it, dripped in concern. He relaxed only slightly at the sight of Adeline sleeping next to Cordelia.

"Everything's fine," I muttered, stepping out of the carriage and onto the dirt path. "I need some air."

Malachi brought his large white horse to a stop beside us. He swung his leg over the saddle and landed on both feet beside me. "I suppose now is just as good of a time as any to take a break," he said. "Let's eat something and let the horses rest. We'll be in Paseocan within the day."

"Can't wait," I mumbled.

He gave me a knowing look before handing the reins of the horse to Serefin, who guided it toward the trees around us.

"Come with me," Mal said. "You look like you could use a walk."

A breath of air escaped me. "You have no idea."

With his hand in mine, he pulled me from the small crowd of our crew and into the trees around us. The smell of the forest air brought back so many memories, memories of my home before I ever met Malachi and memories of the two of us together, catapulted into this new life.

I thought of the first week I was with him in Rewyth, when the tiger attacked me in the lagoon. When he brought me through the forest back to the human lands. And all the times he had killed those deadlings for me, protecting me...

Maybe Erebus was right. Maybe he was here to protect me.

It sure felt like it at times, but that didn't make any sense. Anastasia had said something quite opposite of that before...

He will be your downfall...

"What's on your mind?" Mal asked. We paused near a large tree. I let go of his hand and leaned my back against the rough bark, looking up at the leaves above.

"That's a dangerous question," I muttered.

He laughed quietly. "I'm willing to risk it."

Could I tell him? Could I tell him that Erebus had been talking to me, had been telling me these things about him?

My fingernails bit into the palms of my hands.

He was Malachi, my husband. My other half. He deserved to know.

"Erebus has been speaking in my mind more often than Anastasia," I stated.

Malachi's face didn't show a single sign of shock or distaste. In fact, he stared at me unblinking for what felt like minutes, staring into me with those soul-seeking eyes of his. "And this bothers you?" he asked.

I shook my head. "It doesn't bother me that he speaks to me, it's what he says."

Mal shifted on his feet. "And what is it that he says?"

Another beat passed between us. Birds chirped in the distance, mixing with the subtle wave of wind and nature that nearly fooled everyone into thinking this forest was safe, was peaceful. I knew better than that, though. Something so beautiful always held a darker side, a deadlier side.

It was the beauty that drew you in. That got you killed.

"He claims you are my protector, that you were gifted with your magic and your wings so you could protect me when our fates collided."

Malachi considered this. He considered this for some time, actually, until I was certain I was going to have to scream to get him to say something in response. To say anything, to tell me that he wasn't angry. That he was okay with this curse if it meant he could protect me when the time came.

Slowly, his sharp features morphed into an amused smile.

"What?" I asked. "You're not upset?"

He stepped forward, nearly closing the distance between us as I rested on the tree behind me. "You think I would be upset about protecting you?" he asked, eyes seeking my face in a way they so often did.

"No," I replied, "but I know you've been alive a lot longer than I have. You've had to live with this... this *gift* for a long time before you met me, Mal. Your magic hasn't exactly made life easy for you, and neither have your black wings."

His smile grew. "It's all been worth it," he whispered. "Every kill, every war, every torturous mission from my father. The Paragon. The Trials of Glory. I would gladly go through it all again if it meant I could protect you, Jade."

My stomach blossomed in a warm wave of love so deep, so pure, I would never be able to put it into words. "Do you mean that?" I asked. "Because if you want out of this, if you want to change your fate, I wouldn't blame you for it."

His left hand came up to brace himself on the tree trunk behind me. He brought his face so close to mine that if I moved forward an inch, we would be touching. "You are a damned fool, Jade Weyland, if you think for even a second that I would *ever* leave you in this world. That I could ever spend even a single day away from you, not knowing where you were. Not knowing when I would see you next."

I couldn't help but smile, reaching out and sliding my hands up the sides of his torso, pulling him that last inch closer to me. "My dark savior," I whispered, pushing myself up on my toes to brush a soft kiss against his lips.

He let out a slow breath. "My saving light."

That shadow of Malachi's power inside of me sparked to life, fueling my body with adrenaline and magic and desire. Desire for Malachi, desire for...for more. Of what? It was hard to tell. Being close to Malachi like this always stirred up these feelings. At first, I had quickly brushed them off as my longing for my husband, my need for more of him. But now?

Malachi kissed me back, his lips slowly moving against mine in a gentle yet claiming way. His black wings whipped outward, shielding us from the sun that filtered through the branches over our heads. My protector. My husband.

My downfall. No matter how hard I tried to push it down, Anastasia's voice came screaming back into my mind.

I pushed Mal's chest, sending him a step backward and breaking our kiss. He stared at me in confusion.

"What's wrong?" he asked.

My fingers brushed against my lips, feeling for the ghost of our kiss. How was something so perfect for me supposed to be my downfall? Erebus had said it himself; Malachi was made for me. The darkness to my light, the death to my life. He was my equal in nearly every way.

So what was Anastasia talking about?

"Nothing," I lied. "I'm sorry, I just thought I heard something."

My power flared again, roaring deep in my stomach.

"You can tell me, Jade. I don't want you to go through this alone." *Damn him.* He was right. Of course, he was right. Malachi always had a calm, sensible way about him, the way that made me not want to lie to him anymore.

I exhaled, giving up all the secrets I had been hiding. I was so, so tired of keeping secrets. Of telling lies.

I rubbed my aching eyes with the palms of my hands and finally let my shoulders hang. Malachi was next to me in an instant, holding me up much more than the tree behind me. "You can tell me anything. Let me carry some of this for you."

Some of this. I knew what he meant, even if he didn't say the words. Some of the darkness. Some of the power. Some of the burden.

If Erebus was right, perhaps this was our burden to share. Perhaps we were supposed to share the weight of this.

But if Anastasia was right...

I shook my head and looked at Mal, blurting the words out before I could stop myself again. "*You are my downfall,*" I said. "Anastasia keeps telling me that, but I don't know what she means. It can't be true, right? I mean, you're here to protect me, so that can't be right."

Mal's mask of strong emotionlessness vanished for just a moment, long enough for me to see his nostrils flare, his eyes swarm with shadows. His soft hands went rigid on my shoulders, but only for a flash, before he recovered back to himself.

So sneaky, my husband. But I knew him too well.

"You believe her?" I whispered, not caring that my voice cracked. Not caring that my knees weakened.

Mal was already shaking his head, urging me to look at him. "No, not for a second," Mal whispered. "That could never be possible, Jade. I'm here for you. I'm always here for you."

He stepped back, running his hands through his unruly black hair, the same thing he always did when he was stressed out. I could feel it, too. Deep in my soul, I could feel the dark flush of power, fiery and hot, as unsettled in me as it was in him.

"Then why would she say that?" I asked. "Why would

she keep saying that, reminding me of it every time I might forget it? It's driving me mad, Mal, I–"

I rubbed my eyes again, trying to get rid of the chaos, the uncertainty.

Calm yourself, child, Anastasia said. *I did not tell you of this so you could lose control.*

"Then why did you tell me?" I asked, only realizing I said the words out loud after they had left my lips.

Malachi let that shield drop once more as he searched my face, showing me the pain and love and regret.

You forget, child. I was tied to a fate very similar to yours, many, many moons ago. You are not alone in this. You mustn't worry.

Tears fell down my face. Not necessarily tears of sadness, but more of exhaustion. *I was so damn tired.*

"Make it stop," I said to Mal, barely over a whisper. "Make the voices stop, Mal. I can't do it anymore. I can't keep hearing all these riddles."

He wrapped his arms around me, pulling me to his chest. "You're going to be okay, Jade. You're strong. You were made for this."

I nuzzled myself into him, wanting to escape into his arms. Maybe he could shield me from the voices, hide me from this fate.

He will be your downfall.

Anastasia wasn't going to explain herself. She wasn't going to make it any more clear. My life had been out of my hands for longer than I could remember. I rarely made my own choices, rarely designed my own future. But this? *This* I would control. Malachi was not going to be my downfall. He was my strength, my better half.

He may have wielded death, but he gave me nothing less than life itself.

I wasn't sure how long we stayed that way, wrapped in each other's arms and hiding from the world around us. I would have stayed there forever, too, if it weren't for Adeline's scream ripping through the forest, scattering the birds that surrounded us.

I jumped from Mal's arms, and the two of us were running before we even knew what had happened.

It took ten seconds to reach the carriage, and less than one to see the entire thing in flames.

CHAPTER 11
Malachi

Adrenaline had always been a weapon, perhaps just as lethal as a sword. Just as powerful as a fist. There were many times in battle when that extra burst in my veins saved my life, or helped me save others.

And hearing Adeline scream? I was going to kill whoever laid their damn hands on her.

Jade rushed beside me as we halted in the clearing. The carriage—or what had once been the carriage—was now nothing but a ball of flames, heat radiating into the sky and crackling into a fiery mist.

"Adeline!" I yelled. Many of my men were picking themselves up from the ground, also trying to get a hint of what had just happened here.

"Adeline!" Jade repeated. "Cordelia!"

If they were still in that carriage…

Jade stepped forward, closer to the burning mess in front of us. She thought the same thing I did, that there was a chance they didn't…

Another scream rippled through the air. Adeline's scream.

I exhaled. She wasn't in the carriage.

Jade and I both jogged around to the other side of the fire, where Adeline stood in absolute horror.

Serefin watched a few feet away, his hands out in front of him as he slowly approached her.

"What's going on?" I asked, drawing my sword. Cordelia, Lucien, Adonis, and Eli all waited nearby, similar looks on their faces as Serefin.

"Adeline?" Jade asked, her voice dropping to a soft whisper. Adeline snapped her eyes in our direction.

"She can't control it!" Cordelia called out.

"Can't control what?" I asked.

A second later, we saw what terrified them. Flames—literal burning flames—leaped from Adeline's hands. She screamed as they grew, only stopping when they sputtered out a few moments later.

Adeline was wielding fire magic.

"Holy Saints," Jade mumbled.

Adeline had magic. Adeline, my sister, who had never wielded a single type of power in her life, had magic.

And it was a damn powerful one.

"Holy Saints!" Jade said again, this time with a bubbled laughter that she could hardly contain. I smiled, too. I couldn't help it. Everyone else might have been terrified by this, afraid that she would burn them all into ashes, but not me.

My sister finally had some damn magic.

I relaxed, lowering the sword I didn't remember drawing. Serefin stood up, his wild eyes snapping between me and my sister as he tried to figure out what to do.

"Finally," I said aloud. "I was starting to think Jade's entire sacrifice was going to be for nothing."

Jade walked—or ran, rather—up to Adeline and threw herself into her arms, not caring if she was going to burst into flames. Not caring that Adeline had burned the tall grass around her, not caring that the rest of the crew clearly kept their distance.

And if it were in any way possible for me to love her more in that moment, I would have.

Adeline wrapped her arms around Jade, too, letting herself cry.

"It's okay, Adeline," Jade whispered, patting her back as she continued to hug her. "You have magic, now! This is supposed to be a good thing!"

"How is that possibly a good thing?" Adonis yelled. "We don't have a carriage anymore!"

I sauntered over to him, clasping him on the shoulder. "Oh, come on, brother," I teased. "Are you jealous that our dear sister got her power before you did?"

His eyes darkened. "Careful, brother," he joked. "You might be the King, but I could still kick your ass."

Lucien cleared his throat next to us. "Adonis is right." Unlike Adonis, his voice held no hint of joking. No cues of amusement. "How will we complete this journey without a carriage? It's too far to fly, and the two of them don't even have wings."

"Sharing is caring, brother," I said to him. "You can ride with Cordelia. Trust me, she's very kind and generous."

Cordelia half-growled at the words, giving Lucien a death-glare that only he could return with such hatred. "If you even think about touching me," she started, "I'll gut you."

For the first time in a very, very long time, I saw Lucien smile.

"Good luck," I whispered to them before walking over to Serefin. "At least nobody got hurt," I said once I was close enough.

He looked at me with a worry that I understood all too well. "This time," he said. "It all happened so fast. First, she was arguing with Cordelia about Saints knows what, and the next thing we knew the carriage exploded."

"Jade will help her," I said. "And if she can't, I will. We're all in this together, Ser. We'll get her through this."

He nodded, but he didn't look convinced. "She scared the shit out of me," he mumbled.

I threw my head back and laughed. Serefin had always been so reasonable, but this? Falling for my wild, arrogant, stuck-up sister? It was a challenge for him. It didn't fit into his perfectly planned, thought-out life.

"You have quite an uphill battle on your hands here, Ser," I said. "You better pray to the Saints that you get some sort of water magic, because trust me," I nodded to Adeline, "you're going to need it."

Jade had stepped back from Adeline now, but talked to her in a hushed whisper as she wiped the tears from her face with her thumbs. I didn't have to eavesdrop to guess what she was saying to her.

Breathe in, breathe out. Feel the power in your body, but do not give in to it. Command it. Lead it. Control it.

Adeline would be the first of many to regain the magic that once flowed through these lands.

But she would not be the last.

Jade's hips settled between my thighs as our horse fell into line near the back of the group. I had grown used to this, used to the flush of her body against mine. What I wasn't used to, though, was the fire inside of me at the connection of our magic.

I could feel her power reacting to me, reacting to our closeness. And when she leaned her head back against me...

"You're taunting me," I whispered, low enough so only she could hear. Each slow, torturous step that the horse took caused Jade's hips to roll back against me. I remind myself not to moan aloud at the blatant pleasure of it. "And you know it."

I felt the vibrations of her laugh through her shoulders nuzzled against my chest, but she didn't move away from me. "I am not," she replied, "but I delight in it all the same."

Jade immediately stiffened away from me as the horse in front of us reared, nearly sending Cordelia and Lucien both flying in our direction.

"Will you stop moving?" Lucien shouted. "You're going to kill us both!"

"I wouldn't have to move if you kept your damned hands to yourself!" Cordelia growled back at him.

I coughed on my own laughter. "How are things going up there?" I yelled.

"Don't you dare say a single word, brother," Lucien shouted over his shoulder. "If I end up dead before we reach Paseocan, blame this witch."

"Half-witch! And don't give me any ideas, *prince*. I'd do just about anything to not have to share this horse with you for a second longer."

I pulled back, giving them space as they eventually calmed their horse.

I had to admit, watching Cordelia with my brother was at least entertaining. If anyone could put her in her place, it was going to be him, just as wicked and brutal as she.

"You're loving every moment of this, aren't you?" Jade whispered to me, turning in the saddle so I could see the smile on her face.

"Perhaps slightly," I replied. "We only have an hour or two before we reach Paseocan. We could use all the entertainment we can get before then."

The smile on her face slowly faded. "Do you think they'll be happy to see us?" she asked.

Of all the kingdoms on our tour, Paseocan was not one I worried about. They had been our rival at times, but they were nothing like Trithen. And Carlyle may have been enemies with my father, but he was my ally. He was more than that, even. He was my friend.

"You have nothing to worry about," I assured her. "Once they discover that they'll be getting magic very soon, they'll be thrilled."

"I hope you're right," she said. "The last thing I want is to start any more wars. We're here to protect them. We just need to make them see that."

A wave of caution in my veins reminded me that was

not all we were doing here. That was one of the goals, yes, but there was also another, more important reason we were visiting each of the surrounding kingdoms.

A chill washed over my body as the realization hit me once again. We would be forcing each kingdom we visited to submit.

Take a knee to the peacemaker, or forfeit your life.

CHAPTER 12
Jade

I felt the presence of Paseocan before I saw the gates. There was a quietness that surrounded the kingdom, one that could almost be confused for a calmness.

But I felt the sharp, tricking edge that warned me to stay alert. Perhaps that was part of my new power, to feel these things much more intensely than before.

"Carlyle knows we are coming," Mal whispered against my ear. "You have nothing to fear."

I wanted to believe him. Saints, I wanted to. The times I had talked to Carlyle were pleasant, and I didn't think of him as a specifically violent man. Still, he was the leader of his own kingdom. And in anyone's eyes, we were outsiders. We were a threat.

Malachi may have been a threat before, but now? With me?

We were unstoppable.

Nobody talked as we made the final leg of the journey. Even Cordelia and Lucien had shut up, falling into the quietness of the group as the horses clicking on the dirt pavement became the only audible sounds around.

The front gates to Paseocan came into view.

Massive, black iron gates surrounded the entire kingdom. They were tall, tall enough that the fae would need to use their wings to fly over the sharp spears that lined the apex of each iron segment.

I ripped my eyes away, focusing on what lay within the iron gates. From what I could see, a large stone castle hid far behind those royal boundaries. Far enough that they would be alerted to any attacker, but not too far so they could not respond in time.

Interesting tactic.

The iron gates shook and creaked as we approached, and before Serefin and Adeline's horse at the front of the group even came close, the gate was swinging open.

It was now or never.

Nerves tickled my body, putting every sense of mine on alert. I felt the nerves that laced Malachi's power, too, although his also had a tone of confidence and control. His arms, which held onto the horse's reins in front of me, fell a little tighter around my body.

Always my protector.

"Bring the horses toward the castle," Mal announced to the group. "They should be waiting for us beyond the stone wall."

Of course he would know. This wasn't his first time here in this kingdom. My chest ached as I remembered Mal's past life, the life he had come so far from. The life he had been forced to live, the man he had been forced to become.

A killer. A weapon.

That's who he had been the last time he entered this kingdom.

"I can feel what you are thinking, my queen," he whispered, his lips brushing the space directly behind my ear. "And I love you for caring about me, but you do not need to worry. All I'm concerned about now is you and your safety."

I brushed him off. "That doesn't mean I can't be concerned for your feelings," I said. "Are you honestly not the least bit worried about returning here?"

He sighed against the back of my neck. "Without you, maybe I would be worried about my past reputation, but not anymore. We come with good news, not bad news. We're bringing them word of magic, not of war."

His voice hardened at the end of his sentence. He knew just as well as I did that entry to new land could easily be seen as an act of war, especially since he was a new king.

But we had made it this far, and this kingdom would be the first stop of many. We had no other choice than to trust that Carlyle saw our intentions for what they were—pure.

We stayed silent as those large iron gates closed behind us. The horses even seemed to tense up at the new territory. We did not see a single soul as we approached the large stone castle, but I knew they saw us. They likely had hundreds of eyes on us at any given moment, anticipating our arrival.

Watching our every move.

Every one of the guards now rode their horses with straight backs and solid shoulders. Nobody joked now. Nobody got distracted.

Once we were close enough to the castle, we could see a small, tunnel-like structure built into the wall.

"Through there," Malachi said, although his voice seemed to echo. One by one, we rode through that arched opening. One by one, we officially entered the threshold to Paseocan.

The tunnel was dark, dark enough that I could barely see the white horse beneath me. As soon as we reached the other side, though, I had to squint to keep the sunlight out of my eyes.

"Welcome!" Carlyle's voice chirped. "Come in, come in! We've been waiting for you all, you must be exhausted!"

I scanned the small crowd of armed men, all dressed in black military uniforms, and found Carlyle. He wore a cloak, too, shielding himself from the chilled temperatures. His hair had grown longer over the months, but the smile he wore was as genuine as ever. His look was even finished with a golden crown sitting atop his head, the clear signal that he was the king here.

Not Mal.

Still, when Carlyle outstretched his hand to me, I took it. "King and Queen Weyland, it is truly a pleasure to have you and your men in our home today. Please, let me help you!"

Mal's hands slid off my hips as I let Carlyle assist me off the saddle. Once I landed on the ground, Mal swung off the horse and placed a protective hand on my shoulder. "Carlyle," he replied with a wide smile. "It's been some time. You've been more than generous with us, it's time we came to visit you in your kingdom for once."

Carlyle dipped his chin in gratitude. Of all the kings we

had met so far, of all the royals, even, Carlyle was my favorite. He had a certain grace about him that became comforting over our few interactions. He was loyal; he was intelligent. I trusted him, and that mattered more than anything around here.

"I believe you two have quite the story to tell me," Carlyle started. "You must tell me everything over dinner this evening. My men will bring you to your rooms to rest before then."

"We sure do," Mal said. I followed his lead as he turned with Carlyle and began walking across the stone courtyard. "Thank you, Carlyle. For everything."

Another nod of the head, and Carlyle was off greeting the rest of our men. He even scooped Serefin into a large, bear-like hug.

"This way," one of the guards announced. "We have a special wing cleared out for you."

An entire wing? I glanced at Mal, who only raised his eyebrow at me. Carlyle really was generous. That, or he wanted to get on our good side. Either way, my body now ached from riding on the horse for so long, even if I had Mal to support me the entire time.

I jogged forward, catching up with Adeline. "Hey," I started. "Are you feeling okay?"

She let out a shaking breath but shook her head. "As good as I can. Although fearing that I might blow up this entire castle doesn't exactly put me at ease."

I smiled at her. "I used to fear that all the time," I said honestly. "My magic would come out when it was the least convenient, and when I really needed it, it was nowhere to be found. But you're fae, you were made for magic. I'm sure you'll have perfect control in no time."

She gave me an attempt at a smile. "Where's Esther when we really need her?" she joked.

"You have Cordelia if you need her," I added. Adeline rolled her eyes. "I'm serious," I hissed. "She could be a great asset in helping you control this. She'll be needing to help a lot more than just you here shortly, anyway."

"Still," Adeline retorted, glancing over her shoulder to where Cordelia followed in the crowd. "She's not exactly inviting."

"I can hear you two!" Cordelia yelled from our backs.

I hooked my arm through Adeline's as we laughed, continuing to follow the guard into the massive stone structure.

For a royal castle, it was very comfortable. Fabrics and linens covered most of the stone walls, creating a relaxing and inviting feeling throughout. We walked into a large hall with red velvet armchairs lining the walls, accompanied with massive works of art and candles to keep the place well-lit, even though the sun still filtered through beautiful large windows every few feet.

"Here you are," the guard announced. "There should be plenty of rooms for everyone. Each room is stocked with clean clothes and anything else you all may need, but if you are in need of anything else, please send word. The King has prepared a feast in your honor this evening, we will send a guard here to lead you to the dining hall when it is time."

He bowed at the waist, and then he was gone.

We spent the next few minutes sauntering through the halls, in awe of how large it really was. When the guard said

Carlyle reserved an entire wing of the castle for us, he wasn't lying. Bedroom after bedroom lined the structure, perfectly decorated and truly filled with anything we might need. Fruit baskets, bathing chambers, dresses.

Carlyle had thought of it all.

"Is this what it's like to travel as a royal?" I asked Mal, who said nothing as I took in the beauty around us. Most of the group had settled into their chosen bed chambers by now, leaving Mal and I alone in the hallway.

Mal laughed quietly. "In the decades that I have known Carlyle, I have never had this much royal treatment from him. Trust me, Jade, you make quite the impression. I'm sure each kingdom on our tour will be more than happy to accommodate the peacemaker, even if that means clearing an entire wing of their castles."

Damn.

"Here," Mal said as we reached the end of the hall. With a hand still solid on my lower back, he guided me into the last bedroom. Which also happened to be the largest bedroom. A large bed on massive iron posts stood in the center of the room, so large it did not even touch a single wall.

To think that Tessa and I used to share a tiny bed shoved into the corner of our father's house...

"Wow," I managed to say. "Carlyle has truly outdone himself here."

Mal shut the door behind me as I sauntered in, taking in the beauty of the room.

"He has quite a talent for flare," Mal said, but something else laced his words. I turned to face him.

"You've known Carlyle for a long time," I stated. "You

trust him, right? I mean, he would never try anything stupid."

Mal shrugged, his eyes leaving me to scan the room around us. "Carlyle is a good man," he said. "But nobody has seen anyone as powerful as you, Jade. We can't know how he'll react to you. And if their powers start to develop like Adeline's, we need to be on alert. I don't anticipate Carlyle trying anything, but that doesn't mean his men will grant us the same courtesy."

I nodded. With powers coming to light around us, we needed to be on alert. Always.

"The good news is that if anyone tries anything, Adeline will be there to burn them to ash," I added. This joke only earned me a small, tired smile from Malachi. I walked over to him and placed both hands on the sides of his face. "Hey," I said. "I am with you on this, Mal. You are not alone in this kingdom. The burden of our safety is not on your shoulders alone."

His hands came up to cup mine. "I know," he replied. "But I can't stop myself from thinking of every possible way our enemies might challenge us."

Even now, his eyes swam with something fierce and powerful. The King of Shadows, the most powerful fae in existence.

He had nothing to fear.

"Sleep," I ordered him. "I'll wake you when it's time for dinner."

He held my stare for a moment longer before pressing his lips to my forehead in a soft kiss. We both needed to rest before dinner, but Malachi needed it much more than I.

Exhaustion seeped into every ounce of my being as we walked to the dining hall. This was why we were here, this was what we came all this way for.

Tonight, we would feast with Carlyle's people and declare that we had finished the peacemaker ritual. If they hadn't already, they would start to see fae appearing with magic gifts. This would change everything.

Malachi dressed himself in clean black clothes, similar to the rest of the men in our group. I had been given a conservative silver dress to wear, one that contrasted greatly with my black hair, which I tied back into a braid.

"You are the peacemaker, Jade Weyland," Mal whispered in my ear as we walked into the room. "Don't back down from anyone, even for a second."

It was strange that he was saying such things when we were so safe in this kingdom, but I nodded anyway. I didn't need Mal to worry about me, especially not tonight. Still, my senses told me to be alert. To be strong.

It seemed the entire dining hall was already full by the time we arrived. The second Mal and I walked through the door, everyone stood up, silencing all conversations they had been having seconds before.

"Right this way," one of the guards whispered. He held his hand out, waving us to a long table that faced the rest of the room. There had to be hundreds of Paseocan fae sitting in the massive hall. Sparkling stone chandeliers hung from the ceiling, and the firelight flickered throughout, reflecting off the beautiful tapestries on the walls.

Carlyle already sat in the middle of the long, elevated

table. His eyes widened when he saw us. "Friends!" he started. "Come, sit!" That same, warm smile spread across his features.

We obliged, Mal leading me to the seats next to Carlyle. I sat beside him, Mal sitting next to me. The rest of the men arranged themselves around us, all of us facing out to the rest of Paseocan. The nervous tickle in my stomach grew as I looked at their faces, scanning for any signs of distaste or distrust. To my surprise, all I saw was interest.

Interest and something else—hope.

Carlyle held up his glass of wine. "Let me be the first to congratulate Malachi, my old friend, and Jade, the peacemaker, on their accomplishments over the last few months. They have managed to change the world as we know it, and in time, magic will flow through our lands like it did when the Saints walked among us."

The crowd cheered. Mal inched closer to me, his comforting heat radiating off his body as we continued to listen to Carlyle.

"I can honestly say no two people are more deserving of their rule. They have provided a stronghold in Rewyth after the death of the previous king." Silence thickened as Carlyle paused. "However, they have managed to come back even stronger than before. Even more powerful. And with the help of this one," Carlyle held his hand out. I placed my palm on his, and he raised our clasped hands to the air. Mal's hand fell onto my back, reminding me that he was there just in case I needed him. Always. "These two will rule the fae!"

Another chilling pause filled the air, one I thought

would never end, before someone in the back of the room began to cheer. And then the entire room erupted.

"Thank you," I said to Carlyle. "You and your people have been too generous."

"After the sacrifices you've made," he said quietly, "you deserve not a single ounce less than greatness."

Malachi lifted his glass next. "Thank you, Carlyle, and the rest of Paseocan, for being so welcoming to us. When Jade and I married not long ago, we had no idea she was destined for this life. We had no idea she was to become the peacemaker, chosen by the Saints to save us all from our own demise."

I glanced across the room to see everyone staring at Malachi in admiration.

"Today, we are here to announce that we have completed the peacemaker ritual. The Saints have spoken to Jade, have guided her to this moment, have given her the same power that they themselves once wielded. The Saints have released the hold they had on our powers, and we have proof that fae powers will be restored once more. No longer are the days when only a handful of fae and witches possess gifts. Now, every fae will possess some amount of magic."

Everyone in the room—including me—clapped for this. I fought back tears as my throat burned, a pride I had never felt before washed over me as I stared at Mal, his chin high and his shoulders back. In a room full of silver-winged fae, my husband held the power.

"Let us eat and celebrate!" Carlyle announced over the applause.

And that we did.

No longer affected so fiercely by the fae wine, I

drank. Some of the best food I had ever tasted was provided to us, and we all ate until we couldn't possibly eat any more. Malachi and I filled Carlyle in on everything that had happened under the mountain, including the trials. His empathy and warmth radiated from him as we told him of our losses and our struggles. He asked as many questions as he could, including how we possibly managed to escape the grasp of Silas, and we did our best to answer them.

I allowed Malachi to do the talking when it came to the Paragon and Silas, but he had no issues explaining every detail to Carlyle. Clearly, he did not feel the need to hold back.

And when we told him of the peacemaker ritual, when we told him of the Saints that spoke to me and of Adeline's magic, he could hardly contain his smile.

I didn't blame him. Adeline, and everyone else who would soon turn out similar to Adeline, created something great. They created a sense of hope, a sense that great things were coming to us.

"It seems that this tour of yours to visit the kingdoms is also one to see the magic that has breached the surface of our lands so far, is it not?" Carlyle asked.

I nodded. "That is part of our tour, yes. We are interested in seeing the fae's gifts and helping them control their magic in any way we can while we are here."

"Well," Carlyle said, wiping his mouth with his dinner cloth and pushing himself into a standing position. "It seems it is my turn to present you all with a gift."

"A gift?" I repeated.

"Trust me," Carlyle said, sending me a small wink, "this

is a gift you will like very much." He waved his hand, signaling something to the guards.

I took this moment to glance down both sides of the table, ensuring the rest of our crew was enjoying the feast as much as we were. Everyone seemed perfectly content, even Cordelia, who finished laughing at something Lucien had said.

Malachi's hand fell onto my thigh below the table, squeezing gently.

We watched as seven fae entered the room, lining up in front of our long table. They turned to face us, standing equal distance apart from each other.

"What's this?" Malachi asked.

"This," Carlyle announced, "is what you have come all this way to see. This is what you've done for us, Jade Weyland. This is magic being returned to our world, one by one."

The seven fae still looked at us, waiting.

"These fae have gifts now?" I guessed.

Carlyle nodded. "Would you like to show the King and Queen of Rewyth your new powers, ladies and gentlemen?"

The entire room was silent. My heart began to beat in my chest, loud enough that I was certain Malachi could hear it. His grip on my thigh tightened.

The fae on the far left, an older man with smaller silver wings, took one step forward. He finally looked up from the floor and met my gaze.

A lightness flickered there; one I knew all too well.

He held his hands out before him, and the entire room waited to see what type of power this man could wield, what type of gift he was blessed with from the Saints.

I nearly yelped in surprise when all of the wine in the room—including the wine in our glasses at our table—raised into the air. The man held it there, too, controlling the liquid with a big, knowing smile on his face, before he let the wine drop back into the glasses with an astonishing amount of control.

My jaw could have hit the floor.

Cheers and applause ripped through the room. The look of joy on the older man's face was worth the entire journey over here.

This was what we did this for—so fae who were otherwise normal could possess something special, something curated to them in a way that would create value we could not even comprehend yet. Who knows how many ways this man's power could be used? Who knows how many people could be helped with this gift, as minuscule as it might seem to some?

This would change lives forever. This would change…it would change *everything*.

Five more gifts were displayed to us, each one as unique and special as the last. Air magic, more water magic, and even the ability to move at shockingly quick speeds around the room.

But the best part was seeing the look on each of their faces. These were not power-hungry fae. These were not fae that held malice in their hearts, these were not fae who would use this new gift for evil. No, each of these fae would cherish these gifts with everything they possibly could. They would use these gifts for nothing but good, and the world would be a better place because of it.

I believed this with every ounce of my being.

Until the last fae stepped forward.

I felt the difference, like a storm rolling through the air around us. Even the look in this woman's eye glinted with something different, not the same sparkle of lightness that had been seen in the other fae's faces. A recognizable darkness lingered there, one of power and one of need.

I recognized it all too well.

Carlyle stiffened beside me. I only noticed it because we sat so close. Nobody else would have been able to tell how he tightly held onto his wine glass, much tighter than before.

"Nari," Carlyle started. "Please demonstrate your magnificent power to the leaders of Rewyth, the leaders who have given you the opportunity to possess such a gift."

Malachi stiffened next to me. Carlyle hadn't given an introduction like that to the other fae.

This one was different.

I sat up a little straighter in my seat. My own magic, that lightness and darkness that mixed together with the sense of Malachi's power, seemed to be on edge, too. It buzzed in my veins, creating the heat of anticipation that would have anyone reaching for their weapon.

We waited.

Even Cordelia leaned across the table, placing her elbows on the wooden surface as she focused intently on what we were about to witness.

The fae—with fierce, dark eyes and silver rings decorating her fingers—held her hands out. The fae beside her began to move, parallel to her own actions. It took me a second to realize truly what was happening.

She flicked her hand, and the fae standing beside her

stumbled forward, unable to stop. She raised her hand and he jumped, she lowered her hand and he dropped to the ground.

My breath nearly stopped. This was dangerous. It was wrong.

Nari's magic controlled his body entirely.

CHAPTER 13
Jade

I didn't hear Eli until he had already taken a seat on the chair across from me. He exhaled deeply as he sank into the fabric, his face lighting up by the lanterns scattering the room of the hall.

"You should be asleep," he said. "Everyone else sure is."

"Not you, though," I stated. I took a sip of my wine. After the events of the evening, I had snuck out of the room and found myself here, filling my own glass and doing anything to numb my thoughts. They were becoming too much to bear, too much to keep.

"No," Eli laughed. "Not me. I figured I would come talk to you while you were alone. You've been busy."

"Yes, I have. Is everything okay with you?"

Eli nodded, his eyes flickering across each of my features. It had been ages since I had spoken to Eli. Saints, I knew fae aged slowly, but Eli seemed to have grown by twenty years in the last few months. Those immature, boyish features were replaced with harsh lines of worry and strength.

And he looked exhausted, likely a mirror of myself.

"It's not me I'm worried about," Eli replied. "It's you."

I nearly spit out my wine, coughing once before I recovered from the shock. "I have to say, hearing Malachi's brothers worry about me still surprises me. It wasn't too long ago that I thought you all wanted to kill me."

Eli smiled softly and shook his head. "Yeah, we were all pretty ignorant back then. Especially Adonis and Lucien. They care, too, you know."

"I'll take your word for it," I replied. "I think what they really care about is my power. I'm sure you're all just waiting to see what powers you might possess yourselves."

"Yes," Eli responded, "but that doesn't make us care about your safety any less."

I met his eyes, only to find him staring intently back at me. "What makes you say this, Eli? What's changed?"

"Things have been different for a while now," Eli said. "When you two left to go with Silas to the Paragon's temple..." He paused, shaking his head. "We didn't know if you two would ever come back. That said a lot about Malachi's love for you, but it said even more about what you were willing to do for us. I mean, we weren't exactly *welcoming* when you first arrived in Rewyth."

I smiled as I remembered the first few interactions I had with them. Malachi's brothers had been fierce and intimidating and deadly, but now? They weren't my best friends, but they were there, always having my back. Ever since we returned to Rewyth from the temple, ever since Malachi and I had forced Seth's men to bow.

Before then, even. When we rushed into battle together.

Malachi's brothers had certainly had a change of heart.

"Well," I started. "After what you've been through, I think you deserve someone to fight for you, too."

Eli flinched, and my chest tightened. I had been so worried about myself and Malachi, it was easy to forget what everyone else in this kingdom had been through, too. Especially the rest of Malachi's family.

They had lost a father, too. They had lost a brother. They had, in many ways, lost Malachi at times.

And they were still here. Still standing. Still fighting. Even if that fight was fueled by anger, even if it was fueled by hatred at times, or by retribution, they fought.

And that meant something, even to me. Family wasn't supposed to be perfect. I knew more than anyone how cruel family could be at times.

This family was no different.

"Our powers will come soon," Eli said softly. "And when they do, I want you to know we're on your side. All of us. Even Lucien."

"Thank you," I replied. I took another sip of the wine. "Sometimes I feel like I've lost myself in the darkness somehow, like I've gone way too far to ever find myself again."

"Impossible," Eli said. "We've seen darkness, Jade. We've seen Malachi's darkness, we've seen the darkness in others, as well. You don't even come close."

I wanted to believe him, but he didn't know that dark voice in my mind. He didn't hear the dark thoughts I had, especially when I got the taste of power.

Sometimes I didn't recognize myself, didn't recognize my actions.

"You're doing it again," Eli interrupted my thoughts.

"Doing what again?"

"Getting lost in whatever world you've created in here," Eli said, tapping his temple with his finger. "You'll get lost in there if you keep doing that. Be here, Jade. With us."

"It's harder than it sounds."

"I know exactly how easy it is to allow yourself to fade off into those thoughts," Eli said. His voice hardened, laced with pain and grief. "But you can't. People need you, Jade. People need you now more than they ever have, and I'm not just talking about Malachi."

I stared at him, breathless. "That's a lot of pressure," I said honestly.

"It is," Eli stated. "And if anyone can handle it all, it's you, peacekeeper."

I took another drink of my wine, gulping the sweet liquid and letting it calm my nerves once again. Eli did the same with his own glass, and we sat like that for some time, reveling in the silence.

Those thoughts came back, dark and desperate, but I listened to Eli's advice and pushed them away. I didn't have time to wallow. I didn't have time to pity myself, to get lost in that darkness.

"When did you get so wise?" I said after a while.

Eli smiled half-heartedly. "I was a child before I lost Fynn, I can see that now. But that pain changed me, that grief made me realize what was really important in life."

"Yeah," I said. "I know the feeling."

Eli and Fynn were much closer than any of the other brothers. They were nearly as close as Tessa and me.

I knew what he felt more than anyone else here.

"I'm sorry, Jade," Eli said.

I snapped my eyes to him. "For what?"

"For not being able to protect your sister. We should have been there for her; we should have had her back when you weren't around." His voice cracked in hidden emotion.

I had to swallow back my own tears, feeling a new wave of grief that I had never expected to feel. Not for Tessa, though. For...for Malachi. For his family. For my fae friends who had also lost something that day Tessa died.

"I'm sorry, too," I replied. "For your brother. His death —" I stopped to clear my throat before continuing, "His death was not necessary, but it was courageous all the same."

Eli smiled, tears glistening in his eyes. "Thank you," he said. "I don't know how in the Saints you've managed to remain kind when you have lost so much, but thank you."

That was the final straw.

I let the tears I had been holding back fall freely, tumbling past my emotional barriers and down my face. I stood from my sofa and crossed the room to Eli, sitting next to him and throwing my arms around him. He stiffened at first, clearly surprised by my affection, but eventually returned the hug.

"We're family, now," I said as I tightened my arms around him. "It's time we start acting more like it."

He laughed against me and didn't let go. We stayed like that for a few minutes, until both of our tears and dried up, our grief fading to a low dull and morphing into something much deeper that connected us beyond words.

"Go get some sleep," Eli said, finally pulling out of my embrace. "Malachi will kill me if he thinks I kept you up all evening."

"Fine," I said. "But you know where to find me if you need me. I mean it, Eli."

"I know," he said with a smile.

I stood up and walked out of the common area, heading to the hallway where Malachi would be fast asleep, like everyone else.

But as I approached in the darkness, something made me pause. I still had my human vision, even if the rest of my senses seemed to be getting stronger. And something didn't feel right...

A hand shot out from the darkness and gripped my bicep, pulling me against the wall. I would have screamed if it weren't for a large, warm hand clamping over my mouth.

"Shhh," someone cooed. "It's just me, Adonis."

He removed his hand from my mouth.

"What are you doing?" I hissed. "Are you trying to scare the shit out of me?"

A silent beat passed.

"I heard what you said back there," Adonis whispered.

"Eavesdrop much?"

I thrashed my arm from his grip, and he easily let me go.

"I just wanted to say thank you," Adonis whispered. The words were kind, but his tone still held the fae harshness that he always carried with him. "For saying that to him. He's been hurting since we lost our brother, and...and the rest of us aren't as gentle as you are. So, thank you."

Wow. Was everyone losing their minds today? Or were the Weyland brothers simply learning to trust me after all this time?

I nodded. "You're welcome," I whispered. "He knows I'm here for him."

My eyes adjusted to the darkness of the hallway, just enough so I could see his jaw tightened as he stared at me, eyes like daggers piercing into my chest.

I glared back at him, not for a single second thinking about backing down. I began to move away from the wall in the direction of my bedroom when he stopped me again.

"He was telling the truth, you know. About us being on your side."

I kept moving, away from him and Eli and away from the darkness of the hallway, but I stopped for a second to turn over my shoulder. "I know he was."

CHAPTER 14
Malachi

Jade and Cordelia met with Adeline the next day to help teach her control over her fire magic. I was grateful for it, because it gave me a moment to speak with Carlyle alone.

The two of us walked along the outside of the castle, listening to the morning birds and the rest of the world beginning to wake up with the rising sun.

It was peaceful. It reminded me of Rewyth, of home.

"You weren't expecting that type of power to be shown yesterday," Carlyle started. It wasn't a question.

"No," I replied, clasping my hands behind my back as we continued to walk. "I wasn't. I can't say any of us were."

We took a few more steps in silence. Carlyle had always been a kind, gentle man, but he had his moments. Moments where he was hard to read, moments where I didn't quite know what he wanted from me.

"Carlyle," I started again after some time, "I trust that if there is something on your mind for either myself or my wife, you'll come to me with it. We've known each other for far too long to dance around the truth."

He laughed quietly. "That, I agree with."

"If there is something you worry about with her, or with magic returning to these lands…"

"It's not your wife that I worry about, my friend. I know that she is just as fierce as she is powerful, and her love for you and the fae has grown impeccably since my first introduction to her. I have no doubt that she acts with the best interests of us all in mind."

"Then what is your concern?" I asked. At least Jade was not the cause of his worry. That much alone allowed me to breathe a little deeper.

"My concern comes from the unknown. You and Jade are here now, your power is practically radiating off of you both. But what happens when you leave? What happens when my magic is not as powerful as the magic of my people? Will they overtake the throne? Will they use their power for evil?"

The stress in his words became audible. I knew that feeling well, the feeling of not knowing. Of having to hope that others are as pure as heart as you've thought them to be all this time.

When you give angry people power, they rise up. The trick is to ensure they are not angry. Never angry.

We stopped walking. I turned to face Carlyle, this man who I have known for so long. He was my longest ally, even if my father once disagreed.

Carlyle had done his best to help me, even when I did not deserve it. And he was standing before me now, needing my help.

I placed a hand on his shoulder so he would truly hear my words when I said, "We are here for you, Carlyle. You are the King of Paseocan for a reason. You did not become king because you were weak or powerless. Even if your magic never manifests, you will still be the rightful king. That throne is yours, Carlyle. You lead with grace and with truth, and that means more to the people than any gift of magic ever will."

He smiled. "Your words are kind, Malachi, but I can't say they are all true. These people have been waiting on magic for many, many decades. The hope they have now that they may possess some powerful gift..."

"It is good for them to hope."

"Yes, it is." He took a long breath, looking behind me into the sky for what seemed like many minutes. "I only wonder if too much hope will unsettle the balance."

"What balance?"

His green eyes met mine. "The people here who are poor and powerless will manifest magic of some sort. It may not be today, it may not be tomorrow, but it will happen. What happens when they decide they are tired of being poor? Of being stepped over?"

"That's what we are here to do," I assured him. "Jade and I are here to ensure they understand the consequences. Jade is the peacemaker, Carlyle. This is what she was born for."

"Well, it might take a little more than–" Carlyle's words were cut off by a loud, wailing siren that ripped through the air.

"What is that?"

Carlyle's eyes widened, he was already turning toward the direction of the front gates, pulling the sword sheathed at his hip. "That's the war siren," he explained. "We're being attacked."

CHAPTER 15
Malachi

"Attacked?" I yelled, running close after him. "Who would possibly be attacking you right now, Carlyle? Does Paseocan have enemies close by?"

He didn't slow down, not for a second. Other fae began to run toward the front gates, too, but we all stopped when we heard a few screams coming from inside the castle.

All of our attention slid from the gate of the kingdom to within. *Were our attackers already inside?*

Jade. I had to get to Jade.

I didn't wait for Carlyle. I sprinted ahead, shoving through the other men and women running inside and following that tether of magic in my soul, the one that tied me to her.

I had to get to her. She had to be okay.

My feet pulsed against the dirt pathway until it turned into the stone floor of the massive building, guiding me to her. She had to be inside somewhere, she would be with Adeline and Cordelia. They would protect her.

Who was I kidding? Jade didn't need anyone to protect her anymore. She was more than capable of eliminating anyone standing in her way.

Still, my heart ached to be near her, to know for sure that she was okay.

"What's going on?" Carlyle yelled behind me, following close on my heel. His voice was no longer the kind, gentle fae I had grown to know. He spoke with the commanding, chill-igniting voice of a king.

"They're in there!" someone yelled.

I snapped my attention around the room but saw nothing. "Where?" I yelled.

Another scream. Female. *Was it Adeline? Cordelia?*

My magic hissed with anticipation, waiting for me to command the movements. Waiting for me to make the first move.

And I would. Saints, I would end anyone who hurt them. *Any* of them.

Serefin ran into the room, almost knocking me over entirely. "Have you found them?" he yelled.

"No," I said, pushing forward. "This way, I can feel it."

Along with Carlyle, Serefin and I barged into the secondary dining hall of Carlyle's castle. Unlike the dining hall in Rewyth, this hall was dimly lit, separated by partially-built stone walls that looked as if they could fall at any minute.

And in the back of the room...

"Malachi," Jade called out, her voice low and smokey. I felt her, too, as she said those words. My power reacted to her like a wild animal on a leash, lapping at any signal we were getting from that magic connection.

"Jade, is everything okay?"

"Stay back, everyone!" Carlyle called out. "Leave the dining hall until I command otherwise!"

The lingering fae obeyed his order, bowing their heads as they ran past us and out of the room.

I didn't pay them any attention. My eyes were glued onto Jade. She faced me at the far end of the room, but one of the stone walls blocked my view from what she stared at. I could tell by the darkness in her eyes and the flare of her nostrils that it wasn't good. Not good at all.

I rounded the corner, finally meeting them where they stood, and stopped dead in my tracks.

"Jade," I said again, lower this time. "What's going on here?"

Carlyle froze beside me, and Serefin moved to wrap Adeline in his arms. It was then that I noticed Cordelia brushing herself off on the other side of Jade, clearly shaken up by something. That was very, very unlike her.

What happened here?

"Nari," Jade said, "would you like to explain this? Or shall I?"

The promise of death laced each word. And *damn*, it was sexy.

Nari stood with three other fae, all of them with their backs to the stone wall, rebellious defiance in their faces.

I knew that look. That was the look of a fighter, of a rule-breaker. Whatever they had done, it really seemed to piss Jade off.

"It isn't fair," Nari started. "We have all this magic now. We don't have to take orders from anyone, especially not this human."

Jade's power flared, not noticeable to anyone but me.

"Watch what you say," I warned. "That is the Queen."

"Not my queen," Nari replied.

"Think again," Jade replied before I could say anything, stepping forward with her hand out before her, ready to summon any power she could possibly need. "The four of you think you are smarter than this? The four of you think you can defy your king here? Rise up?"

"What do you care?" the fae next to Nari spat. He hadn't been one to show us his magic earlier, but now I wondered if there weren't more fae than we thought developing powers. "You aren't even part of this kingdom. You're not my leader."

Carlyle stiffened. "It doesn't matter who she is to this kingdom," Carlyle interrupted, anger and sharp emotion cutting the air. "She was chosen by the Saints, you fool. Hand-picked from every soul that walks among us now. Do you understand that?"

Jade stared at the fae, jaw set. He stared back.

"The four of them attacked Cordelia," she explained.

I snapped my attention from Jade to glance at the half-witch.

"I'm fine," Cordelia replied. "I wasn't expecting it, that's all."

Those bastards.

"Do you know why the Saints chose me?" Jade said, taking another step forward. She was dangerously close to them, now. Close enough that if one of them wanted to attack her, they easily could.

I took a half-step closer.

Did these idiots really think they could attack Cordelia?

Part of me was shocked that they managed to catch her off-guard, but the other part of me was royally pissed off that they would even try.

If they were willing to attempt such a thing when we were in the kingdom, what would they try when we left?

Jade gave me a knowing look. "I'm sorry, Carlyle," Jade started. "But I was given very clear instructions from the Saints."

Carlyle's mouth opened. "What are you saying?" he said. "These are my people, Jade. They will not try such foolishness again!"

Jade clenched her jaw, fighting with herself. I knew the choice she had to make.

Let them live and risk more of an uprising, or eliminate the threat.

She closed her eyes and took a breath. I came to recognize that was what she did when the Saints were speaking to her mind. She was focusing on them, talking to the Saints we could not see.

They would be the ones making the choice. Not her. At least, I prayed that would be the case. Bloody hands came with a price.

One I never wanted her to pay.

"Malachi," Jade pleaded. I stepped forward with a hand on her lower back, letting her know I was there. "They hurt her," she whispered. "This has to happen."

"I know it does," I replied. The four rebels on the wall began to squirm, began to realize what they were facing. They were looking death in the eyes.

They had been all along. Their flaw was underestimating her.

A human girl, I'm sure they thought. *What would she possibly do to stop them?*

"Do it," I pushed.

Carlyle moved behind us, but Serefin stopped him with a drawn sword. "Don't move," Serefin ordered. "You know this is right. Let her do what needs to be done."

Jade brought her other hand out, spreading her attention across all four.

"No," Nari begged. "No, this is all a mistake. We didn't mean to attack the witch, we swear! We were simply testing our–" Her words were cut off with a painful scream.

The four of them screeched in pain, pressing themselves as deep as possible into that stone wall behind them.

"The peace must remain," Jade said slowly, her voice void of all emotions. "Above all, the peace must remain."

The light that radiated from her was not one of tranquility, but one of viscous poison. The tendrils did not flow freely into the air like I had seen them do before, but rather pierced so fiercely around the room, I almost flinched away before I saw them encapsulate the four screaming fae.

Carlyle yelled something behind us, but I could not make it out. I was too busy focusing on my wife. My powerful, justice-seeking wife.

When the light disappeared, Jade dropped her arms.

The four fae slumped to the ground. All dead.

My own power twisted in delight within me, clearly pleased with the outcome. Clearly rooting for this death.

Jade breathed heavily beside me. "It had to be done," she said.

"Yes," I said, rubbing my hand up her back. "It did."

"If you wouldn't have done it, I sure as shit would have," Cordelia said, stepping forward.

Carlyle stood there, staring at the four bodies. I took half a step in front of Jade as we all turned to face him, waiting for his reaction. Surely, he would understand. Surely, he would take her side.

It was the Saints will, after all. Not hers.

"I'm sorry for the mess," Jade said.

A flash of an emotion crossed Carlyle's features, his hands tightening in fists for half of a second, before he retained his calm demeanor. "No need to apologize," Carlyle said. "If you say it had to be done, then it had to be done."

Jade nodded, though I could see the tenseness still lingering in her body.

"That is quite a power you have," Carlyle stated through gritted teeth. "You really have been gifted."

I could tell he wanted to say more, but he refrained.

"Yes," Jade replied, so quietly we could barely hear her. She turned to give the bodies one more look as she said, "It is quite a gift, indeed."

"Come on," I started. "We should get out of here. I'm sure Carlyle needs to address his people and explain this little...situation."

I began to guide Jade out of the dining hall, away from the death she had just brought on. Away from Carlyle and from anyone else who might judge her, who might not understand her.

"I had to do it," Jade said again, only to me. Her voice sounded strong, strong enough that I wondered if she was trying to convince herself that she had to.

Only when we exited the dining hall and entered into the stone courtyard of the castle, we froze. A large crowd of fae had gathered, at least a hundred of them, all looking at us expectantly. Some looked in fear. Some looked in anger. Most looked in confusion.

"Is everything okay?" one of the fae asked. "We heard screaming."

There was no use lying to them, they would find out soon enough. I took a deep breath, preparing for the chaos that would surely follow the truth.

Only Jade beat me to it.

"Your friends are dead," she shouted. Gasps rang through the air, murmurs began in the back of the crowd.

Shit.

Jade lifted her chin and looked out amongst the fae of Paseocan.

"I suppose I should introduce myself to you all personally," she started. She took half a step forward, placing herself in front of me. "My name is Jade Weyland, wife to Malachi Weyland and Queen of Rewyth. I was chosen by the Saints to be the peacemaker. For a long time, I wasn't quite sure what that meant. I was confused and angry by this fate, especially considering I was not fae. I was simply a human."

Fae stared at her in awe. Me included. The others stepped out of the dining hall, too, but halted when they saw Jade speaking.

A dark, electrifying feeling washed over me, from the bottoms of my feet up through the back of my neck.

"Kneel," Jade ordered to the fae around us. The crowd did not kneel. They took the next few seconds to look around, watching for who would first submit. And not submitting was a damn mistake. "Kneel or die!" Jade said again, her voice a roar of thunder through Paseocan.

Denying her was death.

Every feral part of my existence begged me to submit, to obey. So I did. My knees hit the ground as I bowed before my queen.

As did every other fae in the courtyard, Carlyle included.

Jade stepped around, surveying the group of fae before her. Her feet clicking against the stone of the courtyard became the only sound. No more murmuring. No more second-guessing her rule.

"I do not wish to command you in your own kingdom," Jade announced, her voice softer but still laced with a deadly force, "but make no mistake, I will eliminate any threat. The Saints command my hand, and if they see you as a threat, you will die. If you stand against me, if you stand against my husband," she reached down and pulled me up from my kneeling position. Even my instincts fought against it, but I stood beside my wife as she added, "you will die."

And damn, every single fae in Paseocan felt that truth.

CHAPTER 16
Jade

"You kicked ass back there!" Eli cheered, bringing his black stallion back to ride beside Mal and me. After the incident in Paseocan, we said goodbye to Carlyle and took our leave, deciding we had done more than enough damage.

I gave Eli a soft smile. "Thanks, but I don't think the entire kingdom of Paseocan would agree with you."

Eli shook off my words. "I disagree. Do you know how safe you probably made them feel? They know you'll end anyone who tries to step out of place, Jade. There won't be any bullies, any power-hungry bastards trying to take over. You saved them."

That was one way of looking at it.

I didn't object when Malachi packed our bags and insisted we leave right away. If anything, I felt uneasy.

But it wasn't because I had just killed four fae. And that scared me—the fact that I wasn't even slightly shaken by it. Rather, it gave me such a rush of power, I wasn't sure I would be able to pull back. Malachi's hand on me was the one thing that reminded me of where I was, of who I was supposed to be.

The peacemaker. Not a killer. Not seeking revenge, but seeking justice.

Your thoughts are loud, Erebus spoke in my mind.

I stiffened immediately, hoping Malachi didn't notice.

So are yours, I thought back.

You did nothing wrong, Erebus replied. *The boy is right. Death suited them. You're worrying your king.*

Why do you care about my king? I mentally snapped back. *Besides, he always worries.*

A dark wave of emotion washed over my body, coming from the origin of that voice.

Damn Erebus.

Eli's horse trotted ahead with the others, leaving Malachi and I, once again, in the back of the group. I noted the way Mal pulled back on the reins, slightly enough where the others wouldn't notice, but enough to where we could have our own privacy.

"You're worried about me," I stated when we were far enough behind the others.

"You're my wife," Mal replied, his voice steady. "I think I have a right to worry."

"Maybe, but you shouldn't. I swear to you, I'm fine."

Mal took a long breath; I felt his chest rise and fall behind me in the saddle. "I know death, Jade. You may not remember, but they called me the Prince of Shadows for a reason. You don't need to hide from me."

I did, though, because how was I supposed to tell him that I was a monster? That I was no longer the innocent human he met who wanted nothing to do with death?

Erebus's laughter echoed in my mind.

"It should have scared me," I said eventually, giving him half a truth. Half was better than none. Half was a step in the right direction, a step to truth. "It should have terrified me, even. I should have been vomiting from the adrenaline and running for the hills."

Mal's hand slid up my arm. "Death should not frighten you," he whispered. "Especially when it is so deserved."

I shook my head. "That's easy for you to say," I replied. "You had hundreds of years to discover who you really are. You're good, Mal. I see it every day. But me? I don't know who the Saints want me to be. On one hand, Anastasia seems to really believe in peace. But then Erebus says things entirely different, and I feel like I'm losing my mind."

"I can tell you one thing," Mal replied. "Watching them bow to you was nothing less than chilling. You commanded everyone, including me, with such force, Jade. I've never seen anything like it."

I brushed him off. "Yeah, well that's hardly saving anyone."

"I think my brother was right. You saved a lot more people than you killed back there, Jade. They will never forget what you did. Carlyle included."

I couldn't keep my laughter back. Carlyle had been terrified as we walked out of his kingdom. He might not have said it, but I could see it in the way he looked at me. That warm smile had a wall built before it. Those eyes had a hint of wariness. It was natural, like a self-preserving instinct that you couldn't deny.

But I saw it in Carlyle, just like I saw it in every damn fae we passed as we left his kingdom.

Two days and two nights passed. I spent my time riding on Malachi's horse, nested safely between his legs, as the crew pushed forward to the next kingdom. The Saints did not speak to me during our travels, although half the time, I craved a little entertainment from their familiar voices.

The nights were cold. Without another inn or a castle to sleep in, we only had each other and a small fire to keep us warm.

Thankfully, we didn't need to fear the deadlings in the thick of the forest. Ever since we had eliminated Silas, the deadlings hadn't been a problem. Cordelia must have been right; Silas was the one controlling them. Without them, they would have no need to attack. No reason to cause chaos.

Hopefully, as time went on, they would grow extinct altogether. *We could only hope.*

On the third day, I was damn exhausted. Exhausted enough that when my instincts told me something wasn't right, I ignored them.

We were just beginning to re-pack our horses from the night, the sun just beginning to filter over the horizon as the world began to wake.

"Did you hear that?" Lucien asked, looking up from the dried meat he ripped apart with his teeth.

"Hear what?" I replied. Granted, I should have been more alert. After the vague warning about rebels at the inn, we all should have been.

But nobody seemed to pay any attention. Nobody

cared at all, really, as Lucien brought up his concerns.

He stared off into the forest around us. "I don't know," he said. "I thought I heard something."

"You're paranoid, brother," Adonis said, walking up and clapping Lucien on the shoulder. "We're all exhausted. You're probably hearing things."

"Yeah," Lucien said, though he didn't sound convinced. "You're right."

I brushed it off, too, walking over to Malachi who was stroking his white stallion. He had been nothing but supportive and affectionate over the last few days, and damn if I didn't want to get him alone as quickly as possible. I snuck up behind him and slid my hands up his back, narrowly avoiding the base of his black, leathery wings.

He hissed in surprise, but immediately relaxed.

"Aren't your terrifying fae senses supposed to alert you when an attacker comes up from behind?" I teased, kissing his shoulder.

"Mmmm," he hummed. "Maybe they did. Maybe they knew you were there all along." He twisted in my arms to face me.

"I don't know," I replied. "What was that you said about having sensitive wings?" I ran my hands across his back again, closer this time.

He stiffened, shuddering lightly at my touch. "Careful," he purred. "I don't think you want to do that again when so many people are watching."

His voice dripped in heat, and I felt it deep in my body. We hadn't had alone time since Paseocan, and we had been so exhausted then, it hardly mattered.

We were still exhausted.

"Get ready to go," Cordelia yelled. "If I have to spend a single extra second in this forest with you all, I might not make it to Trithen alive."

We rolled our eyes and ignored her.

"Ladies first," Malachi said, motioning to the horse. I gave him a tight nod and took his assistance, lifting myself up and onto the saddle.

He followed soon after, and we fell into that familiar habit that now fit us so perfectly. Malachi held the reins, I rested against him, and together, we were ready to make the final leg of the trip.

At least, I *thought* we were ready.

What I didn't know, though, was the fact that we were being watched.

The wind around us picked up, swirling together and picking up the loose leaves, blowing the trees and the branches until the silent air around us roared to life.

At first, we didn't think anything of it. But our horse began to rear, and it took Malachi half-flying us into the air to stay in the saddle.

"What is that?" Adonis yelled over the roar. I barely heard him. "Who's out there?"

"I knew I heard something!" Lucien yelled.

The ones that weren't on horses ducked, shielding their faces from the spiraling wind.

Adrenaline cut through my exhaustion, especially when that voice in my mind said, *You have a visitor.*

The wind continued, pulsing and pushing until not even Malachi's expanded wings could keep us shielded from the flying debris. Our horse panicked beneath us, and within the next few moments, we were thrown off its back entirely. Malachi's wings saved us from hitting the ground too hard, but we still remained helpless in the dirt, waiting for the windstorm to pass.

And when I thought we were going to be entirely blown away along with the trees surrounding us, it all stopped.

One second, we were being pulled into a tornado of wind, and the next second, nothing.

Not even a light breeze.

"Everyone okay?" Malachi asked, tucking his wings back into his shoulders.

A few grunted a response, but nobody spoke. Everyone felt what I felt—the pricking feeling of being watched.

"Who's out there?" I yelled to the forest. "Show yourself."

My hand fell onto my hip where my dagger was strapped. Not that I would need it.

"Relax," a young woman's voice purred. Slight rustling to my right, just behind the tree line, caught my attention. "There's no need for weapons. Don't you agree, peacemaker?"

I squinted until the woman stepped forward. She was maybe my height, and looked to be no older than myself. She wore tight black clothing and thick charcoal lined her piercing green eyes.

And what surprised me the most was the fact that she didn't have wings.

A witch.

"I would agree with you, but it seems you've already deployed your own weapon." I motioned to the settled wind around us. "Who are you?" I asked. "What do you want?"

The woman stepped out further, but immediately stopped when her eyes slid over to Cordelia.

"Lenova?" Cordelia asked. "Is that you?"

"Saints," the witch—Lenova—whispered. "Cordelia?"

A few other rustling sounds in the forest behind Lenova had me reaching for my dagger once again. Malachi did the same beside me, even moving slightly so his body shielded mine. More witches—from what I guessed—stepped out onto the path.

An entire group of them.

"What's going on?" I asked again, ignoring the fact that they somehow knew Cordelia.

Cordelia didn't move, though. Not until the entire group was visible, sizing us up like they had been stalking us all along. I didn't like it.

I didn't like it one bit.

Malachi's power rolled in my body, alerting me to his same level of unease. Witches would be even more powerful now if magic had been unleashed. Esther and Cordelia had some levels of magic, yes, but as Esther had explained to me long ago, it was harder and harder for witches to conjure their powers. Many were too weak since the Saints took the magic of the world with them.

But not all.

"Jade," Cordelia spoke first, not taking her eyes off the witches that now half-surrounded us. "These are Sisters of Starfall."

"You know each other?" Malachi asked.

Cordelia's jaw tightened. "We all lived together for some time," she explained. "This was my old coven."

Out of the corner of my eye, I saw Lucien inch closer. He had been doing that lately, finding himself closer to her when danger was near. I noticed it in Paseocan, and ever since Cordelia had been attacked by those fae and their new magic, he had barely left her side.

Cordelia was powerful, one of the strongest witches in existence according to Esther.

But her old coven?

Dozens of questions began circulating in my mind.

"Well," I started. "Any ideas on why your coven has us surrounded right now, mysteriously coming out of the forest unannounced after invoking a massive windstorm?"

"*Old* coven," Lenova corrected. "We haven't seen Cordelia in years. Saints, we thought you were dead."

"Aw, come on," Cordelia replied, her regular, snarky attitude coming back to life. "You can't get rid of me that easily. Although I'm sure you would all throw a party over my death, anyway."

One of the witches standing behind Lenova sauntered forward, brushing her shoulder as she approached Cordelia. "And it would have been a damn good party."

All of my senses lit up as she stepped out of the forest and threw her arms around Cordelia, surprising me and everyone else in our group as she pulled Cordelia into a tight hug.

Cordelia hugging someone? This was all much, much too strange.

"If we would have known a witch was traveling with the peacemaker, we would have found you all a long time ago.

At least we know someone's around to keep them safe, right?"

The witch pulled away from Cordelia. They all laughed, and I finally found myself relaxing. Maybe they weren't going to attempt to kill us all on the spot.

Not Cordelia, at least.

"Want to tell us what you're all doing out here? If you wanted to see us, you could have made the trip to Rewyth," Cordelia replied.

"We heard the fae had been picking up a few stray witches. Didn't take you as the type to follow someone else's orders, though, I have to admit."

Cordliea laughed again, sending me half a glance over her shoulder.

"Okay," Mal said, his king-voice on full volume. "Someone can tell me what's going on here before I start to get pissed off."

"Calm down, king," Lenova said. "We're here for your wife, not you."

Mal stiffened. "As if that makes a difference to me, *witch*."

"Everyone can relax," Cordelia interrupted. "This coven travels through the forest frequently, like nomads. Isn't that right?"

A few of the witches nodded. "We can't say running into you all was truly an accident, though," Lenova explained. "Especially since you opened the gates of magic back to our lands."

"So?" I asked, hating how defensive I sounded. "What do you want from me, then?"

"It's not what we want from you," she replied. "It's what we want to give you."

"Really?" Malachi responded, sarcasm dripping from his voice. "And what might that be?"

Each one of the witches stood a little taller. I noticed the way a few of them even lifted their chins as Lenova replied, "Our loyalty."

"Are we supposed to believe that?" Malachi hissed. We had congregated without the witches, far enough away to get a small ounce of privacy. "Because I can't say I've grown very trusting of witches lately. And they're clearly powerful."

"What's not to trust?" Lucien replied. "If they wanted your wife dead, they would have killed her already."

"I'd like to see them try," I replied.

Adeline linked her arm through mine. "Why did Cordelia leave the coven, anyway? Aren't witches tight about bonds like that? There's got to be some big reason."

We all glanced to where the witches gathered, now talking in hushed voices with Cordelia.

"I don't see any harm in it for now," I said. "If they want to join us and follow us back to Rewyth, we might as well let them."

"You're too trusting," Adonis spoke up. "You always have been, Jade. No offense. Jade is the most powerful person in our realm." He turned to the others. "We can't risk it."

Everyone thought on these words. "Adeline?" I asked.

She squinted in thought. "I can't say I'm a big fan of Cordelia," she answered honestly, "but she's protected you before. If she trusts these witches, I think it's safe. As much as I hate to say it."

She was right. If these witches wanted to become loyal to me and join us on our journey, we shouldn't get in their way. This was the new world, anyway. The new age. We were supposed to be combining forces and making peace with our enemies all across the world.

Perhaps this was a start.

"Alright," I announced, breaking away from our group and walking over to the witches. "You're welcome to join us. But I have one condition."

The witches waited.

"No violence. No more rivalry with the fae. If your coven wants to join us, that's fine. But we become one. We do this together, and we do this as a team. Everyone. Is that clear?"

Lenova stepped forward, holding her hand out to me. "Our coven is yours, peacemaker." She wore a small smirk on her lips, but the words were genuine. A small tickle of my power in my stomach confirmed she was telling the truth.

"Well then," I said, holding out my hand. "We better get moving. We've got a busy day ahead of us."

Lenova clasped her arm around mine, grabbing hold of my forearm. Her smirk spread to a smile. "Yes, we do."

CHAPTER 17
Malachi

The day passed quicker than the others, likely because we finally had some new entertainment. The sun fell quickly, and before we knew it, we were gathered around the fire.

Rewyth's crew on one side, the witches' coven on the other.

Jade sat across from me, speaking to Adeline about something I could hardly hear.

"We can help you, you know," a new voice made me jump. It was Lenova, the leader of this new coven. She hadn't said so, but I could tell based on how she spoke to the others. They respected her. They looked up to her.

"Help me with what?" I said. I kept my gaze straight ahead into the fire, but I could feel her looking at me from the corner of my eye as she laughed quietly.

"Look," she started, settling into the log beside me. She matched my posture, resting her forearms on her knees as she, too, turned her attention to the fire. "Cordelia tells me you're the descendent of Erebus, the Saint of death. It's no secret that you have a dark power," she pushed, dropping her voice so low that only I could hear. "But I think we both know you have a lot of untapped potential."

Was she kidding?

"You know nothing about me," I retorted. "What makes you say that?"

"You may be a very powerful fae, but you haven't studied the power of the Saints like we have."

"You have no idea what I've studied, *witch*. I learned with the very best from the Paragon. Are you telling me you know more about the Saints than the Paragon?"

"I'm not saying anything," the witch replied. Her calmness only agitated me further. "But if you want to become as strong as you possibly can, I think you might want our help."

"And what could you possibly help me with?"

"You have the power of death," Lonova replied. "Just like your wife now has, thanks to the Saints. Don't you want to explore your magic connection? Push the limits?"

"I've had no problem with limitations on my magic in the past," I spat. "I don't think it will be an issue now."

"Maybe not," she whispered. "But if I were you, I'd be doing everything in my power to make sure nobody could ever hurt the people I love. You were connected for a reason, you know. You were practically born to protect her. Do you feel confident that you could do that? What if another coven of witches decides to harm her? Could you stop an entire coven?"

Yeah, this witch pissed me off.

"Are you suggesting I cannot protect my own wife?"

"I'm suggesting the fact that you are one of the

strongest fae in existence, King of Shadows. That is all. If you don't want my help, that's fine. I was simply offering."

"Fine, then," I spat.

"Fine," Lenova replied.

We stayed that way for a while, listening to the low buzz of the conversations around us mixing with the crackling of the fire ahead.

I knew I was powerful. I wielded *death*. I was, after all, Erebus's descendent. I didn't need any help protecting Jade.

Right?

On the other hand, if this witch was offering me something, I should accept it. She was just as annoying as Cordelia, but at least she couldn't read my thoughts. Not yet, anyway. I wasn't sure what would happen when the new wave of magic reached the coven.

No. We had everything figured out. We didn't need her help. I shouldn't even be trusting her, anyway. We barely knew her, and we barely knew what this coven wanted from us.

"A world full of magic," she said to herself. "Do you wonder what it will look like when it's restored to its full capacity?"

I settled my attention on my sister, who now conjured a small ball of fire in her palms while Jade cheered her on.

Something in my chest lit up at the sight. Adeline was a pure example of what this magic could do for people. Adeline had been powerless at times. My father—who I thought was my father—had used her time and time again, simply in different ways than he had used me.

Adeline was a sweet, caring sister on the surface. But

below the surface? She had been hurt just as much as any of us.

This gave her the chance to fight back.

"If it's done right," I replied, "it will be the best thing to ever happen to us."

"And if it's done wrong?" the witch asked.

I slid my gaze over to Jade, whose smile practically lit up her entire face as she laughed with Adeline. "Then I fear we'll have nothing left to save."

※

Our trip to Trithen was swift. Good, because any unrest in that horrific kingdom would have put us all over the edge, especially Eli.

None of us enjoyed going back there.

Some of the fae we recognized from that day in Rewyth, the same day we killed Seth. The same day Jade declared herself the strongest person in the entire kingdom, in *any* kingdom. The day our enemies, these fae of Trithen, decided to bow.

But not everyone saw her that day in Rewyth. Most of Trithen, in fact, had been living in ignorance since Seth had been killed. His court had heard the news, I made sure of it, along with clear instructions on what to do now that Trithen was under Rewyth's rule.

Our rule.

Still, a quick appearance in their kingdom and a small display of Jade's powers was enough to put them all in their place.

I silently thanked the Saints for that, too, because I was

absolutely exhausted. We had a handful of kingdoms left, but the dreaded part of our journey was over.

"That went surprisingly well," Jade said. It had been hours since we left Trithen, and the terrain of the thick forest was finally beginning to thin out.

"Don't sound too surprised," I replied. "You're only the most terrifying person in the world."

She leaned into me more, resting her hands on the tops of my thighs as I held the reins of the horse.

"That's a lot coming from you," she said. "I think everyone in that damn kingdom avoided you the minute they saw your wings."

I flared my black wings to the side for emphasis. "These black wings?" I teased, tickling her neck with my breath from behind.

She smiled. "Those would be them."

"Next time you talk to Erebus, tell him he could make these a little bigger. That way I would be strong enough to transport us anywhere I wanted to without these damn horses."

"Right," Jade laughed. "Because the Saint of death is very open to suggestions."

We rode in silence for a few more minutes until she said, "I talked to Lenova."

"I'm sure that was delightful," I joked. "Almost as delightful as talking to Cordelia, I'm sure."

"She told me you have more power than you realize. And that she told you this and offered to help you."

Damn, I really hated witches.

"Is that so?"

Jade nodded. "She also said you declined this offer with little to no explanation as to why."

"Hmmm."

"Care to explain to me why you wouldn't want to strengthen your power? Your death power, I might add?"

I let out a long breath. "I'm not sure how much more my power can strengthen. It already kills when I need it to. Is that not enough?" The words even felt false coming out of my mouth. Yes, my power could kill. Yes, my power was strong. It gave me an edge. It forced me to be feared, forced me to become a deadly force on the battlefield time and time again.

But deep down, I could feel it. I could feel the untapped potential. I could feel the extra surge of death that wanted to escape so often.

And these days, especially being around Jade, the need for death seemed to keep growing.

"You're holding back," she said, interrupting my thoughts. "That's not very King of Shadows of you. The Malachi I married wouldn't dare to hold back."

"If it meant protecting people, he might."

"How do you know it's protecting anyone?" she asked. "If you never try, you'll never know."

I shook my head. My power had done more bad than good in the world. It had killed and killed and killed. At the time, of course, I thought that was the right thing. During war, when my father would use me as his own weapon, I relished the way my power could take out hundreds on the battlefield.

It felt damn good at the time. The power. The control. I loved it all. It's what made me a king.

But now? With Jade? I became more and more aware of every kill. I had blood on my hands, yes, but I was trying to stop the blood from transferring to hers. Our magic connection now could not be denied. We were tied together for eternity, and Jade was not a killer.

If I had untapped potential, it wasn't going to be used for good.

I had to control myself. I had to control the death, the killing, the darkness. I had to shove it away, somewhere deep, deep down, so Jade couldn't see it. Couldn't sense it.

But damn. When Jade had her moments of darkness, it took everything in me not to fall to my knees and worship her. She was not the same kind of darkness I was. She was... she was a force. She wielded power like she had done it all her life, a stark contrast to the Jade I knew before.

She was a goddess, wielding death like it belonged to her, like she was the reaper.

Jade ran a hand up my arm, pulling me from my thoughts. Her eyebrows furrowed in question.

"Fine," I said. "If it'll make you feel better, I'll try to wield more of my magic. But if I end up killing more people, I stop."

Her eyes lit up. "Deal," she said. "And you won't kill anyone. I'll make sure of it."

The next few hours became a blur of traveling like every day before. Only, the promise of death grew thicker with every minute, and each of my primal senses buzzed with the thick anticipation of darkness.

CHAPTER 18
Jade

Three days later, screaming pulled me out of my sleep and had me reaching for my dagger before the sun had risen.

Malachi moved before me—jumping to his feet and scanning the camp around us.

We found the source of the scream within seconds, and my heart sank as soon as I saw it.

It was Eli, Malachi's youngest brother.

We all jumped into action, running to where he slept on the forest floor. "Eli!" Malachi yelled. Adonis and Lucien met him there, the three brothers crashing to their knees beside him.

"Nightmare?" I asked Adeline as she ran to my side.

Her breathing came heavy. "I don't know, that's got to be some nightmare."

Cordelia walked up to the other side of us but said nothing. Eli thrashed and thrashed on the ground, even as his brothers tried to pin him down. He was screaming something, but it was hardly audible.

"No!" Eli yelled, evidently in his sleep. "No!"

"Wake up, Eli!" Adonis yelled, trying to hold his head still. "You're having a bad dream!"

"Don't do this!" Eli yelled again.

I wrapped my arm through Adeline's. Her body grew stiff and rigid as she stared at her brother. We were all thinking the same thing: *Eli was probably dreaming of Fynn.*

His dead brother.

Cordelia stepped forward and knelt with the brothers, staring down at Eli who still thrashed against their grasps with his eyes closed.

"Get away from him!" Adonis yelled.

"Let her help," Lucien growled in response.

Cordelia ignored all of them, leaning over Eli and gripping his chin with her hand. She said nothing, but Eli stilled immediately.

Cordelia's eyes grew wide. I even thought I heard her inhale sharply.

Eli's eyes shot open.

"Eli?" Malachi asked. I felt his worry inside of my own chest, thick and desperate as it so often was. He cared so deeply for his brothers, especially Eli. Over the last few months, their bond had grown more than I ever thought possible.

Even if it was hard to understand at times.

But I felt his pain now, his fear for his brother.

Eli gasped for air as he stared at Cordelia, their eyes locked in a hidden communication.

"What's going on?" Adeline asked from beside me.

A beat of silence passed.

Two beats.

Three.

Cordelia answered without looking away from Eli's wild gaze. "Eli's power has awoken. The Saints are showing him our future."

⁂

We sat around the fire as Lucien skinned a rabbit for us to eat. Eli had taken a while to gather his thoughts, but still said nothing about what had made him scream. Even as Malachi and his brothers pushed for answers. Even as Cordelia refused to give us any information.

She had seen whatever was going on in his mind. That much we knew. Whatever she saw, it was bad enough to make her shut up for once.

We all stared at Eli as he cleared his throat. He glanced to Cordelia for confirmation, who sat silently next to Lucien on the other side of the fire. She nodded.

"I thought it was a nightmare at first," Eli started, his voice hoarse and raw from screaming. My chest tightened.

Malachi slid his hand into mine.

"But it felt so real, and it looked...it looked just like this," he continued, holding his hands out and signaling to the forest around us.

"What did you see?" Adeline asked.

He met her gaze. "Death. A lot of it. Fighting. Magic everywhere, some good and some bad."

I tried not to show my shock.

"You saw us fighting?" Adonis asked.

"Yes." Eli took a shaking breath. "But I only recognized us. The others were strangers."

"Could it be the rebels?" Malachi asked. "Would the Saints want to warn you of a rebel attack?"

Eli shrugged. "It's possible. It all happened so quickly, like a sky-view of everything happening in fast-motion. I only saw..." He stopped himself before he finished.

"Saw what?" Mal asked. The sinking feeling in my stomach told me he already knew what he saw.

Eli's eyes slid to mine, and I saw nearly every emotion written in his face. He saw *me*. He saw me fighting. He saw me surrounded by death.

"It's okay, Eli," I assured him, trying to keep my voice steady. "You can tell us."

Cordelia cut in from the other side of the fire. "I think that's enough for now," she interrupted. "We should let Eli rest. Who knows when he'll get another vision?"

She wasn't meeting my gaze, either.

Strange. Even for her.

"Right," Malachi said. "We'll pass the human kingdoms in the next day, and we'll be back in Rewyth before we know it. We can deal with all of this then."

Eli nodded, glancing once more at Cordelia. They knew something else. They had seen something else in Eli's mind, in the vision from the Saints. Whatever it was, they didn't want us to know. The pit in my stomach told me it was *me* they wanted to hide it from.

But pushing them wasn't going to help, either.

I decided to change the subject.

"We're stopping by the human kingdoms?" I asked.

The sound of *human kingdoms* alone sounded foreign falling off my tongue. Kingdom was not the right word for where the humans lived. Granted, I had only ever been to my own home and the small, makeshift town of Fearford. But those two places had been proof enough—the humans all lived in poverty. Against the fae, they had nothing.

"We'll make our appearance, and we'll leave. We won't stay long. I doubt the humans have gotten any magic from the Saints, so we'll announce our reign and we'll be on our way."

"Doesn't that break the treaty? Humans and fae are not supposed to cross into each other's lands."

Malachi shrugged. "Silas and the Paragon were the ones who made those rules. We won't do any harm, I can promise you that."

I nodded, suddenly feeling sick. Malachi would never want to harm the humans, but after Eli's vision...

"Okay," I said. "As long as we're home soon."

The others began to stand from the fire. Malachi slid his arm over my shoulder, tucking me to his side. "I'll never get tired of you calling our kingdom your home."

I took a long breath. "It's funny," I started. "I dreaded going there when I first married you. Now I can't wait to get back."

He pressed a gentle kiss onto my forehead. "We'll be home soon enough, my queen. This will all be over and we can finally relax."

Over. My stomach flipped at the thought. All the fighting, all the death. It would all come to an end soon.

I closed my eyes, taking in the smoky pine scent that

was so, uniquely Malachi. *He* was my home. *He* was my peace.

As long as I didn't let darkness take over, this would all be over soon. I felt it deep in my bones, that the end was coming.

Although the warning from the Saints played repeatedly in my mind as I tried to imagine a peaceful future with Mal.

He will be your downfall.

CHAPTER 19
Malachi

Of all the fae kingdoms we had visited, I was more nervous about the humans. *What a joke.*

It's not that I feared their power. We outnumbered any witch they may have been harboring. They wouldn't have the speed or the strength of the fae. Any fight they started against us would result in their death, I knew that. I was confident in that.

But my heart sank every time I thought of Jade visiting the humans. She wasn't exactly human anymore, although she wasn't a fae, either. She was something else, something in between yet more powerful than any of us.

She didn't belong to them anymore, but they wouldn't see her that way.

"I can feel your worry," Jade whispered. "And while I appreciate the sentiment, it's not necessary."

I stiffened behind her. "They won't like us entering their land," I reminded her. "They might try to fight."

"They won't fight," she said. "Not unless they're truly stupid. They know we'll kill any one of them who tries."

Fearford was now only half an hour away, we would be there before the sun fell. Memories would hit us like punches as soon as we arrived.

Memories of my mother. Of Isaiah. Of Sadie.

Saints.

The crueler version of me had done those things, had killed Isaiah. Had banished Sadie. But I would do it all again if it meant keeping my wife safe.

"You don't need to worry about me going back there," Jade said. "I'm not the same person I was the last time we were in Fearford."

"No," I agreed. "You most certainly are not."

"And I'm no longer the ignorant fool who will trust any human who shows them kindness." Harshness laced her words. She spoke of Isaiah.

"You're trusting. That's not always a flaw, you know. It's one of the things I admire most about you."

"That's a shame," she said with a sigh, "because I'm trying to be less trusting."

We rode in silence for a few minutes.

"Do you think she made it back here?" Jade asked.

Sadie.

Her friend, one of the few humans from Fearford she had built a friendship with. The same Sadie who tried to save her life, but also the same Sadie who defended Isaiah.

And Isaiah had turned on her, had betrayed her. Had gotten Fynn killed.

"I don't know," I answered honestly. I had been so damn close to killing Sadie the same time I had killed Isaiah. For hurting her. For tricking her.

She would be dead, too, if it weren't for Jade. Jade was

the one who forced me to show her mercy. Who forced me to let Sadie escape.

Would Jade do it again? Let someone who betrayed her get away? Or would her new gift cut them down before they even had a clue as to what happened?

I prayed we wouldn't find out. Jade's dark side was growing, and killing Sadie would push her to a place I wasn't sure she would return from.

✺

The ragged, makeshift gates of Fearford came into view.

"That's it?" Cordelia asked. "That's the gate that's supposed to protect them?"

"They do their best," Jade snapped. "They know they are the prey. You don't need to rub it in as soon as we get inside."

"Fine," Cordelia said, rolling his eyes. Apparently, she hadn't been to the human kingdoms before. She was in for a rude awakening.

The horses clicking their hooves against the dry, cleared path became the only sound as we inched closer. I guided my white stallion to the front of the group. It would be better for them if they saw familiar faces, not a random crew of fae breaking into their kingdom.

Only, nobody manned the gates. Nobody stood by. We couldn't see a single person within.

I turned my fae ears to the kingdom, listening for any whisper of hiding humans. Aside from a few animals scurrying in the distance and a few tents flapping in the wind, I heard nothing.

"Hello?" Jade called out. "Is anyone here?"

When we got closer, we noticed the front gate was not even closed. It was cracked open, allowing anyone and anything that wished to simply push inside.

Jade turned in the saddle and gave me a wary look. "This isn't right," she whispered.

"I know. Let's go."

We moved through the gate, the rest of the group falling silently behind us as we pushed onward.

The first thing I noticed was the crumpled buildings. When we had been in Fearford not that long ago, the buildings were barely standing at best. But none of them were downright ripped apart. The buildings now looked like they had been destroyed completely.

Random piles of wood and tent materials lay in piles, not a single human in sight.

"Do you think they left?" Adeline asked. "Perhaps after Isaiah was killed, they decided not to stay?"

"But where would they go?" Jade asked. "They're humans, they can't survive for long in the fae lands. If the deadlings didn't kill them, traveling fae surely would have."

"Not necessarily," I chimed in. "It's possible that they moved somewhere safe, somewhere we didn't know existed."

Jade tensed in front of me. "Maybe."

I turned to my brothers. "Spread out," I ordered. "If you see anything, shout. Make sure this place is really empty before we move on. Maybe there are clues hidden."

They nodded and got moving, beginning to scan the abandoned kingdom for any hints as to what happened.

The hair on the back of my neck stood straight up. Something wasn't right. I just didn't know what.

The others felt it, too. Felt the hesitation and doubt lingering in the air.

"Someone could have wiped them out," Cordelia said. "Forced them to leave."

"The only people who knew this kingdom even existed were us and Esther."

She considered this. "That doesn't mean someone else couldn't have stumbled on it by accident. We aren't that far from Rewyth. Anyone traveling this way could have stumbled across the gates."

She had a point. These humans weren't living on the other side of the wall. Any fae traveling through here could have wiped them out before they had any clue what hit them.

Or, they could have left on their own. Either way, the humans were gone.

Jade slid off the saddle. "What are you doing?" I asked.

"If something happened to them, I need to know for sure." She gave me a reassuring nod before sauntering into one of the nearby buildings, one of the few that was still partially standing.

Saints. I climbed off the horse after her and followed her inside.

I remembered that building. The dark steel walls, the cramped indoors. This was what Isaiah had used as his office. If there were any clues, they would be in this building.

Jade knew this, too. She was already rummaging through random papers that lay on the desk.

"Maybe they left to find other humans," Jade suggested. "Or moved on to a safer area."

"It's possible," I said, taking careful note of the way her voice had tightened. "I'm sure whatever happened, it was for the best. Living here wasn't much of a life, anyway."

She froze from the papers on the desk and looked at me, her eyes fierce with determination and another hidden emotion I couldn't quite place. "This was all they had. This was their home, Malachi. No matter how disgusting it might be to the fae."

So that's what this was really about.

"Hey," I said, approaching her slowly while my boots brushed over the dust-covered ground. "I am not my father, Jade. I'm not here to destroy the humans. If there's anything we can do to help them, we'll do it."

She dropped her head and took a long, shaking breath. "I know you aren't your father. Either of them," she said. "But you're still fae. You always have been. You have no idea what they've been through. And if they've been forced out of their home, out of the only place they've known..."

"We'll find them," I said. "We'll find them and we'll protect them. That's what we do now, right? We protect people."

"Even people who are afraid of fae?" She looked at me with glossy eyes. "I mean, is this what we do now? Are we supposed to protect everyone?"

"If it was fae that drove them out of their homes, then yes. We make it right. We equal out the power." I walked up behind her and ran my hands up her arms. She instantly relaxed into me.

"And what if it wasn't fae?" she asked. "What if something terrible happened to them? Or what if it was the rebels?"

"Why would the rebels kill the humans?" I asked. "If anything, they would be recruiting."

"Humans aren't great allies," she reminded me. "They're weak and fickle. They're no match against the fae."

"Some, maybe," I agreed. "But I happen to know a few humans who could kick a fae's ass."

She turned in my arms and smiled. It was exhausted and weak, but it was still a smile. "Oh, really?" she asked. "Because that's not how I remember it. I remember you threatening to kill me on many, many occasions after we first married."

"Well, I'm relieved I didn't follow through. Life would be awfully boring if I did."

"It sure would," she mumbled.

We were interrupted by that steel door bursting open, sending a flood of light in with it. "Sorry to interrupt, lovebirds," Cordelia sneered. "Adonis found something. You'll want to see this."

Shit.

CHAPTER 20
Jade

"This could mean anything," I said, staring at the dead body. "We shouldn't jump to conclusions."

"Jade's right," Malachi said behind me. "We don't know who did this."

"Well, he didn't do it to himself," Lucien replied.

"I wouldn't be so sure," Adonis sneered. "The humans didn't exactly thrive here."

I shot him a sharp look before returning my attention to the body. It was a man I didn't recognize, but the lack of wings and pointed ears confirmed that he was, in fact, human. Likely a resident here.

Was a resident.

A dagger pierced his rotting chest. The attacker didn't even bother to hide their tracks.

The smell hit me next. I backed up, using my arm to cover my nose.

"How long do you think he has been here?" I mumbled without breathing.

"I'd say two weeks at least. If they didn't even try to bury the body, I'd assume everyone else left around then, too," Adonis replied.

"Two weeks? Where could they possibly have gone?" Adeline paced around the room, looking anywhere except the decaying body before us.

Serefin walked into the makeshift tent and pulled out a box of matches, lighting it immediately.

"What are you doing?" I asked.

He paused for a second and met my gaze with dark eyes. It was rare to see Ser so serious. "Burning the body. He deserves at least that."

And then it was done. Adeline helped, some, with her magic, and we all walked out of the room while the entire tent went up in flames.

"I don't like this," Lenova said once we were outside. "I don't like this at all."

"Maybe it was someone from Fearford?" I suggested. "We can't immediately assume it was an outside force."

"No," Malachi chimed in, "but it's a good start."

"Okay," I said, starting to process the information. "So someone came here, attacked the humans, killed only one, and left the body? Why does that make any sense?"

"It doesn't," Lucien stated. "It doesn't make any sense at all.

"It has to be the rebels," Serefin added. "They probably came here and forced the humans to show their support. It's likely this man was a martyr."

I shook my head. "Who are these rebels?" I turned to Lenova. "Have you heard anything about this? About rebels who want us dead?"

Lenova shook her head. "I heard rumors, but that's it. I didn't think anyone would actually be dumb enough to try and kill the peacemaker. Most of us know what a death sentence that would be."

Her features remained harsh, her eyes locked in mine. She had to be telling the truth. She had no reason to lie to me.

But Malachi was right, I had been too trusting in the past. I had to be careful around this coven of witches. Around everyone, really.

"We haven't seen any signs of them yet," Serefin chimed in. "From the looks of it, they've likely hit this human kingdom and headed east. We may run into them on our way over the human wall."

The human wall. The towering stone wall that was meant to protect my human kingdom from the fae. What it really did, though, was stop humans from wandering into the fae lands to get themselves killed.

And considering Fearford laid beyond that wall...

"Would humans be able to cross the wall alone?" I asked. "Without fae, I mean?"

I remembered back to the time I crossed the wall with Malachi and Serefin to visit my family. Saints, that seemed like ages ago. But it was difficult, even for me. The climb alone was nearly impossible, and Malachi had flown us the rest of the way up and over the wall before bringing us safely down.

Surely, humans would have issues crossing without magic.

"It's possible they've been able to find another way here," Malachi chimed in. "But even that would be difficult.

Especially for humans."

Normally, I would get defensive at a statement like that, but in this case, I knew the truth. "We should move on," I said. "The longer we linger here, the longer we're targets."

"Please," Cordelia chimed in. "You have nothing to fear, peacemaker. One blast of power and any rebel who gets within ten feet of you is dead."

I looked away, turning to the direction of our horses. "It's not me I'm worried about. It's everyone else who would be caught in the crossfire."

Malachi's hand fell on my shoulder. "We're going to figure this out," he said. "We'll find whoever did this and we'll deal with them. We'll find where everyone who lived here went, too. I'm sure they're not far."

The sinking feeling in my stomach told me otherwise, but still. We mounted our horses and pushed forward.

"More," Lenova ordered. Her and Malachi had been training for hours now. The sun was beginning to fall behind the horizon.

From the looks of it, they weren't getting far.

Malachi's hands pushed a little further, summoning a large black shadow of his death magic.

"I can't," Malachi replied.

Lenova rolled her eyes. "You can, and you will. You're afraid you're going to hurt one of us, but you won't."

Mal's jaw tightened. "You can't know that for sure, witch."

I leaned back against the tree trunk, stretching my legs

out before me. "She's right," I shouted. "You don't need to worry about controlling it so much, Mal."

He dropped his hands and ran them through his messy hair, dissipating the magic he held in front of him. "That's easy for you two to say," he said. "You're not the ones holding literal death in your hands."

I shot him a glare. "You're the descendent of Erebus. You have an incredible power, Malachi. Don't do this to yourself. Don't lock yourself in this cage."

Death is the opposite of a cage, Erebus spoke in my mind. *Death is freedom.*

Not when you're stuck with the guilt for eternity.

I expected a snarky response from the Saint of death, but my attention became occupied by a snapping stick in the distance.

Someone was out there.

"Wait," I said, turning my attention to the woods around us. "Did anyone hear that?"

"Hear what?" Lenova asked, breathless, as she paused her training.

I didn't answer. Instead, I stood from the ground and took a step closer to the trees, closer to where I could have sworn I heard—

"Jade, look out!" Adonis yelled from somewhere behind me.

"Kill the peacemaker!" a voice shouted from the trees.

What was–

My thoughts were interrupted by five individuals sprinting out of the woods, heading directly toward us.

Black cloths covered their faces, leaving just enough room for their eyes as they ran forward, weapons in hand.

I staggered backward, Mal instantly finding me as he pushed himself in front, holding his own sword out to defend us.

The attackers instantly halted.

"Who are you?" Mal growled. "What do you want with the peacemaker?"

"Magic is soon to be free," one of them replied. His voice sounded young, too young to lose his life by charging at us like imbeciles. "The peacemaker must die so he can rise."

"Who?" Mal growled. I placed a hand on his back between his wings, reminding him of my presence.

The five didn't answer, though. They simply looked at each other and nodded.

Saints, I nearly laughed out loud. They really thought they could walk in here and kill us? I didn't even have to turn around to know that the others—fae and witches both—were banding together behind me.

Together, we were an unbeatable force.

If they wanted to kill me, they would have to go through them.

Still, one of the five, the smaller one on the right, stepped forward. A girl, I realized, as her long blonde braid fell over her shoulder.

"You're not as powerful as you believe you are," she yelled. "We have power too, you know. You underestimate us!"

I stepped sideways, out of Mal's protective shield. "It would be impossible to underestimate you," I explained, "because we don't think anything about you at all. You're clearly part of whatever little rebellion has formed around here, and that's cute, but you should leave before you are killed."

None of them moved. None of them backed down.

They must really be looking forward to dying, then.

A dark flare of adrenaline ran up my spine. It was Erebus's power, fiery and fierce, alerting me of its presence, ready to protect me.

Part of it felt so familiar, I had felt it through my bond with Malachi many times. But in my own body, on my own will...

Death belonged to me.

"This is your last chance," I yelled. "Back down now and we'll consider sparing your life."

Instead of backing down, the girl on the right leapt forward, hands in front of her. Malachi's presence behind me let me know he was ready to interfere.

And then the wind picked up.

Air magic, swirling around us and blowing my hair across my face.

Is that really all they had? Did they really think that would beat us?

Malachi laughed behind me. The wind died down, and when I brushed my hair from my face, I saw the girl charging at us with her knife held high.

Seriously?

I didn't lift a finger. Malachi's magic dropped them all to their knees before us, including the brave one.

The weapon fell to the side of her as she yelled out in pain, clutching her torso.

Malachi stepped out in front of me. "You five thought you could kill her?" More screams echoed through the forest. "You thought you could get past us, defeat us? With what, this air magic?"

More screams. More pain. I watched in satisfaction as one of them began to roll in the dirt, desperate to get rid of his agony.

It wouldn't stop, though. Not until Mal wanted it to.

I smiled until Mal withdrew his power, ending the fun and leaving the five gasping on the ground.

"If you have any sense at all, you'll return to whoever sent you and tell them to think again. Rebels will die. My wife has strict orders from the Saints to maintain power, anyone who defies her will feel her wrath." His voice boomed through the trees, shaking the leaves and rattling my bones.

Even Lucien and Cordelia stood a little taller.

"Understood?" Mal asked.

The five scrambled to their feet, nodding their heads in fear.

"Not so fast," I said, stepping forward to survey the five. They had come here, likely tracked us, and attacked us. They announced that they wanted to kill me, and they made an attempt on my life. A poor attempt, yes, but it was an effort nonetheless.

A dark, primal feeling fell over me.

Now they would escape with their lives?

No, nobody who threatened me would escape. Nobody would raise a weapon against me—against my kingdom— and live.

I did not hesitate.

Where Mal's magic had just been, mine followed,

attacking each of the five as they were about to turn and run.

What a shame, I thought. *They could never run fast enough to escape me.*

"Jade," Mal started from beside me.

I shot him a warning glance. I knew what I was doing. The rebels, whomever they were, clearly did not understand the first message.

Maybe this one would be more clear.

I pushed more of my power out, wanting them to pay with their lives.

And so they did.

With not even a few screams later, all five bodies dropped to the ground. Silent this time, not screaming and withering in pain. Not moving at all, actually.

All five of the rebels were dead.

Nobody spoke behind me.

"Jade," Mal said again.

"What?" I hissed. "They tried to kill me, Mal. Nobody rises against us and lives, you said so yourself."

He gave me a look I hadn't seen before, one of pity and sympathy all at once. His boots dug into the forest floor beneath us as he walked to the bodies, starting with the girl, and removed the black mask.

Any satisfaction, any darkness, any will for death vanished immediately.

The girl was maybe sixteen, clearly still a child.

My stomach dropped.

I had killed her. She wasn't any older than Tessa had been, and now she was dead.

By my hands.

I didn't realize I had moved until I was kneeling next to the girl, looking at her sun-kissed, freckled skin. So young. So innocent.

Mal moved beside me, revealing the faces of the others. They were older than her, full adults who should have known better.

Why would they let her come with them? Why would they put someone so young in danger like this? Not a single one of them tried to stop her when she attacked.

Did they really think she would succeed? Did they really think this girl was their best chance at power?

I dropped my head.

No. I wouldn't be this person. I wouldn't succumb to this darkness, wouldn't allow death to come so easily.

I could bring her back. I had the power of life, too. I could bring this girl back from this horrible fate.

I laid a hand on her torso and closed my eyes. Please, I thought. Please, bring her back.

She tried to kill you, Erebus's voice spoke in my mind.

Nearly everyone here has wanted me dead at some point. This girl is young. Too young for this fate.

Erebus did not respond. Instead, Anastasia's warm presence washed over me.

Please, I begged her. *Please allow me this. Take this back.*

This gift is not one to use lightly, child, she said to me.

I know that. Allow me to bring her back this one time. I'll control myself in the future, I swear it. I didn't know she was only a girl.

You let darkness overcome you, Anastasia replied. *Erebus's power is not one to be underestimated.*

I know that. I made a mistake.

One you will not make again, she said. The finality in her words shook me, sending a thrill of fear through my body.

She had to bring her back. She had to listen to me.

I shut my eyes even harder, willing all of Anastasia's power to come forward, to resurrect.

Bring her back. Bring her back. Bring her back. Bring her back.

The girl moved under my touch.

My eyes shot open. Someone behind me gasped.

I held my breath as the girl's eyes fluttered open. "What–" Fear filled her eyes as she looked around, seeing the other four still dead beside us.

"It was a mistake to come here," I told her. "Your friends are dead. Go home. Tell everyone that an attack on the peacemaker will result in the same fates as them."

My words were harsh, but I didn't care. Exhaustion ebbed in the corner of my mind, my body feeling the toll of all that power.

The girl sat up with a grunt, slowly moving her body as she pushed herself away from me, away from Mal, away from the dead bodies.

She got to her feet slowly, her hands out beside her, as if waiting for one of us to attack.

"Go!" I yelled again, emotion leaking into my voice.

This time, she didn't wait.

She ran until we could not hear her panicked breathing fleeing through the forest around us.

"Saints," Adeline breathed behind me. I turned to find everyone, including Mal, staring at me with wide eyes. "You are a force to be reckoned with, Jade Weyland."

CHAPTER 21
Malachi

I didn't need to say anything to Jade. I didn't have to. I could feel the turmoil of her emotions as clearly as if they were my own.

She gave into that wicked flare of darkness, and she regretted it deeply.

I should know. I had been there dozens of times before, wallowing in the inevitable guilt that followed after realizing what I had done with that death magic.

Only, Jade could bring them back.

The sun fell over the horizon, casting a golden light over everything we could see.

Jade leaned over, resting her head against my shoulder as she took a long breath. "She was no older than Tessa," she whispered.

"She had no business trying to attack you," I replied. "They were foolish to bring her along, and even more foolish to believe they would be successful."

I meant those words. I was just as shocked as Jade when I pulled off the girl's mask. Fae or not, she was merely a teenager at best, likely brainwashed by the very men who brought her to attack us.

I had felt the darkness in Jade just seconds before she killed them. I knew the feeling very well, had lived in that dark void for years of my life.

But frankly, I would be lying if I said that what I saw back there didn't terrify me. That look in her eyes, that void of emotion, that thrill of the kill. Jade had given into that darkness without even a second of hesitation.

"It was so easy," she said after a few minutes. "I barely had to try."

"Erebus's power is strong. It takes more control not to kill them."

She lifted her head and looked at me, her deep eyes holding so many unsaid words. "I don't want to be this person. I don't want to be the killer. I mean—"

"Jade," I said, interrupting her thoughts. I moved to hold her face in my hands so she could see me, so she could truly understand me. "You are the peacemaker. Just because you kill does not mean you have to be a killer. Life and death, there is a balance. You know this more than anyone."

She shook her head, but I still did not let her go. "How am I supposed to fight this? What happens when I kill again and Anastasia does not let me bring them back?"

I took a long breath. I wanted to comfort her, to tell her that it wouldn't happen again, that she could control it next time.

But that would be a lie. The power of death was addicting, was all-consuming. Jade would have to fight the pull of the darkness every day if she wanted to get away from it.

"You once told me that I was good," I reminded her.

"You told me that I could kill and kill and kill, and I would still be good. Do you remember that?"

She smiled softly at the memory, nodding against my hands. "You are good," she said. "They fear you because of what you can do, but they also respect you."

"Well, it took years before even one person respected me. You already have that. You are their queen, you are chosen by the Saints."

She wouldn't believe my words, but it didn't matter. I leaned down to rest my forehead against hers.

"You have to say that," she muttered. "You're my husband."

I pulled away so she could see me as I said, "I love you, Jade. There is nothing you could ever do to make me stop loving you. You could end the entire world if you wished, and I would stand right behind you. I'll remind you of this every day if I have to, I'll pull you from the darkness myself every single time you slip into it."

A tear fell down her cheek. I quickly wiped it away. "Thank you for standing by me," she whispered.

We turned, watching the sun as it descended past the land beyond, encompassing the orange glow in darkness.

"Always," I reminded her. "I will always stand by you."

CHAPTER 22
Jade

"You're nervous," Malachi whispered in my ear. We were on foot now, walking the last portion of the trip to my hometown.

I exhaled a shaking breath. "Maybe," I said. I rubbed my dirt-covered hands together in front of me, trying to rub away the nerves. "The last time I saw this place was in the Trials of Glory. It wasn't pretty."

He nodded. If anyone would understand what I was going through, it would be him. He knew what it was like to go through those trials and have to face reality on the other side. "If this becomes too much, you say the word and I'll fly you out of here. You don't have to do this alone, Jade."

"No," I agreed, "but I do have to do this. They need to see me. They need to know I'll protect them."

The forest became familiar almost immediately. Just like the trials, I was back home. I belonged here for so, so long. Many years I had spent hunting in these woods, surviving off barely enough food for myself before giving Tessa the rest.

But this wasn't my home anymore. I had nothing here except the old, broken memories of what life I used to live.

Cordelia pushed her way up to the front of the crowd, falling into step next to me. "So this is where the mighty peacemaker was born?" she waved her hand to the edge of the forest, where the barely standing slabs of wood just became visible. "I have to say, I'm impressed."

I shoved her lightly. "Don't be rude."

"No, I mean it," she nodded. "It reminds me a lot of my own hometown, actually. You've risen from the ashes, peacemaker." She placed a hand on my shoulder. I somehow managed to not flinch away from her. "You should be proud."

I saw nothing but genuine emotion in her eyes and gave her a slight nod.

Cordelia was right. This place was nothing. It was worse than nothing. Fighting to survive every single day gave me the edge I needed to live in the fae kingdoms. Without this, I wouldn't have made it.

Of course, I wouldn't have been forced to marry Malachi if it weren't for my drunken father. I would have never fought so hard to survive for Tessa's sake if I weren't the only one she relied on.

But that was my reality. This was my life. I quit feeling sorry for this life of mine when I burned it all down in those trials.

"This way," I said. "I want to see my home first."

The others fell into line behind me as the forest turned

into an open, dirt field with a small row of spaced-out houses. Mine was first, closest to the forest.

I hated that I was nervous, but I needed this. I needed to see what this old life looked like now. Tessa was dead. My father lived in Rewyth.

This house didn't belong to us anymore. It belonged to the old me. The *dead* me.

A few of the others began to whisper behind me as we approached the old, wooden building that used to be my home. The door had fallen from the hinges, now leaning against the hole-filled wall on the outside of the home.

"Wait here," I whispered to Malachi as I stepped forward. "I'll only be a minute."

Malachi's eyes darkened, but he nodded anyway. I could feel his worry within myself, intertwining with my own nerves and creating a sinking feeling in the pit of my stomach.

Memories from the trials flashed through my mind, as real as any other memory I had here. Deadlings everywhere. Burning the place to the ground. Tessa, dead.

I blinked and pushed them away. That wasn't real. *This* was real. The wooden doorframe cracked as I stepped through.

This was real.

It smelled the same. Somehow, after all the time, the light scent of ale and cinnamon still remained. I ran my hand across the dirty kitchen table, now scattered with broken glasses and spiderwebs. How many times had I fought with my father here, begging him to stop drinking? Begging him to return to his family?

I turned to the bedroom. I wasn't sure I would be able

to walk inside. Not at first, anyway. Tessa was everywhere in that damn room, every single inch of it reminded me of her.

But somehow, the pain of Tessa's memory didn't sting quite as badly as it did before.

"You okay in there?" Malachi yelled from the doorway.

"Yeah," I called back. "Just a second!"

I took the final step forward and entered my old bedroom. The bed was unmade, as if Tessa had just slept in it. The quilt that my mother had made for us when we were children lay crumpled on the bed.

Tears threatened my eyes. Not at the pain of the memories, but at all the *change*. I walked to the bed and picked up the quilt, holding it to my nose.

It smelled just like her—Tessa. I used to hate the way she would pull the entire thing over herself at night, but after some time, I quit fighting for it back. I would allow her to cocoon herself in the entire thing during those winter nights.

I didn't mind. Even after the fighting and the bickering, I wanted her to be warm more than I wanted it myself.

The rest of our few belongings were covered in dirt, rummaged through, likely by the animals of the forest.

Malachi's footsteps pulled my attention to the doorway. He stopped at the opening, leaning against it with his hands in the pockets of his now-dirty trousers. "I remember the first day I came here with you," he started, glancing around the room. "I hated seeing this at first."

"Yeah," I sighed, setting the quilt back on the bed. "I can't say I loved it too much, either."

His mouth twitched into a small smile. "Your father

didn't get much of a great first impression when I showed up here."

I thought back to the way Malachi had almost killed my father, his power unleashing in a way I had never seen before. "You were very territorial," I said, matching his smile.

"*Were?*" he asked, stepping forward and away from the doorframe. "Rest assured, my queen, I will still rip this entire world apart for you." He came to stand before me, tilting my chin upward with his finger. "You are mine. I will kill for you any day."

The emotions hit me hard.

The past version of me had no idea what type of love and security waited for her on the other side of that risk, on the other side of that fae wall.

Saints, Malachi was supposed to *kill* me. That's what I thought when I lived here, cooped up in this small wooden shack with nothing but the rumors of humans to keep me occupied.

What I didn't know back then was that Malachi would actually be my savior.

We stayed in that room for a while, taking in the surroundings silently.

It wasn't until Mal and I walked back outside that I noticed something was wrong. Nobody, not even a random stranger in the distance, was to be seen.

"Serefin?" I asked. He crept forward ahead of the group, step by step, up that small dirt path. He held his hand up, signaling all of us to stay put.

Malachi stepped in front of me, protective as always. I didn't need anyone else to tell me that something was wrong, I felt it now, radiating through my body like a blaring alarm telling me to run.

Once again, the memories of the trials came rushing back to me, all too much.

"I'm sure everything's fine," Adonis said as he approached from my side. "I wouldn't worry." His hand fell to the sword on his hip, his silver wings flaring outward.

"You look worried," I muttered. "Besides, I've never heard this town so quiet. There's always something going on here, even if it's nothing good."

I ignored Serefin's warning and followed him up the hill, past the few empty houses that neighbored my own. Malachi and the others followed tightly behind me.

"We should wait for Ser," Mal whispered in my ear. Even so, he didn't try to stop me. He knew just as well as I that something was going on here.

"If something's happened to these people, we need to figure out what."

"I agree," Mal pushed, "but it could be dangerous. If the rebels…"

"If the rebels what?" I asked, spinning to face him. The others walked around us, continuing to follow Ser up that hill.

Malachi bit his tongue, eyes fierce and jaw tight.

"If the rebels come after us, we'll wipe them out. It's that simple, Mal. This is what we're supposed to do. This is our job."

"Did the Saints tell you that? That you have to put yourself in danger anytime there might be a risk?" His words dripped with sarcasm.

My teeth clenched, my fists tightened. "If you doubt my

abilities as the peacemaker, you should come out and say it. You know just as well as I do that I can protect these people."

"Sure," Mal continued, "your power matches anyone's. But you aren't invincible, Jade. If there's a planned attack on you, this could be the perfect distraction. In your old home, in the human lands. You're smarter than this, Jade. You know this."

A dozen rebuttals came to mind, but I took a long breath and pushed them all away. Malachi had a point. I also had to acknowledge how much he had changed recently, too. The old Malachi would have thrown me over his shoulder and kept me far away from danger. The old Malachi wouldn't have let me tour these kingdoms with my power, constantly putting myself at risk.

I was a walking target here. Out in the open, with dozens of structures crumbling to the ground creating a perfect hiding spot for the rebels.

"Wait!" I yelled, calling after Serefin and the others. "This could be a—" *Trap. Trap. Trap.*

Only I didn't get the chance to finish. A loud, ground-shattering boom split through the air around us, and smoke filling my air, lungs, being was the last thing I remembered.

CHAPTER 23
Malachi

It happened too fast.

The strike, the rebels running out, Jade screaming and falling out of my grasp.

No—being *pulled* out of my grasp. First there was nothing, then, everything happened all at once. White, blinding pain came splitting in my mind, overwhelming every one of my senses until all I knew was that pain, that white-hot agony.

I tried to scream for her, tried to scream to the others to help her, to get to her.

Jade. Jade. Jade.

She was all that mattered, all that would ever matter. Not just to me, either, but to all of us.

I dropped to my knees and reached my hands out, unable to see, even with my fae eyes. Unable to see anything but the blinding pain.

"Jade!" I yelled. "Jade, where are you?" The agony lifted, just for a moment. Long enough where my vision cleared and my eyes opened.

"Malachi!" she screamed back to me, but she was no longer right here. No longer next to me, no longer near us at all.

And the rebels...

I pulled at my power, but felt nothing. Didn't feel that flare of heat, of magic, that always rested in the base of my chest. Panic began to take over.

No, no, no. This was not happening. It couldn't be happening.

Every one of my dulled senses focused on Jade, on where she could possibly be.

Those bastards had touched her, had taken her. Had tricked all of us into walking straight into their damn hands.

More screams filled the air, not just Jade but the others, too, all feeling the same crippling pain that I felt.

If I could just get a single ounce of my power, I could flatten these rebels before...

"Malachi, they're taking her!" Serefin's voice roared through the crowd, cutting through all the noise. All the screaming.

In that moment, I didn't care how much pain I felt. I didn't care how crippling it was, or how blinding. I didn't care about anything at all, just getting to her.

Everyone was on the ground, cowering in pain. Adeline doubled over, arms wrapped around her stomach. Lucien lay next to Cordelia, both with their fists to their temples as if they could stop the pain.

And then I saw her.

Everything stopped. I knew nothing else but her—Jade,

my wife—halfway down the hill with men flanking her, half-carrying her thrashing body into the forest.

Blast them, I thought. *Blast them as hard and as deeply as you possibly can, until their skin melts from their bodies and their bones burn to piles of ash.*

Then it hit me. Jade couldn't blast them. Not even close. Whatever these attackers were doing suppressed all of our magic.

Another wave of pain threatened my body, and it took every ounce of strength I had to remain standing. Yelling from behind told me the rebels—whoever they were—were trying to get me back down.

I searched for any trace of my power, anything that might still connect me to her.

But I felt nothing. "Jade!" I yelled again. She still screamed, still fought as hard as she could even though I knew, I knew she was in pain.

I was searching, begging my body for something, anything that might be able to stop this, when Jade glanced over her shoulder and locked eyes with me.

In the flash of pain, I saw something there, something that hurt much worse than any pain those damn rebels could inflict. With eyes wide and brows drawn together, I saw the small glimpse of sorrow.

Jade had given up. She was going with them. She knew they would continue hurting us until they got what they wanted—her.

Someone behind Jade pushed her, breaking our eye contact and causing her to stumble forward.

"On your knees!" a voice behind me ordered. "On your knees, down! On the ground!"

My knees buckled, crashing to the ground beneath me.

"No," I muttered, loud enough for only me to hear. "No, we have to get her back."

"We'll get her back," Adeline said through gritted teeth beside me. The pain was beginning to subside, but I still felt nothing inside me where that heat of power used to be.

"How are they doing this?" I asked, knowing we wouldn't get an answer. I turned and saw roughly five men, all dressed in black with masks covering their faces.

A singular flash of a silver wing told me these rebels were fae, not humans. Then what had they done with the humans? Where was everyone?

"What do you want with her?" I growled in their direction.

One of the men sauntered forward, a large blade swinging in his hand. I thrashed but invisible hands stopped me, holding me back and pinning me to the ground.

What was this magic?

"What we want is this magic. This power." The man took a knee in front of me, coming face-to-face with me.

Staring death in the face.

His head tilted to the side, studying me. Sizing me up. I knew that look, I knew exactly what he was doing. I had been in his shoes hundreds of times.

His eyes fell to my black wings. "Dark one," he breathed. "You must be her husband, King of Shadows."

I bared my teeth anyway. "If you think you can beat her, you are wrong. You'll die for this. You'll all die for this."

The man laughed—actually laughed—and I never in my entire life wanted to rip anyone's head off more. "We're well aware of the power the peacemaker possesses," he said. "And don't worry. We'll take good care of your precious wife."

He stood to walk away, but first, he slid his blade forward, grazing my cheek with the sharp metal. Those invisible hands held me there, forcing me into it. Not letting me pull back as the blood began to drip from my face.

The man laughed again.

He was dead. As soon as I got my power back, they were all dead.

"Don't come for us," another one of the masked men ordered. "Don't look for her, don't follow us. As long as you follow those rules, your wife will stay alive."

Yeah right.

One of my brothers growled on the ground a few feet away, also unable to move.

"You can tell everyone else that power is ours. The peacemaker is no longer welcome."

They sauntered into the forest after the other rebels, after my wife.

The second their magic loosened those invisible hands, my brothers and I were up, charging the space they had followed Jade into. My wings and my feet pumped together, searching desperately anywhere she could be. I even smelled the air as deeply as possible, smelling for the faintest scent of cinnamon.

Whoever those rebels were, they were gone.

And they took Jade with them.

CHAPTER 24
Jade

Anger flooded my senses. *They had actually managed to suppress my power.*

"Drink this," the man dragging me from the right ordered, pulling a small vial of liquid from his pocket.

"Don't tell me what to do," I spat back, using the free moment to attempt another thrash out of his grasp.

"Fine," he barked back, nothing but rough harshness lacing his words. "You want to do this the hard way?"

I inhaled sharply as the guard to my left gripped my hair in a fist and yanked my head back, pulling my chin down and holding my mouth open as the other man poured the liquid inside.

I would have spit it out, would have done anything to get rid of that damned liquid if it weren't for the hand that clamped over my nose and mouth, holding it shut.

"Swallow it, girl," the men growled.

Did I really have a damn choice?

I swallowed the liquid, grimacing as it burned my

throat. A few more men yelled from behind me, running to catch up with us in the forest.

Malachi had to be freaking out. I couldn't feel my magic, couldn't feel that tendril of power that had grown to be a comforting warmth over the months.

Whatever the rebels did, it stunted my power. All of it.

I could really use your help right now, I thought up to the Saints.

How could they let this happen? Shit, even Eli—who barely knew how to use his power at all—had the *vision* of death.

The Saints said nothing in return.

"We don't have much time," a man from behind us said. I spun to look at him, but my vision blurred. The green forest around me blended and morphed into something that wasn't a forest at all.

"He'll come for you," I tried to whisper, unsure if the words even came out. "He'll come for you all. You won't make it a single day alive after this."

One of the men laughed, low and ugly. "He'll have to find us first."

❦

I blinked my eyes open and tried not to panic. *How long had I been out? How long had it been since the attack?*

"Wha—" I tried to talk, but my mouth dried up instantly. I needed water, I needed–

"Here," someone beside me said, making me jump.

"Drink this. Your throat is probably dry as shit right about now."

The masked man to my right handed me a glass of water. I was clearly in no position to refuse, so I accepted it. My muscles ached as I reached forward, grabbing the glass from him and swallowing the liquid.

I took the entire glass down in three gulps.

"Wow," the man sighed, taking the empty glass from me. "You really were thirsty."

"Where am I?" I asked. My damn human eyes couldn't see anything other than the makeshift cot I had been laying on.

"You're with us. You don't need to worry about anything else."

"What do you want from me?"

The fae, with the black mask covering everything but his mouth, tilted his head to the side. "I think you know the answer to that already, peacemaker."

A fresh wave of anger hit me, but I swallowed it down. Anger would cloud my judgment, would blind my vision. I needed a clear, emotionless head.

"Where are the others?" I asked, sounding as casual as possible.

"Your friends, you mean?" he asked. He turned his back and slowly paced back and forth. "They're right where we left them, don't worry. We didn't want anything from your friends. As long as they do what they're told, we won't have any issues with them."

"What they're told?"

"If they come for you, they'll die."

I couldn't bite back the fit of laughter that followed as

soon as I processed those words. "Do you even know who you're dealing with?" I asked. "You're going to die," I stated. "It might not be today, it might not be tomorrow. But the others are coming for me. They'll kill you and all of your rebel friends before you can get two steps away from wherever we are."

"Hm," the man grunted. "You have fire. I've heard that about you."

"Well I haven't heard anything about you," I retorted. "Or any of your rebel friends, for that matter."

The man considered these words for a moment before reaching up and untying the black cloth that covered his face.

"Let me formally introduce myself, then," the man started. His dark eyes and sharp features matched Malachi's, equally as fierce and determined, but not nearly as handsome. My chest ached. He held a thick, calloused hand out to shake mine. I didn't move. "My name is Ky. I'm the leader of this organization you all call the rebels, and I believe you and I are going to become great friends."

CHAPTER 25
Malachi

"She isn't here!" Lucien yelled from behind me. That wasn't the first time he had said those words to me, and it wasn't going to be the last. They were all idiots if they thought for even a second that I would stop looking, stop tracking her.

I turned right, eyes scanning the forest around me. "She didn't just disappear, Lucien," I growled. "And we would find her a lot quicker if you actually helped instead of arguing with me."

"Brother," he pushed. *Damn, I really hated Lucien.* I heard his footsteps approaching before he grabbed my bicep and forced me to spin and face him. "Brother!"

Fists clenched and every single ounce of my being on fire, I looked at him. "What?!"

"Jade isn't here in this forest, but that doesn't mean we aren't going to get her back. Come back to the others. We need to learn more about these rebels if we're ever going to find out where they took her."

A tiny flicker of heat in my chest signaled that my

power was coming back, slowly, like a tiny stream of water. It wasn't going to be enough, and it surely was too late to be useful.

Thanks a lot, damned Saints.

It was gone—that connection that tied me to Jade. That heated presence of her that my magic had grown so used to.

Without my power, our connection was gone.

"Fine," I said, running my dirt-covered hands down my face. "Let's go."

I followed Lucien back to the others, where Cordelia stood in the center of the semi-circle. "I'm just saying," she started speaking to everyone else and oblivious to our approach, "if anyone knows about the rebels, it would be them."

"Who?" I asked. All eyes snapped in my direction. "Who knows about the rebels?"

Cordelia rolled her shoulders back and turned to me. Her jaw was set and determined, but I saw the ounce of pity that flashed across her dark eyes before she answered, "I don't know for sure, but I'm assuming our friends at that inn near Paseocan know something about this."

The inn. Cordelia was right. We may have killed the one person who knew anything of certainty, but someone there was bound to know something. The innkeeper, strangers passing by. Someone knew something. And I had a feeling that people near that inn knew more, not just the man who gave us the warning.

"Right," I said. "Then we'll start there. Those who can fly come with me. The others will climb the wall and take the horses back to Rewyth."

I didn't wait for a response, for an argument. My word was final, and the sharpness of my voice told everyone that.

Cordelia had to run to catch up with me. "Don't you want to wait until nightfall?" she asked. "We'll have cover, we can get in and out of that wretched place before anyone sees a thing."

"I can't wait, Cordelia," I said. "They have Jade. They took my wife!" I didn't mean to yell at her, but she flinched backward anyway. In her own way, she knew exactly what I was feeling, knew the amount of fear pulsing through me.

She could also read my thoughts, still, so she knew I wasn't considering waiting. Not even for a second. Those rebels said they wouldn't kill her, but we had no reason to trust them. Saints, we didn't even know who they were.

I didn't wait to see if the others were following. They would catch up. Before we even reached the edge of the forest, my wings pounded in the air, lifting me up and over the trees.

I hated this damned place. It was bad enough that Jade had lived here, had suffered every single day just to feed herself and her sister. But now, when Jade was revisiting the one place she didn't want to return to, she is attacked? All for what? For trying to help people?

"I'm sorry," Eli said from behind me in the air. His silver wings weren't as big as mine, but they carried him just as quickly. "I should have seen this coming. I should have known something wasn't right!"

I clenched my fists, the wind stinging my eyes as we made it over the wall and into the fae lands. If we kept moving, we would make it to the damn inn in a few hours. "It's not your fault, Eli," I said. "We all should have seen it coming. After Fearford, we should have been on the lookout. We all let her down. *I* let her down."

In the corner of my eye, I saw Eli shake his head. "I saw the death, but I...I couldn't see it clearly enough. I still can't focus on what I'm being shown in my visions."

"Well, nobody died yet," I said. "But they will. Trust me, brother. Every single one of those bastards will die for touching her."

His silence was enough. Eli had a soft spot for Jade, he always did. Adonis and Lucien were harder to read, but Eli wore his emotions plain as day on his face. "We'll get her back," he said. "I won't stop until we find her."

"Damn right we'll get her back."

The woman at the inn was just as surprised to see us now as she was the first time she saw us. I, however, did not return the pleasantries.

"Tell me what you know about the rebels," I demanded, bursting through the front door of the rickety inn and slamming my palm on the counter. "And don't think for a second you can get away with lying."

She stammered in shock, putting a wrinkled hand over her chest as she processed the words. "Rebels?" she repeated. "What rebels?"

To my right, in the dining room by the bar, a few men casually got up. Ale mugs half full, they dipped their heads and headed for the back door.

They were two steps from exiting when Lucien kicked

that back door in, sauntering inside with Adonis behind him.

Trapped.

Nobody was leaving this damned inn until I got my answers.

"So," I announced to the entire inn, clapping my hands together before me. "Some of you may know who I am, but if not, I'll remind you." The men reluctantly looked up from the floor. I saw something there, something dark and defiant lingering in their eyes.

Oh, yes. They knew who I was.

I smiled. "My name is Malachi Weyland. I am the King of Rewyth and the King of Shadows. You decide which is worse."

Adrenaline mixed with anger and a well of emotions that poured into my blood, awakening my power to full force once more. I sent the tendrils of death—more powerful than ever—in the direction of the men, but pulled back right before the magic hit its target.

"Would anyone like to tell me what they know about the rebels?"

"Malachi!" the woman behind the counter squealed. I felt bad for her, I really did. If I would have known she was harboring men who wanted to hurt my wife, I would have killed her a long time ago.

It was a shame, really.

"You don't have to hurt them!" she stammered, clearly shocked by the violence. "Boys, tell the King of Rewyth what he wants to know!"

The two men looked at each other, hands in their

pockets and brows drawn together. They knew something alright.

"We don't know anything about any rebels," one of them answered, spitting onto the floor.

"Is that right?" I asked.

They both continued to stare at the floor.

I drew back my power entirely, causing them both to exhale in relief.

Idiots. All of them.

"Adeline," I said. She stepped up beside me, a hand on her hip.

"Yes, brother?"

"Perhaps you could entice these men here to help us in our endeavors to find my wife."

She smiled. Adeline and I were not related by blood, but she shared that devious need for justice. I saw myself in Adeline more times than not. "I would love to, brother."

Adeline stepped forward, taking her time as she sized up the men. Their wings were small. Their arms were thin. Saints, Adeline nearly surpassed them in height as she moved to stand behind them.

They both cowered, but did not open their mouths. They did not offer any information about the rebels.

Big mistake. Big, big mistake.

With one swift motion, Adeline placed both of her hands on one of the fae's back and released a rush of her power, her fire. Her grip remained tight on his body, even as he screamed in pain and dropped to his knees. Adeline's smile of satisfaction matched my own. She was learning to wield her powers quickly and efficiently.

Cordelia pushed past me from behind and stopped a

foot in front of the men. Her and Adeline together were a sheer force to be reckoned with.

The stories of us together would be told for generations to come.

"Pity," Cordelia said, sending a swift kick between the standing man's knees. He fell to the floor beside his friend. "I thought I was going to miss all the fun."

"Don't worry," Adeline said, finally stepping back from the man as the smell of burnt flesh filled the room. "I saved you some."

"Have they said anything yet?" Cordelia said, turning to me.

"Not a word," I answered. "Claim they don't know anything."

Cordelia smiled and turned back to the men. "Now, now, boys. We're all friends here. We all want the same thing."

The men shook as she approached, her black boots stopping just before them as they looked up at her. "W–we do?"

Cordelia nodded. "We sure do. You see, we want to get our peacemaker back. We want to save the world and fulfill the prophecy of the Saints, etcetera, etcetera. Sound familiar?"

The two boys looked at each other.

Cordelia knelt, gripping the chin of one with her long, piercing fingernails. He squirmed backward, but Adeline was there, meeting him with fire in each hand and a smile of vengeance on her face.

"What do you know about the rebels?" Cordelia asked, any hint of humor or sarcasm now gone from her voice.

"Who are they? Where do they come from?"

"I already told you I don't know anything!" The man kept trying to squirm away, but Cordelia only held tighter. Her concerned look morphed slowly into an evil, stomach-churning grin. *Damn, she was good.*

"You don't have to tell me," Cordelia said. "Your mind has already said plenty."

It took the men a second to realize what she meant, but by the time she stood and wiped her hands on the sides of her legs, they were staring with wide eyes and open mouths.

"What do they know?" I asked her.

"They've met a few rebels. They're regulars here and they live nearby. We can't be far from them, which means we can't be far from wherever they took your wife."

I nodded, then tilted my head in the woman's direction.

"No," the woman stammered. "No, please! I'll tell you anything you want to know!"

Cordelia took my hint and stepped toward her. "You already had the chance for that," she said. "My friend here, the King of Shadows, has a tendency to show some people mercy. We share a lot of traits, him and I, but I'm afraid showing mercy is not one of them."

Really good.

"I've seen a few rebels here before!" she said, her words coming out like a rush of wind. She pressed her back to the wall behind her with her hands out in surrender. As if that would stop us. As if that would stop me.

"You knew the rebel who came to us the night we stayed here," I guessed. "Who was he? Did you let him in?"

She closed her eyes and attempted to press herself further into that wall. "Please, Malachi," she breathed.

"It's King Weyland," I corrected her, taking a few steps closer and meeting Cordelia. "And it would be wise of you to speak up now. Cordelia here is not very patient."

She shot me a smile filled with vengeance.

"Okay, okay! He was a rebel, yes. They swing by here from time to time to meet in a public place. I didn't know they were rebels at first, I swear! And once I heard the term 'rebel', I had no idea what it meant! I didn't know they were going to hurt your wife, Mal–King Weyland! I swear to you!"

"Where are they?" I barked.

Her hands shook. "I beg of you–"

"WHERE. IS. MY. WIFE?"

"That way!" she screamed. I let my shadows pulse out, grazing her cheek. "That way, that way into the forest! There is an abandoned building hidden underground just past the river. Please, you have to believe me! They would have killed me if I told–"

One pulse of magic, one rapid beat of my heart, and the woman's dead body slumped to the ground, sliding down the wall with a satisfying thud.

Dead.

I turned to the men, once again sending out a heartbeat of power. Two heartbeats.

Thud. Thud.

Both dead.

I did not care that I had given in to it, had momentarily let myself lose control. If killing was going to lead me to my wife, then I would kill every damn fae I saw until she was safe in my arms again.

"Let's go," I ordered the others. "It seems we have to pay our friends a visit."

"Dammit," Adeline mumbled, stepping over the two dead bodies. "I wanted to do that part."

"Don't worry," Cordelia said as they exited the inn. "I have a feeling we'll get plenty more chances tonight."

CHAPTER 26
Jade

"I'm not putting those on," I demanded, looking at the cuffs Ky held in his hands.

"If you want out of this cramped, dark room, you will. We can't have you igniting your magic at the first whiff of trouble."

I smiled coldly. "Now why would I do something like that? Why would I ever need to use my Saints-given magic in a situation like this?"

He pushed the cuffs further. "Put them on," he said. His voice sounded more final this time, but I still wasn't afraid. Even without my magic, without the one thing I counted on to keep me safe, I was not going to be afraid of this rebel.

"Fine," I said, eventually holding my hands out so he could cuff them. As soon as the metal touched my skin, I flinched. It felt cold and empty and so, so wrong. "What is that?"

"Laced with blocker magic," he said. "Special gift from

some of our friends. It will stop you from using your powers, no matter how close to those Saints you are."

He fastened them tightly around my wrists before backing up and taking a long breath. "Let's go," he said. He opened the door and the light flooded in. I had to squint to keep my eyes open.

"If you want me dead," I stated as I stepped out of the tiny, cramped cell, "you should just kill me. You're wasting your own time here, and frankly you're wasting mine."

"I told you, Jade, I do not wish to kill you. That's the opposite of what I want to do with you, actually."

He led me down a long hallway, guiding me toward the light that flooded in from the far end where a staircase appeared. "Then what do you want with me?" I asked. "Because if you think I'm going to help you, you are poorly mistaken."

The man laughed. I clenched my fists further, hating the way those damned cuffs felt. I began to feel a hunger deep in my core, the same place I was so used to feeling my magic and Malachi's.

I missed that bond so, so much.

"That's what I'm here to show you," Ky said.

He held his hand out and waved up the staircase. "What's up there?" I asked.

"I suppose you should head upstairs and check it out, peacemaker."

I really hated his guy. He was arrogant and cocky, two things I would wipe directly off his face if I had even a tiny ounce of my magic back.

"Fine," I said. "But don't think these cuffs will stop me if you decide to really piss me off, rebel."

He nodded, but that mask of arrogance cracked for just a second as he sent one final glance down to my cuffs. "Noted."

I ascended the stairs, my legs burning as I took each step. My mind raced with the possibilities of what was waiting for me. Ky was right. If he wanted me dead, he would have killed me when I was unconscious. Then, or when he put these cuffs on my hands.

But he knew I wasn't going to help him. Him, or any rebels, in that case. *So what did he want?* Why go through all this trouble just to keep me alive?

I reached the top of the staircase and turned, finding a long, empty corridor. A few dozen fae seemed to be scattered throughout the room, eating whatever they had in their plain, grey bowls. Everything in the room was grey, actually. Grey and dark and colorless, a mixture of wood and metal combining as the walls ascended upward, sunlight flooding in from dozens of small, rectangular windows at the very top of the walls.

Alarms blared in my mind. Every instinct I had told me this place was bad, was wrong. "What is this?" I asked. "Where are we?"

"This is our headquarters," Ky explained, stepping up beside me as I gawked at the room.

"Are we..." I could hardly get the words out. No, it wasn't possible. We would have heard about this before. This wasn't a simple tent filled with a couple rebellious fae. This was an entire organization. I looked closer, finding weapons strapped to every single fae who sat in the room. Weapons and armor and masks. This had clearly been happening for quite some time, long before I was ever named the peacemaker.

"Yes," Ky said, finishing my question for me. "We're underground."

"It's nothing personal," Ky explained. I had found myself at the end of one of the tables at the far end of the room, listening to Ky and another rebel explain their goal of this entire situation. "We've been expecting the peacemaker for some time now, Jade. We didn't know it would be you, but that changes nothing. Our plan would remain the same no matter who the peacemaker was."

"But I'm not fae," I explained. Ky's story didn't make any sense to me. He told me about how years ago, when a fae began to expect the fulfillment of the prophecy coming, they had built this place. A few fae at first, and then the group grew and grew until a few dozen were coming together almost daily to get the work done, and they all wanted the same thing.

To stop the prophecy before it ever came to fruition.

"I'm nothing like the Paragon, I'm not one of you. I'm here to restore the balance, do you not understand that?"

Ky nodded and looked at his partner. "Yes," Ky said. "We understand that you are not fae, but you must understand our concerns. You're the most powerful person in the world now, Jade Weyland. It doesn't matter who you are or who your husband is, that's the truth. That goes against our ultimate goal. It's as simple as that."

"And what is your ultimate goal?" I pushed. "To have chaos? To let power-hungry, vindictive fae take over?"

"Isn't that exactly what you planned on doing?" Ky's friend asked.

"I'm. Not. Fae." I slammed my shackled hands down on the table. They both flinched, and I couldn't deny the wave of satisfaction that rolled through me.

Perhaps I had a few more fearful qualities than I once thought.

"Right," Ky stated. "We've picked up on that."

"Look," I said, not able to hide my annoyance from my voice, "I understand that you think I'm going to try and take over the world, but I assure you, I am not. I did not want this fate. I didn't ask for it. Saints, if I would have known that all of this trouble came from being this chosen one..." I let my thoughts trail off. "The point is, you've got this all wrong. Did your little friends tell you that I also met the Saints?" They paused. "All of them."

"You met the Saints?" Ky's friend questioned, leaning forward across the table.

I nodded. "It was part of the ritual to become the peacemaker, yes. They speak to me frequently and they guide nearly all of my decisions."

"And where are they now?" Ky pushed. "Your *Saint* friends, where are they? What are they telling you about us, about this situation?"

He raised an eyebrow in a way that sent a rush of fury down my spine. He thought of me as weak. He thought of me as powerless without them. But I wasn't going to admit that they hadn't helped me, even if that's what he wanted me to say. I couldn't give him that satisfaction.

"They don't like you," I blurted instead, slapping the best sarcastic smile I could muster onto my face. Even the small movement made my lips crack.

"Well," Ky replied. "The feelings are mutual then."

I squinted my eyes at him. *Why would anyone not like the Saints? Why would anyone want to be on their bad side?*

The three of us stared at each other for a couple minutes, nobody saying a word. I hated Ky. It's not even that I simply hated him, but it was as if every ounce of my body repelled him. Even with my magic being restrained by those cuffs, I felt a warning deep in my body to stay away.

Noted.

Not like I could do much about it now.

"So what?" I asked, breaking the silence. "You keep me here forever? If you don't want me to be the peacemaker, why bother with keeping me alive?"

Slowly, a wicked smile grew on Ky's face. His yellowed teeth flashed against the light coming in from the upper walls. "If I'm being honest with you here, peacemaker," he started. His friend began to smile, too, as they both stared at me. I kept my face free of reactions. "There is another motive I have for your presence with us here."

"Oh really?" I pushed. "Care to enlighten me?"

He nodded, placing his folded hands on the table before him. "Your husband is the King of Shadows." It wasn't a question.

"He is."

"You see, I have met your dear husband before, but of course, he would not recognize me."

My blood ran cold. "You know Malachi?"

"*Know* is not the word I would use for it. But yes, I

know of him. We fought against him when he invaded our kingdom and murdered hundreds in cold blood, not caring who was hurt. Innocents. Woman. Children."

Shit, shit, shit. "No," I said, leaning forward. "No, you don't understand. That wasn't Malachi's doing. His father forced him to do those things."

Ky sat back in his chair. "I have a hard time believing a fae so powerful would need to take orders from his father. Especially orders so cruel."

"It's true," I pushed. I didn't care that I sounded desperate, I needed him to understand me. I had a deep, sickening feeling as to where this was going. "He isn't the same man he was back then, Ky. I swear to you."

"Either way," he said. "Your husband killed my brother."

Those eyes sharpened, finally hitting me with the anger and betrayal and regret that lurked behind them. I had seen eyes like that; viscous and full of vengeance. Eyes like that would do anything to make that pain go away, to make that anger subside.

No, I knew what was coming.

"What do you want with him?" I asked once more.

"A life for a life," Ky said. "Your husband will come for you, Jade Weyland. And when he does, I will kill him."

CHAPTER 27
Malachi

"Is this a good idea?" Adonis asked, running to catch up with me. I didn't dare rest, didn't hesitate for a single second before darting in the direction of the river. It would be hard to find, that much I knew. If these rebels had gone undetected for more than a few weeks, they had to be hiding themselves to some extent.

"Is *what* a good idea?" I snapped. "Saving my wife?"

"No, that's not what I mean and you know it. I heard what those rebels said, brother. If you come after Jade, they'll kill her. They'll try to kill you, too."

I snorted. "Consider this me calling their bluff. If they were going to kill Jade, they would have done it back there. They want her for something. They might be draining her magic, sacrificing her in some crazy rebel ritual, I don't know. But I do know I'm going to get her back."

Adonis grabbed my arm and forced me to stop walking. I spun to face him, fist ready to go, before I saw the others standing behind him. They clearly thought the same things he was saying. "You all agree with him?" I asked. My attention slid to Adeline. "Even you?"

"I want Jade back too," Adeline said softly. "But maybe it would be safer if we had some sort of plan first. We can be back in Rewyth before midnight, and we can meet with the others to discuss what might be happening. We can rest, gather more fae to fight with us. Those rebels were strong, Malachi. It would be a risk to run in blind."

"I can't believe this," I muttered. "Jade needs us. She's probably locked up without her magic, waiting for us to bust into wherever the rebels are hiding and kill every single one of them."

"Or," Cordelia said, stepping up. "She knows that we're coming and she's trusting our timing. She has the Saints to help her, too, Malachi. You know she'll be okay."

I hated every single one of them for being right. "Fine," I said after a minute. "We go to Rewyth to gather the others, but I'm not resting until we get her back."

"I would expect nothing else," Lucien mumbled under his breath. "Let's get moving. We can think of a game plan on the way."

I couldn't believe we were so close to her, and we were turning back. I was beginning to feel it, too, that small tether of power that connected us. I had lost that feeling after they had taken her, when whatever shield of magic they were using blocked our power, but it was beginning to reform again. If she was in danger, I would feel it.

At least, I prayed to the Saints I would. They were the ones that had connected us, right? Wouldn't they want me to know if she was in trouble?

My wings cut the air as sharply as a knife, pumping me

into the sky with the rest of the group and bringing me home. None of us complained when our backs began to burn, our muscles aching from flying for so long. Nobody said a word when rain pelted our faces, making the flying that much more difficult. They all knew better, and they were on my side, whether or not I wanted to believe that.

We were getting her back.

❦

L enova and the other witches had just made it back to Rewyth when we arrived. Everyone else from the castle looked surprised, to say the least.

My boots landed on the dirt of the kingdom, just inside the gates of Rewyth. Guards circling the castle immediately gave their salute, straightening their backs in shock when they realized who it was.

"Who has seen my mother?" I asked, ignoring everyone and brushing through the gathering crowd at the front doors of the castle. "Where is Esther?"

"Here," Esther said, rummaging through the crowd. "This way, son!" The urgency in her voice told me she already knew what was going on. Witch magic, maybe, or simply her uncanny intuition. Either way, we had no time to waste.

I turned to one of the guards beside me. "Get a small army ready," I ordered. "Anyone with magic gifts, skills, or a sword. Our mission is to save our queen."

He nodded and was off, making his way to the soldiers.

Esther was pulling me through the crowd, leading me to the study where we could talk. My brothers all trailed behind me. "They all had magic," I whispered to Esther. "Strong magic. Enough to put us all on our knees, Jade included."

We filed inside, Esther closing the study door behind us. "Rebels?" she asked. "Have you learned anything about who it was? Where they came from? Surely they were not fae we knew."

"No," I replied. "We were warned that rebels may want to attack Jade, but we didn't possibly think anyone would be stupid enough to actually do it. Turns out, the rebels aren't as stupid as we believed. They absolutely ravished us, Esther."

"What happened?" she asked. "Tell me everything, don't leave out a single detail."

So I did. I relived the events in acute detail, filling Esther in on everything that happened, including the empty kingdom of Fearford and the warning we received at the inn. She didn't interrupt, nor did she seem surprised when I filled her in on the uncanny abilities of our attackers.

"The poison is the only thing I've heard of that limits my abilities that way," I explained. "But it wasn't just that. It was as if someone was weighing us down with invisible ropes."

My brothers, Cordelia, Adeline, and Serefin, waited silently while I explained, nodding along to the details of the attack.

"It wasn't just him," Cordelia added after I was finished. "Even I was stripped of all abilities. I couldn't see into their minds; I couldn't see where they were taking her. It was as if I were a mere human."

"Have you heard of anything like this before?" Adonis

asked. "Have you heard of a power that can strip everyone else's? I mean, why would the Saints even allow something like that to happen? And to the peacemaker, of all people.

Esther remained quiet for a chilling amount of time. In the weeks we had been gone, she had changed. I couldn't quite put my finger on why or how, but something was definitely different about her.

"We knew some people wouldn't be happy about the peacemaker's presence. That much is not a surprise."

"Who are these rebels?" Eli asked from behind the group. "What do they want with her?"

"She's a witch, brother," Lucien said. "Not a Saint. She doesn't have all the answers."

Esther smiled softly. I crossed my arms over my chest and waited, trying to ignore the lingering panic that laced every single muscle in my body. It felt so, so wrong to be this far from her.

"They dulled your powers and they took her with them," Esther repeated. "But they didn't kill her. They want something from her."

"What could they possibly want? Her power is hers alone, they cannot take it. They cannot use her power as their own," I replied.

"No, but they can try. Power-hungry individuals do idiotic things all the time. If they think Jade is going to give them a step-up, if they have thought that she can provide them with more power than they ever had before, they'll surely take it."

"And their gifts? I can't imagine how we'll be able to penetrate the rebels' hideout if they have magic like that."

"It could be a shield," Esther explained. "A powerful

one. And to hold it against Jade's magic, they must be strong and skilled."

"Well," Lucien added, "I'm sure the Saints' unleashing of magic in the world only made them stronger."

We all took a long breath, glancing around the room.

"I'm open to ideas," I said after a few moments. "If anyone has any thoughts on how to kill the rebels as soon as possible, let me know now."

Again, a few silent beats passed.

It wasn't until Esther stepped forward that our attention resettled on her once more. "Actually," Esther started, "I have something you all may want to see."

CHAPTER 28
Jade

"Sorry about this," Ky explained as he shoved me back into that dark room. "With your power, we can't take any risks. This is the only room reinforced with the shielding magic. The longer you stay here, the weaker you'll be."

"Great," I mumbled. "How thoughtful of you."

He removed my cuffs once I was inside, but the weight of the room had already dulled any flare of my abilities I was beginning to feel, stripping me of all connections to my power.

And all connections to Malachi.

I waited until he had closed the dark, steel door behind him, leaving me alone in the room, before I collapsed against the cold wall.

Kill Malachi? Saints, I should have known. They didn't care about me! They wanted me dead, just as much as any other power-hungry fae who saw me as a threat. They were going to kill me, too, I was sure of it, right after they eliminated Malachi.

I couldn't let it happen.

He was going to come for me. I knew he would. With any luck, he was gathering an army right now to tear this place to the ground.

"Anything you can do right about now would be great," I whispered, turning my eyes up to the dark ceiling. My human eyes were still adjusting, but I could make out the four corners of the tiny room. A cot, a bucket, and a small cup of water.

How welcoming.

The Saints would help me, right? They would have to. They wouldn't put all of this work into creating me as the peacemaker just to let a group of rogue fae end us all, everything we created.

No, I wasn't going to let it happen.

The enchanted force of the wall began to ache in my bones, pulling all of my magic and then some, stripping me of my strength, my fire.

My legs began to ache. My arms felt weak, hanging at my sides.

I couldn't fight anyone this exhausted. I couldn't fight off Ky at full strength, let alone with this damn magic pulling every ounce of force from my body.

I hated it. I hated that I was here, I hated that those bastards blamed Malachi for something that wasn't his fault.

He had killed hundreds before. I knew that. I used to fear that part about him, but now? I knew what it really was. I knew who he really was, and he wasn't a killer. Not really.

He was a king. A man. A husband.

He was given this incredibly dark gift, and had been manipulated into wielding it for so long.

But now? He wouldn't use his power against innocent people. No, he would only use it on those who deserved his wrath.

Ky didn't understand. Malachi may have killed his brother, but that was the old Malachi. The one in pain, the one tied to his father in ways he could never understand.

Exhaustion began to weigh down my eyelids, making it hard to form coherent thoughts.

I would fight. I would find a way out of this damn room and I would fight, if not for myself, then for him, for Malachi. But I was so, very tired. Just an hour of sleep, and then I would feel better. Stronger.

Just...an...hour...

I only awoke from my dreamless sleep when I heard the steel door beginning to creek open. I hadn't even made it to the cot, no. I had fallen asleep slumped on the ground next to the steel wall.

The door cracked open quietly, silently.

Much too slow to be Ky. He would swing the door open with the arrogance he couldn't put aside.

"Jade?" a female voice whispered. "Jade, are you in here?"

I shot to my feet, hand moving to my hip where my weapon no longer existed. "What do you want?" I asked, my voice a low growl.

"Saints," the female voice whispered. My eyes were still

adjusting, but I made out a female frame as a woman came inside, shutting that steel door behind her.

Wait...I knew that frame. I knew that voice. I knew that girl.

As soon as the steel door was closed, the woman pulled me into her arms.

I hugged her back, finding the strength to lift my arms only for a moment to pull the woman into my embrace. "Sadie," I breathed.

"I can't believe it," Sadie whispered into my hair, not tightening her grip on me for even a second. "It's really you! I never thought I would see you again, Jade. Never, not after..."

"Wait," I said, interrupting her. I used every ounce of strength I had to pull myself from her embrace and look into her shadow-covered face. Any feelings of warmth or kindness I had for my old friend vanished as a new feeling washed over me, one of betrayal and darkness and anger. "You're a rebel?"

CHAPTER 29
Malachi

Esther walked with a purpose, one I hadn't seen her walk with in quite some time. There was something else lacing her movements, too. *Nerves? Excitement?*

"Where are you taking us?" I asked for the third time.

"You'll see," she answered, also for the third time. She walked us through the dark, nearly empty halls of the castle. Everyone we passed parted ways, gawking at myself and my brothers as we brushed passed. I nodded at a few of them, but otherwise didn't pause.

And then we began heading down to the dungeons.

"Please tell me you haven't been locking prisoners down here," Adeline sighed from behind me. "This place creeps me out."

I hadn't been to the dungeons since, well, since Jade. Since Isaiah and Sadie. To be honest, it creeped me out, too. We rarely had a need for the dark, underground tunnels of the castle, and I couldn't imagine why Esther was dragging us down here.

She had been locked up here once, too.

"This way," she said, turning the corner and taking us down the stiff staircase that led to that dark place.

I glanced back at my brothers. They only gave me a knowing look with raised eyebrows.

And then we followed.

Esther had lit many more lanterns than usual, making the darkness of the dungeons somehow brighter. At least that part was comforting.

We barreled through the underground, following quickly as Esther practically flowed through the dark tunnels.

"Almost there," she said.

"Almost where?" I asked. My nerves, agitation, and slight panic of being away from Jade mixed together in a rush of emotion that was beginning to bubble to the surface.

Esther stopped in her tracks at the end of one of the tunnels and turned to face us, an eerie, lit up smile playing on her lips.

"Dragon."

She waved her hand out, signaling us to head into the last room at the very back of the dungeon.

Dragon? She had locked that poor child up in these dark, dirty tunnels?

With an instinctive hand on my hip, I followed Esther's signal and rounded the corner.

Just as I thought, Dragon sat in the far corner of the room, lit up by the fire in the lanterns around him.

"Careful, now," Esther called from behind us.

My brothers, Serefin, and Adeline filed into the room

behind me. Adeline gasped, either from excitement of seeing him or of pure shock from the conditions he was being kept in. Ripped clothes, dirty feet, just as we had found him in the Paragon.

"Dragon," Esther said, filing in after us. "Remember what I taught you. Deep breaths, keep your emotions calm."

Dragon shot up to his feet, his face lit up in excitement. "You're back!" he yelled. "Oh my—Adeline! I never thought I would see you again!"

"What's going on here?" I demanded, my voice booming off the walls around us. "Why is Dragon in the dungeons?"

Dragon began bouncing on his bare feet, barely able to contain the joy.

"Dragon," Esther warned. "Stay back."

"Nonsense," Adeline pushed. She shoved herself to the front of the crowd and dropped to her knees, her arms out on either side of her. Dragon didn't hesitate. His excitement was nearly palpable now as he took the few steps, nearly about to throw himself into Adeline's arms when—

The air in the dungeon shifted. A breeze that should not be possible entered the cramped space around us, blowing so hard I nearly stumbled backward.

"What in the—"

And then, right before my eyes, Dragon began to change. Shift. His features morphed, slowly at first, and then all at once.

He was...he was changing. Shifting into something else, something not fae nor human. I saw the wings first, forming in the wind that gathered dust and blew it all around him. Dragon was lifted off his feet, right before Adeline, and thrust into the air as the change continued.

Someone screamed.

A flash of fire filled the room.

I covered my eyes with my hand as a flash of light, so bright I could have sworn it came from Jade herself, filled even the darkest corners of the deep, underground dungeons.

A few flaps of wings smacked the air, then the stone walls of the room, before a loud, primal, animalistic roar filled the space, wanting me to submit. Wanting everyone in the room to submit, to kneel.

I took my hand away from my eyes.

Dragon had morphed into a...a....

"A dragon," Adeline muttered in awe, still on her knees before him as she looked up at the creature, now three times the size of the small boy. Black wings with sharp talons filled that now much too small corner of the dungeon.

I couldn't move. Couldn't think.

This was impossible. This had to be a dream, a nightmare, a vision. Anything but reality.

And then the dragon opened his mouth. The cool air of the dungeon instantly heated, a small ball of fire became visible in in the back of the beast's throat as–

"Take cover!" Esther screamed from behind us.

But it was too late.

The dragon unleashed the fire that burned within, encapsulating all of us. Adeline, Lucien, Adonis, Eli, Cordelia. Everyone.

I closed my eyes again, shutting them tightly. If I was

going to die, I was glad it was by this. By a mystical beast who shouldn't even exist anymore.

But the heat never came. The fire never hit me. I blinked my eyes open again to see Serefin standing in front of us all, an invisible shield of...no, it wasn't glamour. It was something else, like a wall that existed there, protecting us all from the fire that began to fizz out.

Serefin had shield magic.

Dragon was...a dragon.

Everything began to settle as the beast backed itself into the corner, once again calm. Serefin's shield sputtered out before disappearing completely.

"Well," Cordelia sighed from the back of the room. "I think we have quite a bit to unpack here."

Holy. Shit.

CHAPTER 30
Jade

"Jade," Sadie said, holding her hands up in surrender. "Jade, listen to me. Don't freak out, let me explain."

"I don't need to listen to anything you say."

I couldn't believe what I was seeing. After everything I did for her...I trusted her, I thought she trusted me. We worked together, I thought she was on my side.

She knew I was the peacemaker.

And this entire time, all this worry and time spent hoping she was okay, she was one of them. Working with them behind my back.

"I'm not a rebel, Jade!" She whispered in a hushed voice, as if worried that someone would hear her. "I wouldn't do that to you, I wouldn't betray you like that after everything you did for me!"

My anger turned to confusion. "If you're not a rebel—which I find very hard to believe—why are you here? Why are you living with them? Did you know they were trying to kidnap me this entire time?"

"No, Jade! I swear it!"

"Then why?"

Sadie took a long, shaking breath and dropped her hands, letting her shoulders fall and her head hang back. She looked...exhausted.

No, Jade. She's *not* exhausted, and you can't trust a single thing she says.

"I made it back to Fearford, after days of running through the forest. Malachi, after what he did to Isaiah..."

"No," I interrupted. "You don't get to say his name. Not after this."

"I found my way back to Fearford and life returned to normal, nobody talked about the peacemaker. Nobody even mentioned the fae. We were simply trying to survive and rebuild ourselves after Isaiah died."

I flinched at the sound of his name off her tongue.

Sadie took a deep breath. "And one day, they came. It was quick and unexpected. They only had to kill a few humans. The rest, they overpowered with their strength. We didn't stand a chance."

Okay, maybe she wasn't lying.

"What do they want? Why would they invade a human kingdom?"

"None of us knew at first. That...that had to be weeks ago, now. We didn't know who they were or what they wanted, just that we had to follow them. Follow them or die. They brought us back here, told us to keep ourselves inside, so that's what we did. That's what we've been doing ever since."

I could hardly believe what she was saying. Correction —I *didn't* believe what she was saying. "You had no idea they were rebels? You conveniently never found out who your captors were the entire time you were here?"

"After a few days, we began to hear things. Whispers of the peacemaker and of her dark husband."

I grimaced.

"But I swear to you, Jade, I had no idea what they were planning to do. I heard yesterday that they had taken you here and had locked you in this cell. It won't be long until they find out I've come to talk to you."

"Then why did you?" I asked. "They could kill you without even blinking, Sadie. Why risk coming down here?"

She stepped forward and placed both hands on my shoulders. I tried not to flinch away. "Because," she started, "you're my friend, Jade. You might not believe it right now, and that's okay. But you saved my life once. So did Malachi. If I can repay the favor in any way, I'll do it."

She smiled at me, and I couldn't help but give her a small nod. Did I trust her? No, not in the slightest. I didn't trust anybody here, human or fae.

But I did need a way out. And Sadie was the only option I had come across.

"Okay," I said. "Do you have a plan?"

Sadie left without anybody noticing, thanks to a guard that had taken a particular liking to her. When she left, though, I found myself craving her presence. The darkness of the steel, magically enforced room grew thicker and more lonely with every passing minute.

I had wondered for so long if Sadie ever made it back to Fearford, ever found peace. Ever recovered from the loss of her friend, Isaiah.

But here she was, living with the rebels.

At least she was alive, I told myself. Somebody here wasn't actively trying to kill Malachi, at least I knew that.

And she wasn't alone. She had been talking to the humans, some from Fearford and some from my home. They were all being kept here, being told nothing other than the fact that they were to stay indoors.

If I didn't hate the rebels before, I definitely did now.

I lost track of time in that dark room, not being able to tell if the sun was up or down. Not hearing anything, not even a footstep, from the hallway outside. I had no idea how long it had been since Sadie left, or if an entire day had passed.

I knew nothing.

I tried to keep my thoughts off Malachi. Tried and failed.

He was likely planning a way to storm the place, maybe he was right outside tracking the movements of the rebel guards.

Keep him safe, I thought up to the Saints. *If anything else happens, please keep Malachi safe.*

The steel door creaked open.

"Sadie?" I whispered, barely audible. But it wasn't Sadie's lean figure that walked through the door, no.

"Your friend isn't here," a male voice boomed. "You have no friends here, actually."

He left the door cracked as he pushed his way inside. I slid off the cot and immediately backed into the wall behind me, every single instinct alert. Every instinct on fire.

"What are you doing here?" I asked. "What do you want?"

The man became familiar, my eyes adjusting with the filtering light from the hallway. It was Ky's friend, the one who had been with us earlier.

"Ky believes we should leave you alone down here," the man said. "He says you're too dangerous to be messed with."

I held my breath, not daring a response. This fae was twice my size, and without my magic or a weapon...

"I'm here to find out how much of that is true, peacemaker."

I didn't have time to flinch before the fae sent a fist straight into my stomach. Pain and shock both erupted, taking up every single one of my senses. I doubled over, trying to suck in a breath.

But the fae wasn't done.

He sent an elbow into my back, pain ripping through my upper body. I fell to the ground, unable to catch myself as my weak limbs crashed to the cold floor.

"You're not so powerful without your magic, now, are you? Just another dumb, weak human. It's a shame, really."

Another kick to my curled-up body, one I couldn't begin to deflect. I didn't have the energy. Couldn't fight against the erupting pain that now encompassed every single ounce of my being.

Please, I thought up to the Saints. *Please, make it stop.*

But it didn't. I thought he would be done after the

fourth kick, or maybe the fifth. In fact, I prayed to the Saints every single time that it would be the last.

But it wasn't. Eventually, the pain became too much to bear, too much to hold. So I let it go, let it take over entirely, let it morph with my soul and with my being until all I knew was the pain.

CHAPTER 31
Malachi

"How is this possible?" I asked Esther. After a lot of chaos and yelling, Dragon had finally shifted back to a boy right in front of us. I had never seen anything like it, it was...it was lore, it was not supposed to exist. Yet here he was, right before us.

"I didn't believe it, either," Esther started. "I assume Silas and some of the Paragon knew, hence the name he was given. It suits him, I'll say that much."

"I can't believe this," Adeline breathed. "This whole time, shifters have been real? *Dragons* are real?"

"Dragon is the first I've met, the first I've heard of being real, actually," Esther answered.

"What does this mean?" I asked. "Does this mean other dragons exist?"

"I certainly wouldn't rule it out," Esther replied.

"That explains why I couldn't read his mind before," Cordelia added. "He's not like everyone else." She stepped forward and lowered herself to meet Dragon's eyes. "You're different, aren't you?"

Dragon shrugged. "I guess so. Silas told me not to tell anybody."

"Of course he did," I muttered. "Can you control it? Do you shift often?"

"We've been getting better," Esther explained, "although like most magic, it's difficult to contain with any rush of emotions."

Adeline stepped forward. "Shall we also discuss whatever just happened to Serefin? I mean, he practically saved all of our lives just now!"

We all shifted our attention to Serefin, who stood with wide eyes. "Don't look at me," he said. "I have no idea how I did that."

Esther laughed quietly. "It's shield magic. You protected your friends from Dragon's fire."

Serefin held his hands out before him and looked at them intently. "Shield magic?" he asked. "Are you sure?"

Esther nodded. "After what I just saw, I'm very sure."

Adeline squealed in excitement, and I moved to clap him on the shoulder. "You're a protector now," I said to him. "That's very fitting."

Serefin just smiled. "Always, brother," he replied.

Suddenly, my vision blurred. My body stiffened. I wasn't quite sure what was happening, even my power seemed to stir inside of me, waiting for some sort of attack.

And then there was pain everywhere all at once.

Pain like I had never felt before, burning me from the inside out.

I looked at my friends, but they all seemed fine. Someone shouted my name, but their faces blurred together in my tunneling vision.

Pain in my chest, my stomach, my core, over and over and over again until it stayed.

I hadn't realized I had fallen to the ground, doubled over without breathing, until Cordelia rolled me onto my back.

Someone yelled in the background, I couldn't hear anything over the ringing in my ears.

It hurt, *everything* hurt.

"Malachi?" Adonis yelled over me, leaning across from Cordelia and staring at me.

Saints, I wanted to scream. Wanted to tell them to *go, go, go*.

But I couldn't even take a breath, let alone speak.

I wasn't sure how long I stayed like that. My vision blurred in and out, the darkness taking over for small amounts of time before it all began to fade away.

"Malachi?" Adonis yelled again, shaking my shoulders. "Tell us what's happening!"

"It's her," I managed to get out. I couldn't say anything else, gasping in breaths and fueling my lungs.

Cordelia knew, though. Could see exactly what I was thinking.

Her eyes widened. "It's Jade," she whispered, barely a breath. "They're hurting Jade."

I bent over and coughed again, this time feeling the breath escape from my lungs as if it were my own. And somewhere in the pain, laced deep and deliberately, was a trace of something else.

Something *dark*. Something *familiar*.

Something so filled with her, with Jade's essence, it nearly overtook me entirely. It was our bond coming back full-force, trying to alert me that she was in trouble, that she needed our help.

After a few moments, the pain faded. As soon as I could, I jumped to my feet. "She needs us," I yelled. "We have to go to her! We cannot wait any longer!"

"I'll fetch the others," Adonis said, running back into the depths of the dungeon.

"What about Dragon?" Adeline asked. "He can help us!"

"Only if he can control himself," I replied, "and by the looks of it, I'm not sure he can."

"I can!" Dragon yelled. "I swear to you, I can do it! Let me help her! Let me help get the peacemaker back!"

Well, I wasn't going to argue with that.

I nodded and turned on my heel, following Adonis out of the dark hallways.

Serefin's hand fell on my shoulder. "I'm with you, brother," he whispered.

"No," I replied. "You need to go with the others. If anything happens, you can protect them with your shield magic."

"I'd rather protect you. Let me fly by your side, we can find the rebels before the sun rises."

Serefin, not my blood but just as connected to me as anyone who might be my real brother. Serefin was brave, many times braver than me. He had fought directly by my side in battle, had killed for me. Had stood up for me. For years and years of my life, Serefin was the only person I trusted.

But now, I cared about a lot more than my own

survival. I had the entire kingdom at risk. I had brothers and friends and... dragons.

Somehow, a handful of witches even fell into the group of people I needed to protect.

"Please," Serefin pushed, sensing my resistance. "You need protection just as much—if not more—than anyone else. I'm not even sure I'll be able to pull my shield out again so soon, but let me try."

I stopped walking and turned to face him, soldiers and witches now running in every direction, around us and through the castle, preparing for our upcoming battle.

"I love you, brother," I started, patting him on both shoulders. "You know I do. I know you want to come with me, I know you want to protect me. But this?" I waved my hands out, signaling to the castle around us, to the people we cared about. To Eli, Adeline, Cordelia, the others. "This is what we've always wanted for Rewyth, Ser. This is what I've fought so hard for. This is what we've always deserved. I want—no, I *need* you to protect that. Protect the integrity of what we've built here. I'll be okay on my own, but them?"

I glanced down the hall where the others waited for us near the castle door. "They need you now, and I need you to protect them."

"They need you, too, Mal," Ser whispered. "We all do."

"You don't need to worry about me."

"Well, I do. You'd do anything to get Jade back, and we know that. But I also know you'd give your own life for hers in an instant if it meant making her safe, if it meant bringing her back home."

His words didn't hurt me as badly as the pain in his

eyes. Serefin was great at masking his emotions. He had kept our relationship respectful and professional for as long as he could, only letting me see his true concern or emotion when it was absolutely necessary.

I loved him for that, but I also knew I wasn't going to pull back for Jade.

"Go," I said, nodding in the direction of the others. "That's an order."

Before anyone else could stop me, I ran outside and launched into the air, over the castle wall, over the trees that surrounded Rewyth, over everything I had known. That tug of Jade's power pulled me, guiding me, laced with a pain and a desperation that only made me pump my wings faster and faster.

Jade needed me. I felt it like I felt the air in my own lungs.

And I would stop at nothing to get her back.

CHAPTER 32
Jade

The darkness became worse than the pain.

After the fae left, satisfied with the amount of punches and kicks he had given me, I was left alone in the dark, cold cell.

At first, the hope was the worst part. Hope that someone had heard. Hope that Sadie would come rescue me. Hope that the fae would see he had hurt me enough.

But that quickly faded. Hope was a dangerous, dangerous game, I knew that more than anybody. I tried not to feel it at all, like when I was first sent to marry Malachi. The lack of hope made me strong, made me brave. Forced me to look death in the eye without backing down.

Now, though, hope was around every corner. Every distant sound, every yell echoing off the steel walls.

Malachi. Malachi. Malachi.

I placed a hand on the center of my chest. For a split second, when I was sure the fae attacking me wasn't going to stop until I was dead, I thought I felt it; that familiar, magical bond that made him eternally mine.

But now, sitting back in the magically-enforced steel, I felt nothing. Not a shred of magic, not a flicker of power.

I must have been imagining things, imagining the connection being re-formed in my panic of survival.

"Shouldn't the magic of the Saints be stronger than some damn wall?" I whispered to myself.

I waited for a reply, but again, none came.

My breathing, slow, steady, and shallow, became the only sound I heard as I drifted off again, being claimed by the inevitable exhaustion.

CHAPTER 33
Malachi

Faster. Further. Higher.

My thoughts revolved around Jade and did not stop, not once. The others would catch up, I knew they would. But they wouldn't beat me there.

Good. I didn't need anyone trying to stop me. First, we had to find where the damn rebels were camping out. I had a feeling that wouldn't be as easy as it sounded.

What had that woman at the inn said?

Past the river and...

It didn't matter. When I got close enough, I would be able to feel her.

And I prayed to the Saints that it wasn't her pain I would be feeling again.

I knew one thing, though. I was going to find whoever laid their damn hands on her, and I was going to rip their head off.

I flew and flew and flew, until every single beat of my wings burned through my body, until I was sure I could not fly any more, and then I finally saw the river.

I dove to the ground without a second of hesitation, my boots grinding against the dirt forest floor. The trees were thinner near the river, creating less coverage for my identifiable black wings.

I crouched near the flowing water, catching my breath. Letting my heart rate slow to its original pace.

I had to focus. Losing focus could mean death, not only for me but for her, too.

Please, I thought up to the Saints. *If you do anything else, please help me get her back.*

I wasn't sure if I was half-delirious from the exhaustion of the long flight, or if I truly was losing my mind, but a male voice boomed through my head. *You have everything you need to get her back, King of Shadows.*

I flinched at first, hand immediately falling to my hip where my sword remained strapped. "Who are you?" I said aloud.

You know who I am.

Yep, the voice was definitely in my head.

No, I do not know who you are. If anything, you're a figment of my imagination. You aren't real.

A rumble of my power flared in my chest, burning my entire upper body in a wavelike flare of heat.

What in the...

"Did you do that?"

You know exactly who I am.

"Erebus," I breathed. My mind ran through a hundred different questions for the Saint of death. *Where are you? Why did you give me this gift? What do you want from us, from Jade? Why did you let her get taken?*

But I asked none of those.

"Where is she?" I asked aloud, keeping my voice at a hushed whisper as I scanned the trees around us. Nothing aside from the natural flow of wind caught my attention.

She's close, Erebus replied. *Use your gift to find her.*

I've tried, I thought back. *It's not strong enough. I don't feel her; I haven't felt her since I got a glimpse of her pain back in Rewyth.*

You're holding back, he said, a hint of irritation lacing his words. *Unleash your full power and you will find her. It is the only way.*

It isn't the only way! You can help her!

The Saints can only do so much. We gave you both what you need to live, to take control. Now it is up to you.

Shit.

How? How do I unleash the full potential of my power?

Stop holding it in, stop fearing for the lives of others. Be unstoppable. Be deadly, if you must, but do not fear who you are, Malachi Weyland. Blood of my blood.

As those words hit my mind, my body erupted in chills. My power flared up like a wild animal, ferocious and merciless. A newfound energy washed over my body, fueling my muscles with energy and my lungs with breath.

I felt...I felt *unstoppable.*

Is this what he wanted? For me to not hold back, to not worry?

Another flare of my power lapped at the surface, and I didn't fight it. Didn't try to control it.

I was sick and tired of controlling myself, anyway. I knew what rested deep within, I had witnessed it only a handful of times.

Death. Destruction. Power unlike any I had ever seen,

besides the one in my wife. It was there, hidden away and shoved so far deep in my soul that I barely remembered its existence.

That was the power that scared me. The magic that turned me into something else, something unlike any other fae.

But I wouldn't hold it in any longer.

I let my head fall back and my palms raise toward the darkening sky as I let go.

Thunder boomed nearby. The vibrations only fueled my power even more. A rush, like unstoppable waves of the sea, escaped from me. I closed my eyes and let it go, let it find Jade. Let it finally move from its resting place deep within me.

And when I opened my eyes again, I saw no sunlight. I saw nothing, actually, even with my fae eyes. Black smoke—no, *power*—rushed from my palms quicker than I had ever seen it, filling the thin forest around me with a dark cloud of doom.

I laughed; I couldn't help it. To feel so free, it wasn't in my nature, not usually. But this? It felt so right.

Black nothingness, black death. I could not even see the glistening river in front of me as I stepped out of my cover behind a thick tree.

Eli had been right with his vision of the future. Death was near.

CHAPTER 34
Jade

The entire building shook, rattling from the very steel walls that entrapped me.

A storm? Someone losing control of their powers?

I placed my hands on the cold walls and waited for the rattling to stop. No, I knew exactly where that world-shattering boom had come from. I felt it in my soul, even with the exclusion of my magic. I knew it was him.

He was coming for me.

Through the steel walls of my enclosure, I heard panic begin on the outside. Men's voices yelling, footsteps as soldiers began to run.

"They're coming!" someone directly outside my door yelled. "Everyone get ready! Someone get the girl!"

Shit. Shit. Shit.

I stood up and backed myself against the wall, as if I could hide from the fae. As if I could disappear entirely.

But a few seconds later, that steel door was bursting open. Not slowly and carefully like it had been opened before, no. Someone kicked the door with such force that it slammed against the wall behind it.

"Let's go!" the same fae who had assaulted me earlier screamed. I hated the way I cowered away, crossing my arms over my stomach for instinctual protection.

But that didn't stop the fae from storming forward with a piercing hand around my neck, his fingers digging into the sensitive skin as he half pulled, half-pushed me out the steel door and into the hallway.

It was not empty like it was the last time I had seen it.

Instead, soldiers ran back and forth, chaos filling the room as orders were yelled, fae panicking and pulling weapons from their belts.

"What's going on?" I asked.

The fae answered by forcing my neck down, causing me to hunch over as he dragged me down the hallway. "You don't speak!" he yelled. Although I could hear the lace of panic in his words.

They weren't expecting this, whatever it was. Did they think Malachi would come quietly? Did they think he would show up without a fight, without a show?

Malachi, the King of Shadows, was not going to show up without a fight.

And they had taken the one thing he cared about the most: his wife.

I was forced down the hall, following the rest of the soldiers filing up the stairs and into the open room of the underground building. I saw a few of them running up another set of stairs.

That must be the stairs to the outside. That would be my ticket out of here.

I just had to get rid of this damn fae.

I squirmed under his grasp, trying to loosen his grip, but that only made him angrier.

"Stop moving!" the fae growled, baring his teeth. "You'll only make this harder on yourself, peacemaker."

It was then that I felt it, like the fog being lifted from every inch of my body all at once. It was powerful and hot and forceful, so very *him*. Our magic bond snapping back to life, channeling Malachi's emotions into me.

And mine into him.

And what I felt through that tight bond of magic was nothing less than absolute fury and the promise of death.

Good, I thought. *They deserve to die. Every single one of them deserves to die for this.*

"Where are you taking me?" I asked again. "There's nowhere we can go where he won't find me!"

This seemed to piss him off further. He gripped my upper arm, almost piercing my skin, as he began forcing me through the dining hall.

The more pain I felt, the stronger my connection to Malachi would be.

"If you think you can possibly escape," the fae started, "you are sadly mistaken. Fighting will only make it worse. You're coming with me and we're getting away from the building. Now go."

He gave me a harsh shove toward...towards those steps, the ones that led up and out of the building.

Was he really stupid enough to bring me outside?

I ducked my head and moved in the direction he ordered, trying not to look too pleased by where we were heading.

Suddenly, all of those lanterns flickered out.

I kept moving toward the stairs, taking the first step on the raised platform when the fae behind me forced me to stop.

A few others began to panic, darkness taking over. Not the type of darkness they could see in, though.

Not the type of darkness even a fae's eyes would adjust to.

Him. Death's awakening, darkness looming. It was all him.

Malachi.

"What is that?" the fae behind me shouted to someone else.

"I don't know!" the other man yelled back. "Get her out of here and keep her hidden! This is the first place they'll attack when they come for her!"

I bit my cheek to keep from smiling, even as the fae's nails cut through my skin, blood bubbling to the surface where he tightened his grip.

"Keep moving," the fae ordered, growling just inches from my ear. His breath brushed my cheek, I flinched away from the disgusting smell.

I wanted absolutely nothing to do with this fae. If Malachi didn't rip his head off first, I would.

I kept moving up the stairs, one after another, until we reached the top.

And just when I thought the world could not get any darker, could not come any closer to eternal death, I stepped outside.

Darkness swallowed me whole.

CHAPTER 35
Malachi

I couldn't see Jade, but I felt her. She was close. I sensed it strongly, pulling me to her with every calculated breath I took.

I needed to cross the river, but flying would be too obvious. Inching out of my hiding spot behind the trees, I crept closer to the flowing water. It trickled quickly but quietly, only making a few splashes as the water fell across the rocks below.

I removed my thick boots and my heavy tunic, dropping them on the ground next to me without a sound, only leaving my trousers and my belt that contained my sword.

And then, with silent motions that not even the closest predator would hear, I slipped into the water.

It was cold and refreshing, igniting every one of my senses as I dipped underneath, pushing the water behind me and propelling myself to the other side.

And when I reached that other side of the stream, I placed both hands on the ground and slid out, as silently as I had slid in.

That power within me lit up again.

Closer. I was getting closer.

The woman at the inn had said something, something about it being...underground?

I took a few steps forward, my bare feet connecting firmly with the cold dirt beneath me. It would make sense if they were underground, hiding away from the rest of the fae that might fly above.

It was the perfect hiding place.

But where were they? And how would I find them?

There would have to be some sort of entrance, one likely hidden with glamour if they were smart, like the entrance to the Paragon.

Shadows—my shadows—still spread through the air, pulsing with every breath I took, darkening even the approaching moonlight from any sort of illumination.

I could see, though. Through the shadows that were my very own, I could see even clearer than before. And I searched for only one thing: her.

I crept forward like that for a few minutes—one foot after the other, not breaking a single twig or cracking the smallest leaf. Silent, like a summer breeze passing through the land. But I felt that pull to my wife like I had never felt it before, one of delight and thrill and fear.

She must have known I was coming. Must have sensed it, maybe even seen my shadows. Saints, I hoped she had seen my shadows.

Entirely unleashed, entirely unchained. Coming just for her.

A few footsteps in the distance caught my attention. I halted again, freezing where I stood and sending another wave of thunderous shadows in the direction the sounds came from.

A few fae shouted.

I clenched my fists. That had to be them.

I sent even more of my shadows out, encapsulating every inch of open air with the darkness. Through that magic bond, I felt a flicker of amusement.

Yes, Jade was close. She was here. She knew I was coming for her.

With the shadows covering me, I inched forward. Their camp had to be somewhere nearby, my magic drawing them out of hiding so they could prepare for a fight.

Like they ever stood a chance.

I silently pulled my sword from my belt. "Come on, you bastards."

They wanted a fight. I would bring them a war.

I moved forward again, not caring as much about hiding the small snaps of each footstep as I aimed toward where I heard movement.

A few more crunches of forest terrain in the distance.

I raised my sword. I pushed more shadows through the thick, humid air.

"That way!" a voice whispered in the distance, just a few feet away and covered by my shadows. "Spread out! Guard the entrances!"

Those poor, poor idiots.

I sent a flare of my power out, pushing toward every being I felt with my primal, instinctual senses. The shadows danced with the looming darkness of the trees, creating a deadly smoke as the first fae body fell, the first victim of my unleashed magic.

And then the second fell.

The third.

Soon, five bodies were down. Five enemies eliminated. Five less fae to hurt her.

I didn't care if they had nothing to do with it. I didn't even care if they hadn't laid eyes on Jade. They were equally as responsible.

I took a few steps forward until I saw the bodies through the smoke. All so young, all so hopeful. I knew what it was like to fight for a cause, but for this? What did these rebels think was going to happen?

"Move!" another fae voice, slightly closer, ordered. I crouched in the shadows, completely hidden by my own darkness. I squinted my eyes to see a small flap in the forest floor pushing open.

A hidden door.

But it was not a soldier that exited the hidden hideout. It was not a fae. It was not a rebel.

Jade. My wife.

Any tiny shred of control I had left disappeared entirely, vanishing along with any doubts that I wouldn't be able to get to her in time.

She crawled out of the hidden door, climbing on her hands and knees, looking in awe at the dark shadows twirling in the air around her.

And then the fae from behind her moved, gripping the back of her neck and hauling her to her feet as the door behind them slammed shut.

I could not have controlled the darkness that leapt from me if I wanted to. Thank the Saints that Jade was not affected by my power, because she would have been obliterated, too, as my magic scavenged the several feet between us, landing on their target with a sickening scream.

Jade spun around, watching with wide eyes as the fae behind her loosened his grasp and fell to the ground.

I was on my feet in an instant, half-running, half-flying the short distance to her before I wrapped her in my arms.

"Malachi," she whispered, collapsing into me with a cry of relief. "Malachi, thank the Saints."

I pulled away and held her by the shoulders. "The Saints have nothing to do with this," I mumbled. "It's up to you and I. Let's end these sorry bastards."

Anger fueling my movements, I began to move toward that door.

Jade stopped me with a hand on my chest. "No!" she argued. "No, this is all a trap, Mal! It's a trap, they're going to kill you! You have to get out of here now. Right now!"

"Calm down," I said. "Who's trying to kill me?"

"The leader of the rebels! His name is Ky. He claims you killed his brother in war a long time ago, he's trying to get his revenge."

"That's what this is all about? Some fae trying to get revenge?" I looked back at the door that led to wherever they had kept Jade. "I'm going to kill them all. Then we can go home and we won't have to worry about this again."

"Wait! There are humans in there, innocent ones. Don't kill them all!"

"Saints," I breathed. "They're rebels now, Jade. They deserve to die!"

"Sadie is in there!" The pleading in her eyes made me pause, even if just for a second. "We have to help them, Mal. They're victims here, too."

Deep down, I knew she was right. The humans were nothing but pawns in this fae game. But caring about collateral damage wasn't always my specialty.

"Fine," I said anyway. "The others are on their way. We'll go after who we can, and we'll regroup with them and make a new plan on how to save the humans later. Sound good?"

Jade nodded.

"Are you okay?" I asked her, scanning her face in the darkness.

Through the shadows that danced around us, I noticed the way she held her arm tightly across her torso. Her face had been bruised—freshly, the skin was busted and red and a halo of purple began to color her delicate skin.

"Who did this to you?" I asked, cupping her face with my hand.

"The same people who want you dead. Let's get out of here before they succeed."

I took her hand and guided her through the shadows until we were hidden behind a row of green bushes. We both knelt, hiding ourselves from anyone else who might be exiting that building.

"My power," Jade whispered as we crouched. "It's...it was being suppressed when I was in there. The Saints haven't spoken to me. I haven't been able to use it at all, Mal. Not since we left my home."

"It must be some sort of shield magic," I said. "Which Serefin now has, by the way. It could come in handy later."

"Serefin has shield magic?" Jade asked, a hint of a smile playing on her lips.

I nodded.

"Wow. Of all the power he could possibly get, that suits him best. He'd do anything to protect you, you know."

"And you," I added. "They'll get here soon, Jade. And once they do, we're getting rid of these damn rebels."

"I don't understand," Jade whispered, turning her attention to the forest around us. "They should have noticed your presence by now. Why aren't they attacking?"

"They can't attack what they can't see," I whispered back to her. "Although I wouldn't be surprised if they started battling my shadows with their own magic, soon. If your Saints want to chime in and help us out at any time, just let me know."

Those damn Saints.

We're here, the low, sultry voice spoke into my mind.

I couldn't help but flinch.

"What?" Jade asked. "What is it?"

"Nothing, it's just..."

We are connected now, the voice said. *Because of your connection. The peacemaker's power will return soon. Keep her out of that damn building.*

"Great, thanks," I whispered to the voice.

"What?" Jade whispered, clearly seeing that something wasn't right.

"I think...I believe the Saints have been speaking in my mind. Only once or twice."

"Is it Erebus?" Jade asked, a wave of hope perking her up from our crouching position in the waves of shadows. "Is he going to help us?"

As she said the words, a rush of strength like I had never felt before washed over me, fueling every single one of my senses. The dark shadows around us immediately began to stir, mixing together in a frenzy of death and chaos.

Someone screamed in the distance, meeting their death by my hand.

Erebus's hand.

A satisfied laugh echoed in my mind.

"I think he already has," I replied.

Jade's smile grew wide and wicked. We actually had a chance of making it out of here alive.

"Come on," I whispered to Jade, pulling my sword out and handing it to her. Saints, I always loved seeing her wield my weapon. "Let's give them what they deserve."

CHAPTER 36
Jade

I focused on that spark of power that I knew was there, I willed it with everything in me to come back. To be strong. To protect me.

But the damn shielding magic that had been in that room lingered, dulling my power and weighing down my limbs. Even holding Malachi's sword took more energy than it needed to, causing my movements to be slow and sloppy.

I followed Malachi as he crouched, walking barefoot and shirtless through the forest as we stalked the perimeter. Aside from a few screams after Malachi's power intensified, we had heard nothing. It was likely they had all gotten spooked off, running into the forest to save themselves.

That, or they were hiding. Waiting, just like us, for the right moment to attack.

Not a single bird chirped in the distance.

Not a single tree waved in the wind.

Death was coming. I felt it in every inch of my being,

every ounce of my soul. Eli's vision, the one promising death and retribution, would be coming to light.

"It's too quiet," I whispered up to him.

Malachi's shadows had stilled, too, almost as if in anticipation for what was to come.

He couldn't use his shadows forever. They protected us, yes. They kept us hidden. But they also gave us away.

"Drop them," I whispered up to him. Mal stopped and faced me. "Drop your shadows. They'll think we've left."

He considered this for a minute. "They'll never believe we left without a fight. And the way they haven't come for you yet..."

"They will," I said with absolute assurance. "They'll come for me, Mal. But it'll be you they're trying to kill."

His jaw tightened. "I'll push the shadows toward the way we came," he said. "With any luck, they'll follow the shadows and try to find us. Are you feeling any stronger?"

I nodded. "Yep," I lied.

"I can feel when you're lying, you know," Malachi whispered with a wicked grin. "Even without your magic in full force."

"Fine," I admitted. "But that doesn't mean I'm not ready to fight. Send the shadows. We'll deal with them."

"If you say so, my queen," Malachi muttered, placing a gentle kiss on my forehead. I closed my eyes and took a long breath, trying to take in this moment. Trying to make it last forever.

When I opened my eyes again, the shadows around us were gone, pushing like a cloud back through the forest in the direction we had just come from.

Malachi's pointed ears flickered, no doubt listening for any hint of soldiers moving.

And then, all at once, we were at war.

The first group of fae charged us from our right. With a roar of anger and determination, and with their swords held high, they ran for us.

Malachi quit pushing his shadows out and used all his magic to drop the group of five fae to their knees, screaming in pain.

Malachi was strong, yes, but could he kill every single soldier here? I wasn't sure, but I certainly didn't want to risk it.

Movement caught my attention between a group of trees in the darkness. "Straight ahead!" I yelled. Mal spun on his heel, forgetting the five fae that now cowered on the forest floor and turning his attention to the others.

A crack split through the air. Seconds later, a blazing hot ball of fire whizzed by, narrowly missing my head.

"Shit!" I yelled. "Fire power!"

Another rush of flames came toward us, uncontrolled and chaotic as they came inches from grazing Malachi's body.

"Get back!" he yelled. "Take cover!"

"We have to fight, Mal! They'll keep coming!"

Another ball of fire attacked, even closer this time. Mal and I both ducked to avoid being burnt to ash.

"You aren't strong enough yet, Jade! Get back!" Mal yelled. Something lingered in his voice, something needy and desperate and... terrified.

I did as he ordered, backing up until a few large tree trunks protected me from any balls of fire.

Mal retreated, too, but not as far. He kept his back to me while he took long strides, barefoot and all, and aimed his death power at our attackers.

Come on, stupid power, I thought to myself. *Come back any time now, preferably before we're roasted into oblivion.*

Two fae charged Mal from his left. I jumped out from my hiding position, taking three strides toward them with the sword tight in my grasp. I swung once, a battle-cry escaping me as the weapon met flesh, cutting the first fae directly in half at the torso.

"Jade!" Mal yelled. I spun to face him, losing track of the second fae. Mal was on us in seconds, jumping onto the fae's back and snapping his neck in one swift motion.

For two full seconds, Mal and I stood there, eyes wide and staring at each other, our chests rising and falling in unison.

For two full seconds, I let myself feel fear. Fear of not being good enough, of not having my power. *Of Malachi.*

And then I pushed that fear away, swallowing it whole, and tightened my grip on my sword.

Malachi and I turned, back-to-back, ready for another attack.

And before I could take another breath, before I even had the chance of feeling fear again, we were surrounded.

CHAPTER 37
Malachi

"It doesn't have to be this way!" I yelled to the circle of fae around us. They all wore black fabric around their faces, with green and black paint smeared across their skin to blend easily into the surrounding foliage.

I tried to push more of my shadows into the surrounding forest, but I needed my strength. I needed all of my damn strength if I was going to make it out of here alive.

Alive, and with my wife.

"Yes," a voice called from the back of the group. "It does have to be this way. Such a pity, really."

Jade's shoulders rose and fell as she breathed deeply behind me. *If any one of these damn bastards touch her, they're dead. They're all dead.*

I scanned the line of soldiers that stopped a few feet away from us.

Come on. Come on and attack us already.

In front of me, a couple of the rebels shuffled, creating room for a fae behind them to walk in front.

"Hello, Malachi," he said, crossing his hands in front of his torso. "I would say it's nice to see you again, but it surely is not."

"Who are you?" I asked.

"My name is Ky. I don't expect you to know that, though. I don't expect you to know any of the fae you have gone to battle against."

I waited while the words processed in my mind. *Ky...* this was the fae that hurt Jade.

The one behind all of this.

The one I was going to kill.

I stepped forward, only an inch, and looked him up and down. This was the fae behind it all? This was the one who took my wife from me?

Saints, I nearly wanted to laugh.

"You harm the peacemaker because of past grievances?" I asked. "Do you know how powerful she is? Your men will not survive a fight against her, I can assure you that."

Ky smirked and tilted his head to the side, as if everything I said to him only amused him further.

"She didn't seem so powerful squirming beneath the fists of my men. I heard her cries all the way down the hall, actually."

That did it.

With a single movement, I pulled every last piece of power I had left. I exhaled deeply, pulling and pulling at that heat blooming in my soul and pushing it in Ky's direction, spreading it across the area in front of me. Somewhere in the chaos of darkness, Jade moved from behind me. I heard her say something, but I couldn't make it out over the ringing in my ears.

And I didn't stop. I pushed and pushed and pushed, wishing nothing but death on Ky and his little army of rebels.

Nobody touches Jade and lives.

Nobody even looks at Jade with harm and remains standing.

They would all die.

The sound of metal against metal behind me eventually caught my attention.

Jade was fighting with the others, weapon to weapon. I spun around, not even checking to see if Ky and his friends were dead yet, and began helping my wife.

She had gotten more skilled in combat. So skilled, actually, that she cut three fae down before I even had my hands on one.

"There are more!" she yelled through gritted teeth. "We can't hold them off forever!"

"How is that power of yours coming along?" I asked, snapping the neck of another pale-winged fae.

He fell to the ground before me. I stepped over him before stopping the blade of another, ripping it from their grasp and impaling their torso with the steel.

"Working on it," Jade said, using her black boot to shove a dead fae off her own weapon.

I glanced away for half a second to survey the scene around us.

Jade was right. More were coming. We couldn't hold them off forever, not alone. My power was already depleting. I needed a few minutes to restore it, and that was a few minutes we didn't have.

We kept fighting, fae after fae. Rebel after rebel. Jade's shouts of anger fueled me in my own fight, cutting down as many of those blood-thirsty rebels as possible, until a few began to...began to *run away*.

"What's happening?" Jade asked, not stopping her fight.

A few men screamed as they ran. I looked to find someone pointing up at the sky, past the trees and into the darkness.

I cut one more fae down before following the looks of horror.

Only to find a dragon flying straight toward us.

CHAPTER 38
Jade

"What is that?" I screamed, my voice hoarse from the effort. Thankfully, nobody else tried to kill me at that given moment. Everyone was too busy running away from whatever monster swarmed the sky above us.

Malachi stared into the sky for a few more seconds before a deep, wicked smile spread across his face. He took a few steps toward me before tearing his gaze away. "Believe it or not, that's Dragon."

I glanced up again, seeing black and red scales lacing the underbelly of the beast. And those wings...those were the things one saw in nightmares. This was the type of beast mothers told horror stories about.

"Dragon is a..."

"Yes," Malachi said, cutting me off. "And unless we want to turn to rubble, we better get out of here. Now."

He moved first, pulling me along with him through the trees. I didn't know which way we were headed, I didn't care.

If Dragon couldn't see us…

"Dragon doesn't know we're down here," I said, more to myself than to Malachi. I repeated it again, louder, so he could hear me. "He doesn't know!"

Malachi was already sprinting, his bare feet practically gliding over the forest floor as he dragged me along with him. The grip he had on my hand tightened. He knew, he had to know. With the chaos going on around us, Dragon was certainly going to…

A loud roar, one that shook the trees around us and vibrated the bones in my body, split through the air.

My stomach dropped. Mal stopped running.

There was nothing we could do but stare at the world around us as Dragon engulfed the entire forest in flames.

CHAPTER 39
Malachi

I had never been more certain that I was going to die. Maybe once, in the middle of war, surrounded by my enemies without even a sword to fight with. But that was different. There was always a slight sliver of hope, a fraction of a plan that would save my life.

There was always *something*.

Now, with fire coming directly at us from a dragon that shouldn't even exist, I knew death was ours.

I wrapped Jade in my arms and flexed my wings around us, any last shred of hope leaving with my final breath.

And then I waited.

Waited for the heat, the flames, the ash that would surely result from the blow of the dragon.

But it never came. Even as soldiers screamed abruptly around us, until their screams were cut off by something I couldn't see, we were still alive.

I blinked my eyes open, only to find a glimmering shield around us.

"What the—"

"You really should have waited for us," Serefin insisted, standing with his hands held out in the air, a shield of protection stopping Dragon's deadly fire from killing us.

The blaze ceased.

Serefin dropped his shield.

Jade and I both stood, a mixture of adrenaline and relief swarming my body and sending her emotions through our magic tether.

"Saints," Jade whispered as I pulled my wings back from her body. "We almost just died."

"Yes," Serefin said, his face blank. "You did."

"You...you just saved our lives, Ser," Jade stuttered before throwing herself into his arms.

His eyes locked with mine for a split second, long enough for me to see the fear and relief and love swarming beneath them.

Serefin *had* just saved our lives.

"Where are the others?" I asked.

"On their way. They figured they'd wait for Dragon to take out most of the soldiers."

We glanced around the forest. Nothing but burnt tree trunks and piles of ash remained.

"Ky is dead," Jade whispered. "There's no way he survived that fire."

"Then we get the humans and we kill the rest of the rebels. It's the only way."

The three of us locked eyes with a silent promise, one made with unsaid words.

"We might not be able to use our magic in that building," Jade suggested. "It's enforced with something, or one of the fae is working overtime to stop us.

And whatever powers they used on us during the attack when they kidnapped me? I'm sure we'll run into them, too."

She was right.

Going into that building to get the humans would be a death-trap. It would be so, so easy to walk away. To leave the humans and return to Rewyth, considering this a victory against all rebels now that their leader was dead.

But that was the dark side thinking, the death and the destruction and the chaos. That was the self-preservation taking over, telling us to run from danger.

The Saints did not gift Jade with this destiny for her to turn away when things grew dangerous. They gave her this power to fight, not just for herself and for Rewyth, but for everyone who may need it.

She met my gaze and nodded.

We didn't have an option.

"The others will be here for backup," Ser insisted. "Do you know how to get into the building?"

"This way," I said, turning to the door that led to the underground hideout. "Get ready."

We walked over the burnt forest floor, my bare feet stepping over the charred bones and ash as we made our way to the hidden door.

The forest grew eerily quiet.

Not a single soldier yelled in the distance. Dragon's wings made no sound now that he was out of sight. No birds chirped. No wind howled.

Nothing.

"Here," I said, bending down and flipping the hatch open to the underground. "I don't know what we're going to find down there, but we can't let those bastards think they've won."

"No," Serefin said from behind me. "We can't."

Jade smiled and stepped forward. "I'll go first," she said. "I know the way."

"Absolutely not," Ser said from behind her, grabbing her arm. "It's too dangerous. I still have the shield magic, I'll go first in case we're attacked."

"Your magic is new," Jade explained. "How can you be sure it will even work when you need it?"

"It's better than nothing," Ser replied. Saints, I didn't want him going first, but with my power depleting and Jade still without the help of the Saints, we didn't have many other options.

"Stay together," I ordered, holding the door open for Serefin. "If anything bad happens down there, we regroup up here and we wait for the others. Understand?"

Jade and Ser both nodded, and *Saints*. I never felt more love for them in my entire life.

I pushed away any thoughts of finality, any thoughts of one of us not coming back up to the surface.

And I followed Serefin down the stairs.

CHAPTER 40
Jade

I held my breath as we descended the stairs. One step after the other, I anticipated the attack. The rush of magic. The deadly force that would certainly be the end of us.

But step after step, it never came.

And before I knew it, we had made it to the end of those dark stairs.

Not a single fae stopped us, not a single fae even lingered in the area.

Maybe we had gotten lucky. Maybe the fae had all left, abandoned the underground hideout and gone to the surface to fight...

But when was I *ever* lucky?

"This way," I whispered. "They're keeping the humans somewhere down here."

Our breathing echoed across the steel walls of the underground fortress. How they even built this place was beyond me, entirely beneath the ground and designed to survive an attack from...well, apparently a dragon.

We walked down the dark hallway, past where I had been kept in that small room. "Hear anything yet?" I asked, motioning to their fae ears.

Mal and Ser both stiffened at the same time, turning to one specific room.

"Over here," Ser ordered. He moved without hesitation, pushing open one of the many doors in the hallway and halting at the door frame. His mouth hung agape, just for a moment, as he surveyed whatever was inside that room.

"What is it?" I asked, pushing forward to see for myself.

I halted, too, unable to form words as I took in the scene in front of me.

Humans, at least a hundred of them, shoved into the small steel room and sitting without even an inch of space between them.

"Saints," I mumbled. Men, women, children. It didn't matter. They had apparently been shoved into this room with no chance of getting out. "How long have you all been in here?"

"Jade," Sadie's voice caught my attention. I turned my head to find her standing from her crouched position in the stale room. "They forced us into here without telling us why."

I pulled her into a hug. Her skin gleamed with sweat. "We're getting everyone out of here," I said. "The rebels won't be a problem anymore."

A few gasps filled the room. "The peacemaker," one of the humans in the back said. "You're real?"

Mal placed a hand on my shoulder. "The peacemaker is very real, and she's here to save your lives. The fae who forced you out of your homes did so wrongfully, and you won't have to live in fear like that. Not anymore. Jade is here to protect you."

I lifted my chin. Hearing Mal say those words sent a fire in my chest, one that flared my power from the inside.

Finally, I began to feel my magic again.

"Can you lead them out of here?" I asked Sadie. "Our people should be here soon. Lead them as far away from this place as you can. We'll find you on the outside."

Sadie nodded and immediately began helping the others stand. Mal, Ser, and I backed up, letting them file out of the dark room they had been held in.

It was inhumane, at the very least.

"I can't believe this," I muttered. "Herding humans as if they are cattle."

Mal's thumb rubbed against the back of my neck. "Never again," he whispered into my ear. "Because of you, Jade. You are their savior."

I relaxed into him, finally letting myself breathe. Finally letting my clenched fists fall. Sadie moved up the stairs in the distance, the file of humans following after her.

We saved them. We actually saved them.

I was finally starting to feel that hidden, dangerous flicker of hope when pain erupted over my entire body. My vision blurred, my legs collapsed beneath me.

Someone was attacking.

Mal and Ser both fell, too, onto their knees next to me as pain washed over us, leaving the three of us incapacitated on the ground.

I moved my hands to my head, scratching at the agony, trying to let out that fire inside me.

My body burned, killing me slowly from the inside out.

A scream escaped me, mixing with the torturous cries of the fae next to me.

"That dragon of yours was a surprise, I must say," Ky's voice interrupted my screams. The pain let up long enough for me to glance up at him approaching. "But this fight of ours is not over."

CHAPTER 41
Malachi

Ky was supposed to be dead.

Deader than dead.

Ash on the forest ground that I stepped across with my bare feet.

More pain erupted in my mind, blinding my thoughts. I tried to reach for Jade but could not even manage lifting my hand.

Whatever magic this rebel was using, it was strong.

Serefin needed to use his shield.

"You want to kill me," I managed to cough through gritted teeth, "just do it already."

Ky, the rebel, knelt before me. I wanted so badly to wipe that look off his face with my fist. "And end the fun so soon?" Ky muttered. "That isn't what you did to my brother, you know. He didn't get the mercy of a swift death."

Saints. I didn't have the energy to deal with this again.

Jade moved next to me, just barely. She was moving toward Ser.

Good. He could shield her from this. I just had to distract him long enough so they could fight back.

They had a chance.

I closed my eyes, just for a second, and thought about my death magic coming out to absolutely slaughter this man. I pictured the way he would be the one falling to his knees in pain, begging me to kill him just to make the burning inside his body stop.

But when I opened my eyes again, nothing had changed.

Jade let out another scream of pain beside me.

"Let them go!" I yelled to Ky. "They have nothing to do with this!" The rest of my breath was pulled from my lungs, making it impossible to keep talking.

Pain. So much pain.

Ky laughed. "And why would I let the peacemaker go?" he asked. "After all the work I've done to get her here?"

More pain split through me, erupting in my chest.

He could kill me, that was fine. But he wasn't laying a finger on her.

Serefin tried to stand and ended up falling, half-catching himself on my shoulder. Ky and Jade both flinched at this movement, but I took the split second of distraction to make my move.

"Get her out of here," I whispered to Ser before releasing him and launching myself at Ky.

It took every last bit of energy I had, every last ounce of strength.

And I launched myself at Ky.

He was shocked, at first. So shocked that he let his magic grip on the three of us falter, just for a second. Long enough for me to throw my shadows at him, full force. He never saw it coming as the darkness pierced his body, radiating all around him.

"Go!" I yelled to Ser. I pushed Jade in the direction of the humans that were still filtering out of the building, now panicking and beginning to shove each other up the narrow stairwell. "Get out of here! Find the others on the surface!"

Ser hesitated, but he knew. He knew I would never forgive him if something happened to her. He knew I couldn't live with myself if she didn't make it out.

It was the only option.

Only, when I turned to face Ky, to finish him off once and for all before he could cause any more trouble in this world, I was met with a long sword through my flesh.

CHAPTER 42
Jade

"MALACHI!" I ripped myself from Serefin's grasp and tore my way back to Malachi, where Ky's blade still impaled him. I felt that sharp pain in my own body, too, through our magic bond that also allowed me to feel his shock as he looked down to see Ky's weapon.

Anger, pain, and pure hatred mixed together inside me, creating a deadly storm of emotions I wouldn't wish on anyone.

And I wanted Ky dead. I wanted him dead more than anything. Mal fell to his knees beside me. I gently lowered him to the ground while Ky pulled the weapon out of Mal's body.

"No," I muttered. Ser drew his own sword, now yelling through his own pain.

Ky might have powerful magic, but he wasn't as angry as us.

My magic rumbled, unable to be contained, begging for a target to relieve some of the pain I was feeling.

And I let it.

I threw everything I had at Ky, at the fae who had hurt Mal, at the one who had caused all this damage. Whatever magic the stupid walls of this place had kept from me was back now, laced with a fiery need for blood. For vengeance.

Serefin yelled something behind me, but I didn't stop. I threw the ball of magic at him until it poured from my fingertips. I wanted nothing but his death, nothing but his bones burning to ash before me.

And so they did.

And I watched in satisfaction as his scream stopped in his throat, his entire body vanishing before my power as I poured and poured and poured.

And just as quickly as it all began, it was over.

I was left panting and sweating, staring at what was just Ky, but was no longer.

I spun around to find Ser half-holding Malachi as his blood poured from his hands. I joined him, dropping to my knees in front of Malachi.

"No," I whispered to him. "Stand up," I ordered. "We have to get out of here and then we'll be able to stop the bleeding."

Mal's eyes were already cloudy, but not from pain or anger. In fact, any anger that had been in his gaze before was gone now.

"You did it," he whispered. "You killed him."

"Yes," I replied, "but there will be more like him. I need you, Mal. This isn't over."

Ser held all of his weight now, grunting under the pressure. The humans were almost all above ground now. Just a couple of minutes, and we could...

"Stay with us, brother," Serefin mumbled. "Jade is right. We need you, Mal. We don't win this war without you."

I gripped Mal's face in my hands. Already so pale, so cold. Blood dripped onto the floor beneath us. "Please," I whispered, ignoring the way my voice cracked. "Please don't leave us now, Mal. We are so close. We are so close to having everything."

Mal smiled. Actually smiled. "I already had everything," he whispered to me. He brought a bloody hand up to brush a tear from my cheek. "I've had it this entire time."

"Don't," I argued. "Don't you dare give up on me now!"

His eyelids grew heavy, taunting me with every blink. This wasn't happening. This couldn't possibly be happening. The mighty, dangerous King of Shadows was not going to be killed by a mere fae, not after everything we'd been through.

Not after everything *he* had been through.

Serefin lost his grip on Mal's shoulders and he fell forward, falling straight into my chest. I fought to lift him up, holding him with all of my remaining strength, which wasn't much.

"It was all supposed to happen this way," Mal muttered, just inches from my face now. I cried violently, tears running freely down my face and dripping from my chin.

"You can't possibly think that," I replied.

"You know it's true, Jade. I was always going to be your downfall. Now, I don't have to be."

He blinked a couple more times.

And then his entire body collapsed.
Malachi Weyland, King of Shadows, died in my arms.

CHAPTER 43
Malachi

I had many regrets in my life, but none hurt me as badly as seeing the look on Jade's face as I slipped into the darkness.

She had to understand. If it were up to me, I wouldn't leave her. I would *never* leave her. But I tried so hard to fight, to stay awake, to make it through. At the end, as long as Jade was safe, that's all that mattered.

Serefin would protect her. He would get her out.

The pain from Ky's weapon disappeared, leaving me floating in a void of darkness. It did not feel cold or frightening, though. It felt comforting, exactly like I had expected.

A slight breeze caressed my skin, tugging at my awareness.

"Hello?" I called out, though nobody was nearby. I felt that solitude deep in my soul, an expansion of the solitude I felt inside of myself for most of my life.

Until I met her, anyway.

"I must say, I did not think we would get the chance to meet so soon," a familiar voice spoke through the wind.

I did not panic. I had no reason to. I simply turned my head to the side and searched for the source of that voice. "Erebus?" I called out. "Is that you?"

The wind picked up slightly, and when I blinked, I began to see a shape forming within the shadows of the darkness. Not just any shape, but a person.

Erebus, forming from the shadows of night.

"Of course it's me," his gravel voice answered. *"I am the Saint of death, after all. And you're dying."*

"I don't want to die," I answered honestly. "She needs me back there."

Erebus stepped forward in mid-air, walking on nothing but shadows. I glanced around, too, realizing I was doing the same thing within the vast void of emptiness.

"She's brought you back before, King of Shadows. Anastasia will not grant her this again."

Erebus's features came into view, sharp and clean. His face was pale, nearly iridescent, actually, which was a sharp contrast from his black curls and grown facial hair. The black linens he wore reminded me of the Paragon, yet when Erebus wore them, they radiated strength.

I suddenly felt the need to bow my head.

"I didn't see you the last time I died," I noted. "Why now?"

A chilling silence passed between us. I felt the weight of his words before he even said them. *"Your last death was not final. I'm afraid this one is."*

I supposed I had already been brought back from death

once, when Jade had resurrected me in the trials. Once was already too much.

I was dead. After all these years, after all those struggles. It was finally here.

"You have nothing to fear," Erebus continued. *"Life is a fickle, reckless thing. You will find death to be much more peaceful."*

"Of course you would say that," I muttered. "You are the Saint of death."

The feeling of laughter fell over me before I heard Erebus chuckle. *"And as my descendent, you should feel the same way."*

I lifted my head and looked him in the eye again. As dangerous and terrifying as he was, I recognized something there, a sort of longing I had felt my entire life.

"Was this what you meant?" I asked. "Was this what Anastasia meant when she said I would be her downfall?"

Erebus smirked. *"Welcome home, Malachi."*

CHAPTER 44
Jade

It started as panic—pure, horrifying terror that pulsed through my heart, taking over my body, stronger than any adrenaline. More powerful than any magic.

Malachi's body grew cold beneath my hands as I pounded on his chest, begging his heart to start beating again.

The blood from his abdomen had already slowed.

"NO!" I screamed. "You can't die! You can't die, Malachi!"

I hit his chest again.

And again.

"Bring him back!" I yelled, this time to the Saints. "You have to bring him back!"

Serefin leaned over me, pushing onto Mal's wound. As if that would save him. As if that would bring him back, would start his heart again.

Serefin couldn't help. He couldn't bring Malachi back, but I could.

I had done it before, in the Trials of Glory. That was a test, yes, but it was also so, so real. If I could do it then, I could do it again.

I grabbed Mal's face in my hands and closed my eyes. "Please," I mumbled. "Give me the power to bring him back, and I swear I will do no harm. He's my protector. I need him."

The power deep in my chest flickered. Yes, that was it. That was a start. I just needed more, more power, more magic. More life.

And then I could bring him back.

He could come back, yes. I just needed....

"Please," I begged again. "Anastasia, I know you can help me. I just need a little more."

There is a balance to everything, peacemaker. We have told you this before. It is very delicate, very fragile.

"I don't care about the damn balance!" I yelled aloud.

Serefin flinched next to me.

"I just want to bring my husband back! Bring him back, Anastasia! I know you can do it! I know you can help me!"

Just because I can does not mean I will, or that I should. He will be your downfall, Jade Weyland. I have warned you of this fate.

"NO!" I screamed. "I do not accept this! Bring him back, Anastasia!"

But the Saint of life did not reply.

The panic came back in a wave, crashing over every bone in my chest and tightening, like fingers in a fist. Tightening and tightening and tightening until I couldn't breathe, couldn't think. Couldn't move.

"BRING. HIM. BACK!"

Serefin yelled next to me, still pressing onto Malachi's open wound. The same wound that could have healed by now, could have been healed by now.

"Why?" I asked. "Why did you bring me back but not him? Why now? He's better than me, I swear it! He's stronger and smarter and he's—he's–"

My vision tunneled, everything around me swarming and contorting until I blacked out entirely.

A white light pierced through the darkness. A familiar presence washed over me, warm and welcoming, but somehow still dreaded.

When my eyes adjusted, I saw Anastasia standing before me.

"What am I doing here?" I asked. "I should be with him! I should be, I should be bringing him back!" My breath came in fast, rapid pants, my lungs needing more oxygen than they could handle, than they could take. I clawed at my chest, at my throat.

Anastasia looked at me with a straight face, so different than that comforting smile. In fact, nothing about her was comforting. Not anymore.

"I can't," she said.

"Yes, you can."

She stepped forward, her perfect, smooth forehead wrinkling as she repeated, *"No, Jade. I cannot bring your husband back. Not this time. I warned you of this, I warned you he would be your downfall."*

I shoved my hands over my ears. I couldn't hear this. Not now. Not when everything was at risk.

"The balance is too far gone," Anastasia said. *"Bringing him back will only make it worse. It's not possible, Jade. Not this time. Get yourself out of there before you die, too."*

CHAPTER 45
Jade

To my surprise, all pain I felt disappeared. I no longer felt the fatal blow of Ky's sword as if it were my own, radiating pain from my chest and taking over every sense, every thought.

No, all I felt now was a lethal, chilling numbness. One that welcomed me, wrapping me in its arms and swallowing me whole. One that surrounded me entirely, engulfing me within and hiding that pain, hiding those thoughts.

Serefin pulled me away from Mal once I quit screaming.

"Why isn't he coming back?" Ser asked, turning his attention to me. "He isn't waking up, Jade!" Panic laced his words.

"I know," I breathed. "They...they won't let me bring him back."

A silent beat passed.

"What did you just say?"

I met his eyes so he could hear me this time, so he had no confusion about my words as I spoke them. "He's dead," I started, forcing the words out like poison. "They will not revive him, Serefin. They will not let me."

The voice that spoke was not my own. It was a voice so empty, so foreign, that I did not recognize it. I raised my bloody hands in front of me, surveying them. Mal's blood —red and warm—dripped from my fingertips onto the floor of pooled blood next to him.

Malachi was dead.

The thought did not even sound real in my own mind. How could it? The idea of Malachi, of my savior, my everything, being dead was so absurd, I could not even fathom it.

I was the one that should be dead. I was the one that deserved this fate, not him.

It was never supposed to be *him*.

The emptiness inside of me spread until I couldn't feel my own limbs, couldn't hear Serefin talking to me. I saw his lips moving, though, saying something over and over again and trying to get me to hear him.

What was the point?

Mal was dead. This was all over.

My other half.

My king.

All of it was for nothing.

I couldn't lead Rewyth alone. I couldn't fight this war, wouldn't be this person.

My emotions became too much, too thick. Too heavy. My power swirled, somehow restored from everything and back in full force, shattering everything around me and somehow literally shaking the ground, rattling the steel walls around us.

"Jade!" Serefin yelled. "Jade, we have to get out of here!"

I couldn't think. Couldn't move.

Serefin shook me hard enough to catch my attention, his fingers digging into my shoulders so hard that I actually felt the pain through my numbness.

Serefin picked up Malachi and threw him over his shoulder. "Come on!" He began running, climbing those stairs up to the surface.

I should have stayed. I should have let the shaking walls crush me, swallowing me entirely. It would have hurt less. Dying would be easier, would be safer.

To face them on the surface would be impossible.

Even so, I watched as Serefin climbed those stairs, Mal's bloody, lifeless body in his arms, and I couldn't help but hope.

This could not be the end. It couldn't.

So I picked myself up, pushed myself onto my weak, wobbling legs, and followed Serefin to the surface.

I climbed the stairs, one by one, somehow finding the strength to keep going, to not give up.

The ground around me continued to shake, matching the turmoil inside, feeding the darkness. We were a perfect match, those crumbling walls and I.

And when we got to the surface, not even the moonlight could have illuminated that darkness.

"Serefin!" Adeline's voice cut through the air. My eyes adjusted, too, until I saw them all. Adeline, Cordelia, Adonis, Lucien, *Saints*. Even Esther. They were all here, and they came with an entire army of fae.

No, I couldn't face them. Not when Serefin carried the body of the man they were all here for.

Adeline ran forward, only to realize the cruel reality of

what had happened. She stopped a few feet in front of us. "No," she said, shaking her head. "No, this can't be real. This can't be happening. He's okay, right? He'll be okay?"

I opened my mouth to explain, to make her feel better, to say anything, but no words came out. Serefin pushed past her, toward the army in the tree line.

"Where are the other rebels?" he asked.

"Dead," Lucien called out. "There were only a few, but we took care of them."

"Malachi?" Esther shouted, stepping out of the group and walking toward Serefin, who knelt and laid his body in the ashen dirt. "What happened?" Esther asked, surveying the scene.

She knelt next to his body.

"A sword," Serefin explained. "Jade tried to bring him back, but..."

Esther's eyes found mine. "But *what*? What happened, Jade? Why can't you bring him back?"

I stepped forward, too, not feeling my feet as they moved. "They wouldn't let me," I finally explained. Saints, my mouth barely moved. "They couldn't do it, they said the balance was too delicate."

"The balance?" Esther repeated, her eyes going adrift as she thought. "We can fix this," she mumbled. "Cordelia?"

Cordelia was at her side in an instant, already knowing her next thought. "We can't," Cordelia said, shaking her head. "If the Saints will not allow it, it cannot be done. Jade has already tried."

I stared at them, that numbness growing with every passing second.

No, they couldn't bring him back. Anastasia had been

very clear about that. Even if they could, she would not help them.

Cordelia's eyes widened. "Esther, don't even–"

"It's not up for discussion!" Esther yelled back, baring her teeth and straining her neck, making even Cordelia flinch at her words.

"What's going on?" Serefin asked. "Can you help him?"

"Yes!" Esther yelled. "I can and I will. Right, Cordelia?"

Cordelia hesitated for a second, long enough to make me wonder what exactly Esther was going to do to help.

"Right," she said eventually. "We can bring him back."

Cordelia called out to Lenova and the other witches, calling them forward. I stepped back, giving them more room. Adeline hooked her arm through mine, violently sobbing at the sight before us, but I couldn't bring myself to care. To think. To watch.

No, it was all too much.

Having hope would break me, would shatter me entirely.

But together, the witches began to chant.

They held hands, Cordelia and Esther leading the group as they looked up to the moon and begged, pleading in a language I did not understand.

It had to work. Even through the numbness, even though I didn't want to feel any hope, I still held on.

It had to work.

They chanted and chanted around Malachi's body, every single one of the witches speaking in a desperation only someone who had lost so deeply would possibly understand.

Did they? Did they understand what was at stake if Malachi did not come back?

Thunder rippled in the distance. Dark and beautiful, reminding me of him.

Saints.

It had to work.

Adeline gasped and gripped me harder as Esther stepped forward. I didn't see the dagger in her hand until it was too late.

And before I could even process the scene around me, Esther was plunging the weapon into her own chest.

She fell to the ground beside her son, bleeding out just as he did.

And dying, just as he did.

The rest of the witches carried on, louder now. They had re-formed the circle where Esther stepped out, not a single one even looking away from the moon to witness what happened. Unless I was losing my mind, unless everything I was seeing was simply a delusion.

But the chanting stopped.

The witches dropped their hands, breaking the circle.

And—in a way that absolutely ruined me—Malachi took a breath.

CHAPTER 46
Malachi

One entire week passed.

An entire week with no fighting, no battle.

An entire week with no whispers from Erebus, with no summoning from the Saints.

An entire week home with *her*.

Jade and I woke up in bed. I was still getting used to it—waking up beside her. Everything felt surreal, felt like it was too good to be true.

Erebus welcomed me home, and now I was back with Jade.

But Esther wasn't.

"You don't need to keep staring," I said. "I swear to you, I'm fine."

My eyes were closed, but it didn't matter. I could practically feel Jade's gaze burning me with concern. It had been like this the past three nights; every time I woke up in bed, she was already awake, staring.

"I know," she replied. "I just want to be sure."

I blinked my eyes open and rolled over, finding her lying

on her side with her head propped on her hand. She always looked so beautiful like that; undone, with her messy black hair falling over her shoulder.

It was hard to find her like that.

Unguarded.

I reached down and grabbed her free hand, pulling it forward and placing it on my bare chest. My heart beat steadily under her warm touch. "See?" I asked. "I'm alive."

Memories flashed through my mind, the same ones I had been trying to suppress for the last three days. Erebus speaking to me, my own mother sacrificing herself.

Jade screaming as the life left my body.

The memories came to me in chaotic spurts of emotion and power, and I still didn't understand so much.

Jade felt the same. I could nearly hear her thoughts through our bond, though that bond had broken before, it was now stronger than ever.

And I felt her fear, her worry.

Just as I was sure she felt mine.

Her brows furrowed as she pulled her hand from my chest, rolling to lie on her back.

"What is it?" I asked. "What's wrong?"

She shook her head as she focused on the ceiling above. "I can't help but feel angry. Sometimes the anger is too much, it's all-consuming. I don't know if I'll ever get past it."

"Angry at who?"

She shrugged. "The Saints. Esther. Everyone. But mostly Anastasia. She held the power to bring you back herself, Esther didn't have to die."

I agreed with her, of course I did. I had hated Esther for

a long time, but she had saved Jade's life, too. She was on my side, whether I admitted that in the end or not. There was no denying it now.

But we all knew there was a balance. We could kill and kill and kill, but at some point, there was a line.

We had crossed it one too many times.

"She sacrificed herself for me," I said. Saints, it was the first time I actually said those words out loud. Esther died so I could live, gave herself so I could come back to this world.

I had already lived so much, yet Esther thought I deserved more life.

She was not selfish. She was not cruel or untruthful. At the end of the day, Esther was my mother, and I loved her. She gave her life so I could continue living.

I sat up in bed, running my hands through my mess of curls.

Jade followed. She leaned up and rested her head on my shoulder, narrowly avoiding my relaxed wings.

"It's over, you know," she whispered in my ear. "We've won the fight. We've survived the war."

Saints, I wanted to laugh at that. How many times had I thought that? How many times had I believed I had won, just to be right back where I started once more?

I twisted, wrapping Jade in my arms and pulling her back down on the bed. After a squeal of surprise and laughter, she relaxed into my body.

"I never thanked you, you know," I said to her.

She tilted her chin up to meet my gaze. I would never get over her beauty. "For what?"

"For making me save those humans. For reminding me

of my humanity. For always seeing the good in me, even when you can't see it in yourself."

She smiled and reached up, trailing a finger down my cheekbone. "I suppose I should thank you, too," she said.

"Oh, really? May I ask what for?"

The smile slowly faded from her face, the light in her eyes dulling, if just for a moment. She had a way of doing that, of slipping into those emotions that we both fought so hard to avoid. Her brows furrowed as she lifted her chin and answered, "For being the light when I had none."

A knock on the door made Jade jump from her spot in my arms.

"What is it?" I called out.

Serefin's voice replied. "I'm just reminding you of the Sunrise Festival today, your majesties. Wouldn't want either of you to be late."

"Of course not," I replied. "Be right there, Ser."

I waited until his footsteps had retreated down the hall before pushing myself out of bed.

"Can't we just stay in this bed forever?" Jade moaned.

"What?" I teased. "You don't want to celebrate a new world with all of our people?"

"Maybe," she said, dropping herself back onto the bed. "But can't we do it tomorrow?"

"Come on," I said, walking around the tall bed posts and hoisting her off the silk sheets. "It's time we finally had some fun around here."

CHAPTER 47
Jade

Part of me hated that it all felt so normal; the music, the dancing, the laughing. I mean, everyone was celebrating as if we hadn't just been begging the Saints for Malachi's life back.

Of course, not everyone knew that part. But still. It was eerie to think about.

"You're sulking," Adeline said as she approached. Her floral dress swayed back and forth as she skipped toward me, and two flowers tucked her curled hair back behind her ears. "You're sulking at a party. That's unacceptable, Jade."

"I'm not sulking," I replied. "I'm observing. There's nothing wrong with that."

"Maybe not, but you could use this." She handed me a cup of the fae wine. I took it, sipping on the sweet liquid and looking around at the festival. Malachi stood with his brothers—Eli, Adonis, and Lucien—to my left, all smiling and talking in hushed voices. I didn't remember the last time I saw them all talking to each other that way.

Cordelia walked up to them, placing a light hand on

Lucien's shoulder as she casually joined the conversation. She had been upset after Esther died, but I think she understood. Of everyone else here, she would know what Esther was thinking in those last moments. Esther would have wanted us all to be happy, to finally be at peace.

Now, we finally got the chance. The chance to start over, the chance to live this life how we were supposed to live it all along.

Adeline looped her arm through mine as we watched. "You did this for us, Jade," she whispered. "However torturous this fae life has been for you, I want you to know how much of a blessing you were to us."

I put my hand atop hers, fighting the sudden rush of tears. "Thank you, Adeline."

Serefin walked up behind her, placing his hands on both of her shoulders. "Mind if I steal you for a dance?" he whispered.

Adeline smiled, quickly letting go of my arm and letting Serefin guide her to the crowd of dancing fae with an excited squeal.

Serefin met my eyes, too, just for a second, before giving me a silent nod.

We hadn't talked about what happened that day with the rebels. We didn't need to. Malachi was back, and that's all that mattered. Both of us would have done anything to bring him back, but at the end of the day, it was Esther who needed to sacrifice herself.

Not me. Not Serefin.

"So, this is where the fun has been happening," a male voice from behind made me jump. I turned to see my father walking up, dressed in a black jacket and new black boots.

"Father," I said. "I'm surprised you showed up. A fae festival has never really been your version of fun."

"No," he replied, coming to stand in Adeline's place, "but staying cooped up in that castle all day isn't exactly my version of fun, either."

I nodded. "I understand."

"Besides," he continued, "if I want to spend any time with my daughter, I might have to start attending these things now."

I actually smiled, turning to look my father in the eye. He was so different now, so much more clear. "You can see me anytime you want, you know," I pushed. "You just have to send word."

"Yeah, yeah," he said. "When you're not out saving the entire world, I'll let you know."

I smiled again, turning my attention back to the crowd. We stood that way for a while, shoulder to shoulder, taking in the world around us.

"I have to say, this is much better than the worn-down shack we were living in before," he said.

My eyes snapped to his. "You're kidding, right?"

My father shook his head. "Not in the slightest. But I did always know you would be the one to save the world."

I expected him to be joking, but he said all of this with a straight face.

"Well," I replied, "that makes one of us."

I was surprised when my father decided to stick around. The rest of the humans we helped rescue left, journeying back to their lands with a handful of fae to help them rebuild what they had lost.

With time and resources, I was confident we could help

them live better lives. Not ones of poverty or scarcity, but lives of abundance.

Humans didn't need to fear the fae anymore. Not while I was here.

My father smiled, his dull, brown eyes actually sparkling for once, as he put a hand on my shoulder. "You did good, kid," he said. "Even if I didn't."

I placed a hand on top of his. He didn't have to say anything else. Neither of us did. I knew what my father meant, what he had said in those few words.

He was proud of me. He was sorry. He was a changed man now.

We both changed.

"Enjoy your celebration," he said, turning to walk back into the castle. "You deserve it."

I watched him walk away, no longer stumbling like I had seen so many times. Not limping, not cowering. Simply walking. Like he belonged here. Like he deserved to be here.

My chest welled with an emotion I couldn't quite name.

He's right, the soft voice in my head said. I jumped at the sound of it, I hadn't heard Anastasia since the night Mal died. *You deserve this.*

I thought you were done with me, I thought back. *I thought you left for good after Malachi came back.*

A tickling feeling of satisfaction filled my chest from her before she replied, *I've had some time to think, to process what happened.*

You let him come back, didn't you? I asked. *A life for a life.*

A long beat of silence filled my mind.

I thought he would be your downfall, Anastasia admitted. *I thought he would pull you into the darkness, pull you out of the light.*

What changed?

It appears I was wrong, peacemaker. As long as he is at your side, I think darkness bows at your feet.

I smiled to nobody. *I have to agree with you on that one, Anastasia.*

Besides, the voice echoed in my mind, *I think you two have saved enough people. You deserved a little saving of your own. Remember to stay out of trouble next time, okay?*

No promises, I thought back.

A warm rush filled my body, illuminating my senses as my power rolled in my veins. I hadn't realized just how much I missed the presence of the Saints until now. The last week, thinking they had abandoned me, was misery.

But she wasn't mad at all.

And she actually approved of this relationship with Malachi.

Finally, everything fell into place.

"What was that about?" Malachi asked as he approached.

I turned to face him. "I don't know, but it was surprisingly pleasant."

Malachi nodded with a raised brow. "Come here," he said. "I want you to hear something."

I took Mal's outstretched hand, letting him guide me through the crowd to where his brothers stood with Cordelia and Dragon.

They were all smiling, clearly excited about something.

"Go ahead," Mal said as soon as I approached the circle. "Tell her what you told me."

Eli stepped forward, his face lit up with a joy I had only seen a few times. "I can see it all," he said, his eyes focusing on something else.

I glanced at Mal, who only smiled back at me.

"You can see what?" I asked.

"The future, everything. Our lives here in Rewyth."

I waited for him to say more, but he clearly got lost in the thought again, smiling about something only he could see.

"I hope this is a good thing," I said. "And not more death and war like the last time."

Eli laughed quietly, Malachi pulled me against his body.

"No death," Eli replied. "No war. Just us and, for once, peace."

Even Lucien smiled at this, wrapping his arms around Cordelia's shoulders as Dragon bounced around in front of them.

"Peace," I repeated. "That sounds almost too good to be true."

"Get used to it," Mal whispered into my ear. "Because I think I'm done fighting for now."

I leaned into him, relaxing into his body and watching our friends smile, dance, hope. "Me too."

Acknowledgments

Thinking about how this series changed my life has truly left me at a loss for words. First, thank you to my mother, Julie, for believing in me. Without you, my writing career would have ended before it ever started. Our business meetings, which almost always required a margarita, were some of the best inspirational conversations I've had, and I surely would not have been successful in this career without your motivation and support. I live my dream now because of you.

Jess and Kenz, you two have been there for me on those late nights and long weeks when I wanted to give up and rip my hair out. You both have always been the ones waving the flashlight toward the end of the tunnel, showing me the light when I needed help to see it. I don't know how I was lucky enough to find you in this life, but I am certain this series would be crumbled in the trash somewhere if it wasn't for your positivity and endless kindness. The universe sent me you two when I needed friendship the most, and I think about how lucky I am every single day.

To my friends and family, who put up with me cancelling plans to stay home and write, thank you for not giving up on me!

And finally, thank you to Jack, who doesn't read my books but still puts up with me talking about fictional characters ten hours a day. This career empties my emotional well on an almost weekly occasion, and you're always there to help me refill that well when I need it.

When I first wrote House of Lies and Sorrow, I thought maybe ten people would read it. I had no idea it would receive the love and support that it has, and it's all because of you—the readers. Every single time a stranger tells me they've loved these books, it warms my heart. Every time. I never take you for granted, and I'm truly floored by the love this series has received.

Thank you for believing in me. Thank you for loving Jade and Malachi. Thank you for taking a chance on an indie author. Thank you for escaping with me into my twisted, dark worlds.

Thank you.

I'll never stop writing for you.

Love,
Em

Printed in Great Britain
by Amazon